" . . . a fast paced, funny tale."
—Roberta Johnson, *Booklist*

"Funny and cynical . . . aliens as relentless capitalists, and . . . the galactic community as a gargantuan marketplace in which the earth is nothing more than a poverty stricken backwater . . . As broad and breezy as Pohl and Kornbluth's *The Space Merchants*."—Gary K. Wolfe, *Locus Magazine*

"*First Contract* turns the theoretical basis of all those boring high school economics classes into an engaging case study of what happens when Adam Smith's "invisible hand" is actually a slimy alien tentacle."
—*Yuma Daily Sun*

"Space business and humor don't usually mix. Greg Costikyan's *First Contract* may be the first book since Frederik Pohl and Cyril Kornbluth's classic *The Space Merchants* to bring these concepts together and make them fly. . . . An unabashedly comic novel. . . . Costikyan launches plenty of zingers at IPOs, trade shows, and other staples of big business. The million-quatloo question is: when the time comes, will Earth be the Aztecs or the Japanese?"
—Chris Aylott on space.com

FIRST
CONTRACT

GREG
COSTIKYAN

A TOM DOHERTY ASSOCIATES BOOK
NEW YORK

For Betsy

FIRST CONTRACT

Copyright © 2000 by Greg Costikyan

Edited by Debbie Notkin

A Tor Book
Published by Tom Doherty Associates, LLC
175 Fifth Avenue
New York, NY, 10010

www.tor.com

Tor® is a registered trademark of Tom Doherty Associates, LLC.

ISBN: 0-812-54549-4
Library of Congress Catalog Card Number: 00-026243

First Edition: July 2000
First mass market edition: June 2001

Printed in the United States of America

0 9 8 7 6 5 4 3 2 1

ACKNOWLEDGMENTS

The author wishes to thank Johnson Mukerjii, president and CEO of Mukerjii Interstellar, Ltda., and prime minister of the Republic of Tuvalu, for his candor and assistance; Dr. Leander Huff, Ph.D., for not suing; and Mr. Lee Gelber for what little the author knows about sales. Eleanor Lang, Debbie Notkin, and Valerie Smith, as usual, provided invaluable assistance with the text. Thanks to A. E. Brain for suggesting the title. The theme music of choice is the Flying Lizards' rendition of "Money." No warranties are expressly or implicitly stated. If the market does not develop in the anticipated fashion, this may have a marked and deleterious effect on the company's projected earnings. All characters contained herein are fictional, and any resemblance to persons living or dead is purely coincidental. And all merchandise is FOB Earth.

FIRST
CONTRACT

PROLOGUE

PICTURE THIS: YOU'RE WALKING DOWN THE STREET, FOOT-
loose and fancy-free. All right, you aren't exactly footloose:
You've got three kids, a mortgage, and bills to pay. And
maybe you aren't exactly fancy-free; in fact, maybe you've got
a sneaking suspicion that your country is in decline and your
culture disintegrating. Whatever.

The point is, you're happy. Reasonably happy. As happy as
it is given mortal man or woman to be. You're making good
money, the economy is fine, your kids are doing all right in
school, and it's a nice day. All is right with the world. Or at
least, all things taken together, the good with the bad, more
things about the world are right than not-right.

Then, some guy comes along and whangs you on the side
of the head with a 2-by-4. While you're lying dazed in the
gutter, he rifles your wallet. When he's finished, he saunters
down the street, whistling.

And you're left there, with no money, no credit cards, no
way to call home, and a throbbing lump on your head, wondering what the hell happened—and who *was* that guy?

Got the picture?

Good.

That's what it was like when the aliens came.

1

PEACHE$ AND CREAM

THE ROOM WAS BRUTALLY AIR-CONDITIONED; EVEN IN dark, conservative suits, the men and women were almost cold. From one wall hung an original Matisse; the furniture was heavy teak, and the floor was carpeted with a gorgeously detailed Bokhara. Tinted glass displayed an unparalleled view of Silicon Valley: serried ranks of identical office buildings, marching off along the freeway, flanked by what the real-estate agents like to call "the Golden Hills of California"— dry grassland prone to fires.

One Johnson Mukerjii, president and chairman of Mukerjii Display Systems, sat at the head of the table, a portly, dark-skinned man in a Savile Row suit—your servant. I removed a Honduran cigar from one pocket and pointed it at David Greenblatt, our chief technology officer. "Can you update us on the MDS-316, David?"

Greenblatt hurriedly removed a finger from his nose. He wore a polyester shirt of a color never seen in nature; eyes blinked worriedly behind glasses as thick as a bulletproof partition. He was the only one in the room without a suit—one of the perquisites of technical types. Geeks, as we familiarly call them.

"The what?" he mumbled. "Oh! The 3-D thingiewack."

I sighed, and began to take the cellophane off my cigar.
"Yes, David."

"Geez, we've been finished with that for ages," he said.
"R&D is all done. It's been tested up the wazoo, too. Up to
the production guys, now."

"Final Q/A sign-off was within previously defined para-
meterization?" asked Stephen Hsieh, our VP of production.

"What?" asked Greenblatt. He studied Hsieh as if the man
were mad. Greenblatt didn't like jargon, unless it was his own.
"Oh, like, was everything copacetic? Sure."

Hsieh smoothed his Hermès tie beneath his Hong Kong-
tailored suit jacket and glared at Greenblatt with undisguised
loathing. I smiled benignly; *divide et impera*, that's my motto.

"And you, Stephen?" I asked. "How does retooling of our
Bangkok facility progress?"

"I am pleased to report, sir," Hsieh rapped, eyes gleaming
behind steel-rim glasses, "that all systems will be fully opti-
matized by the designated production go-date."

I removed the band from my cigar. "Excellent, Stephen.
However, you do realize that we will need a dozen or so samples by the Consumer Electronics Show—several months in
advance of the ship date?"

Hsieh paled and shot to his feet. He liked to project an
image of absolute competence, and took the slightest problem as a drastic threat, not only to his continued employment
but, seemingly, to his very masculinity. "I—I wasn't informed," he said. "Why wasn't I informed? How many units?
Where? What's the precise date?"

"I'm sure your staff can find these details out," I said. "I
assume there'll be no problem?"

"None," said Hsieh definitively. "Absolutely none. Uh . . ."

"Yes, Stephen?"

"Do I have budget to air-express the units if necessary to
hit the show?"

"Of course, Stephen."

"Thank you," he said, performing a half bow; too much time spent in Japan, I think. He sat down, hands still shaking.

"That's my lad," thought I; Stephen worked three times as hard when he was terrified.

David Greenblatt hesitantly raised his hand, as if this were the sixth grade. "Yes, David?"

"Um, I have an appointment with Huff this afternoon."

"Leander Huff?" I asked.

"Yeah," he said. "You know, the columnist for *Vaporware News*?"

"Why did he call you?" I asked, a little alarmed. Huff was opinionated, arrogant, and universally read; a bad story by him on the MDS-316 could hurt us badly. And press relations were not exactly David's strong suit. Actually, *human* relations were not David's strong suit; he got along much better with hardware. "Perhaps I had better go along," I said soothingly.

"Sure, chief," said David.

I ran the cigar under my nose, sniffing the aromatic tobacco. "Mr. Sharps," I said. "How are the accounts responding to our pending introduction?"

Old Fred Sharps opened heavily lidded eyes and pulled himself upright. He searched pockets for a pipe, before remembering that he'd quit smoking three years before. "Well, now, Johnny," he rumbled. "The reaction looks mighty good. I talked to Rube Stokowski at Wal-Mart—you remember Rube Stokowski?" I nodded; no, I did not. But if I told Sharps that, we'd spend the next fifteen minutes in reminiscence. "Rube was real excited. I wasn't sure it'd be an item for them—they sell mostly bread-and-butter equipment, you know? And this'll start off as top-of-the-line, leading-edge technology, with a price to match. Not for your typical Wal-Mart customer, you ask me. But that demo David's folks worked up was pretty impressive. Stokowski went on and on over lunch, and then—well, funny thing. Me, I ordered my usual Manhattan, and Rube, he says to the waitress—"

"Fred, old man; I'm sure this is a fascinating anecdote, but I do have a meeting in twenty minutes—"

"Oh, sure, Johnny. Anyhow, the long and the short of it is, Wal-Mart is talking five figures."

I frowned. "Is that all?" The MDS-316 had a launch price of a few thousand dollars; five figures in cash sales meant no more than a couple of dozen units.

Sharp looked wounded for a moment; then, his eyes cleared. "Units, Johnny; units, not dollars."

"Tens of thousands of *units*?"

Fred grinned happily. "Of course, they want a deal on dating, but for an order like that—"

"No problem," I said. "Stephen, we'll need to scale up production pretty quickly."

"All contingencies are scenarioed," Hsieh assured me.

"Can we start thinking about retooling the facility in Singapore, as well? We may need more manufacturing capacity than we'd expected."

Hsieh frowned; he didn't like the Singapore factory. Wages were too high there. "I'll explore it," he said reluctantly.

"What else, Fred?" I asked.

"CompUSA, no problem; Sears looks good; some of the independents are balking at the release price, but I tell 'em—"

"Fine, Fred. What's the response from our reps?"

"Very positive. Everyone seems to think we've got a hit on our hands. But it's important we stick to our release schedule; Matsuzuka isn't far behind with their own holographic display—"

"There will be no difficulty," said Hsieh.

I removed a small silver knife from my waistcoat pocket and cut a thin wedge from the end of the cigar. "Tanisha?" I said.

Tanisha Grant, our matronly CFO, sat up and put her hands flat on the table. "Financially, we're in pretty good shape. However, the Bangkok retooling is draining cash—and if we're going to be offering special dating, we won't see any income from the MDS-316 for some while. I think we need to raise some capital."

"Certainly," I said. "What would you recommend?"

"We have two options," she said. "We have SEC approval for a new share offering; and MuniBank has given preliminary approval to a new loan."

"Which do you prefer?"

"Speaking as a CFO? Wall Street would like the equity offering better, right now. Our debt/equity ratio is high; they'd like to see us reduce it, and no one has any doubts about the fundamental soundness of Mukerjii Display Systems. But if you really want to bet on the success of the MDS-316 . . ."

"Yes?"

"Once the new display is released, the publicity, to say nothing of the lift to our earnings, should increase our share price—which has been depressed in recent months by our heavy investment in the display system. By making a share offering *then* we could raise considerably more money—or raise the same amount by selling fewer shares."

"But we need the money now," I pointed out.

"Right," said Tanisha. "So we borrow the money from MuniBank now; and after the MDS-316 has been released, we sell shares and repay the loan."

"Excellent," I said. "Ladies, gentlemen, it looks to me as if we have all our ducks in a row. Development is complete, production is about to begin, the finances are there; all we need to do now is go out and sell the crap out of it."

"Leave it to me, Johnny," rumbled Fred Sharps.

"I'll get MuniBank on the phone immediately," said Tanisha Grant.

"All systems functional," said Stephen Hsieh.

"Can I go now?" asked David Greenblatt.

"Of course, David," I said soothingly.

As everyone filed out, I found my silver matchbox, opened it, and struck a match. I waited until the sulfur had burned off, then ran the flame up and down the shaft of the cigar. I'm not sure of the rationale for that, but it's supposed to improve the taste. Then I held the match to the end, turning the cigar with the other hand, to ensure that the end was evenly lit.

The air in the room was crisp, clean. The chair was eminently comfortable. Beyond those tinted windows spread the buildings and highways of the world I ruled. Already, the traffic flow was heavy; some folk were beating the rush hour home. Smoke curled through the air; I savored its smell. There were millions in prospect with this one, I thought; millions. Tanisha was right; our share price would soar, when this was released, and my net worth with it. Ah, life was sweet.

"AFTERNOON, MUKERJII," BELLOWED LEANDER HUFF. HE was slightly deaf and had a tendency to shout. His body was that of an aging linebacker, draped in a tweed jacket and casual slacks; his gray hair was severely crew-cut, and one hand held an aging briar. The perfect image, in other words, of the Orange County conservative. Which Huff was.

"How do you do, Leander," I said, extending a hand and tensing the muscles. As expected, Huff put my hand through the wringer—probably not from macho competitiveness, but merely because that was what one did in his circle. I withdrew my mangled digits and sighed, wishing, not for the first time, that David Greenblatt hadn't set this meeting up. I had met Huff before, and the experience was always exhausting.

"I'm afraid I'll have to ask you to refrain from smoking," I said.

"What?" he bellowed. "Not another of these antismoking Nazis, are you, Mukerjii?"

"Ah—no," I said. "It's merely that the device we're about

to demonstrate is not a production model; it's fairly sensitive, and smoke might—"

"Yes, yes, all right," Huff shouted. "And who is this?"

Greenblatt had entered, glasses askew, the demonstration model of the MDS-316 in his arms. He scuttled into the conference room and carefully laid it on the teak table. Without meeting anyone's eyes, he dropped to his hands and knees and began crawling around on the floor, connecting cables.

"May I, ah, introduce our chief technology officer, David Greenblatt?" I said.

"How do," brayed Huff to David's rear end. David rose, adjusted his glasses, and made a perfunctory swipe at his untucked shirttails. Somewhat reluctantly, he met Huff's extended hand with his own; Huff mashed it like a bundle of wet Kleenex. David snatched his hand away at the earliest opportunity.

"This is the MDS-316," I said, gesturing toward the table. The device was an open glass cube, about three feet on a side; the electronics were in the motherboard below the opaque bottom of the cube. Cables snaked away to a computer.

"I read *These Stars Are Ours!*," Greenblatt said.

Huff gave the engineer his attention. "Pardon?" he said.

"I said, I read *These Stars Are Ours!*," said Greenblatt a little more loudly.

Huff wrote sci-fi as a sideline. He preened a bit at encountering a fan. "You did, eh, lad? And what did you think?"

"I think it was despicable."

"David!" I groaned.

Huff blinked twice. "What?"

"I'd almost call it racist," Greenblatt said.

"Racist? *Racist?*" Huff was turning red.

"David!" I said urgently. "Do shut up."

Greenblatt blinked rapidly behind his eyeglasses and fingered his pocket protector nervously. "Well, um, what else would you call it?" he said. "Why should humans be superior to other sapient beings?"

"Bosh," Huff bellowed. "Why shouldn't we be? We're the roughest, toughest life-form in the galaxy—"

"There's no evidence for that. And the idea that Americans are superior to other people . . . Isn't that racist?"

"Bosh again!" shouted Huff. "Of course Americans are superior. Has nothing to do with race."

"Huh?" said Greenblatt.

"Mongrel vigor!" said Huff triumphantly. "Take collies. Very trainable breed, rather stupid. Take Dobermans. Rather ferocious animals, often violent. Take any breed you like: It's one extreme of the canine race. Breed 'em, and what do you get? Regression to the mean. Better all-round animals. Healthier, smarter, more vigorous . . . Same with humans. Whites, blacks, Orientals . . . mix up the cultures, mix up the genes, you get something superior. What's the biggest melting pot in the world? America! That's why we're superior."

"That's craz—" David began.

"Another word Greenblatt," I said, "and you'll be scanning the want ads."

He peered at me in a wounded fashion.

"Dr. Huff," I said. "Please, let us proceed with the demonstr—"

"You need to learn some manners," shouted Huff. "One thing if you don't like the book. No need to make an ass of yourself."

"Well, gosh—" said Greenblatt.

"Be quiet! We're here," I said loudly, "to show you the—"

"Damn fool thing to do," said Huff. He mumbled to himself and scowled at Greenblatt.

"Please, Dr. Huff," I said. "May we show you . . ."

"Anyway," said Huff, "not here for this nonsense. What's

all this about your holographic display? Weren't you going to demonstrate? Or is this another of your damnfool vaporware projects, Mukerjii?" He glowered at me.

I sighed. "Not at all," I said soothingly. "Here on the table is the MDS-316, the first such device to sell for under—"

"What's the strobe rate?" bellowed Huff.

"Umm?"

"That was the problem with the model you showed at CES last year," he said. "The display refreshed maybe five times a second. Flickered like a disco strobe light. I'm an epileptic, you know; almost had a grand-mal episode right then and there."

"The display now refreshes a good twenty times a second," I said, "approximately as frequently as an old computer monitor. I would be surprised if you were to note any visible flicker."

"Right, then," said Huff. "Let's boot it up and see how it flies, eh?"

"Go ahead, David," I said.

The insides of the glass cube gradually lightened. Within, the Huntington Library and surrounding gardens appeared. The image was truly three-dimensional; the library building itself, with its ornate columns, rose a foot above the bottom of the cube. Trees, hills, gardens surrounded it.

Huff was entranced by the image. For all his bluster, he was an enthusiastic technophile. Show him a new toy, and he was happy.

The "camera" swooped down toward the Huntington gardens. The cube was filled now with the image of a fountain, the top of the spray even with the top of the cube. Water tumbled down the sides of the fountain toward a circular pool; people sat on the edge and watched the spray. In the pool, a duck circled.

"Fantastic," shouted Huff. "What's the resolution?"

"The system is capable of displaying data at a resolution of one thousand dots per inch," I said. "You understand, three dimensions require vast processing power. On a flat screen, a thousand dots per inch means a million per square inch, in a holographic display, it means a billion per cubic inch."

The camera panned away from the fountain and toward the flowers that surrounded it. Now the entire box was filled with the image of a rose-colored camellia, petals of jewel-like perfection unfolding from the center.

"Amazing," muttered Huff, moving about the display. "Can you construct images on the fly?"

"Sure," said David, "but not so detailed. That's a limitation of the processor, not the display technology. When the new chips are released—"

In moments, he and Huff were deep in a technical discussion that was over my head. I could relax, sit down, and nod and smile at appropriate intervals.

Despite David's gaffe, it was going to work.

Once the demo had run its course, we retired to a nice little bistro not too far from the office. Huff ate like a trencherman, at my expense—a common characteristic of writers, I have noticed. He also imbibed an enormous quantity of Macallan 25; I winced at the size of the bill, but Huff intimated that his next column would contain a glowing update on MDS's new holographic display—something previous experience had led me to believe was worth mid–six figures in additional sales at launch. And what the hell; I had drunk my share of the scotch myself, and whatever the price, twenty-five-year Macallan is superb stuff. We parted in a haze of bibulous good fellowship.

Ah, life was sweet.

SOME MEN IN MY POSITION PREFER THE COMFORT AND ease of a limousine; and it is true that one may work while a chauffeur does the driving. But why own a Jag if not to drive it?

I loved to drive home, speeding along winding roads through the hills above San Jose. The speed limit was forty, but I normally took the trip at seventy. It was nothing to the Jag.

Normally there aren't any cops on the road; it's not much used, a county highway. No state police there; but occasionally, one is unlucky enough to run into county cops.

As I did that day. They were waiting around a turn. I slowed as quickly as I could, but they got me; the cop car's siren sounded, its tires screeched as it pulled onto the road and accelerated behind me. Sighing, I pulled over, wondering whether the scotch I'd drunk would put me over the line on a Breathalyzer.

As the cop car pulled off behind me and the cop opened his door, I found my driver's license. He approached, and I hit the button to lower the window.

"Do you know how fast you were going?" he asked. Mirrored sunglasses glinted in the afternoon sun.

"Are you implying that I was exceeding the speed limit?" I asked blandly.

He snorted. "May I see your driver's license, registration, and proof of insurance, please?"

I handed them to him with a hundred-dollar bill.

He blinked. "Are you attempting to bribe me?" he said.

"Is the amount insufficient?" I asked.

He looked back toward the cop car. "Shit," he said. "I've got a partner."

"Ah," I said. "Then perhaps you would be so kind as to give this to him with my compliments." I handed him another bill.

He took it, looking torn; I wondered whether scruples were bothering him, or the need to part with half the money. He sighed, pocketed both bills, handed me back my papers, and said, "Look, don't speed on this road, okay? This isn't a free-way. There are turns, and . . . look, watch your speed."

"Most assuredly, sir," I said. "I shall take your recommen-dation under advisement." I must have driven that road a thousand times; no turn was likely to surprise me.

He walked back to the cop car, conferred briefly with his associate, and U-turned, presumably to return to his previous vantage point.

I shifted into gear.

Ah, life was sweet.

As I tooled up the drive, the sun glinted off the windows of my house. It was a long, low affair, rambling across the hill. One might term it ranch-style, except that it was on three levels, really, conforming to the topography; hard to build a ten-thousand-square-foot house on a hill and keep it all on a level. Call it California eclectic, with elements of Frank Lloyd Wright. Maureen had designed the thing.

She waved to me from the patio as I drove up. Michael was waiting to take the car to the shed. "Pleasant day, sir?" he inquired.

"Indeed," I told him, and tossed him the keys. By the time I got to the living room, Maureen was waiting for me with a gin and tonic.

"How are you, Johnny?" she said, bending a bit to kiss me. I grabbed her and gave her a squeeze. Maureen has a great deal to squeeze.

I went to our bedroom and changed my suit for swimming trunks, then went to the pool and swam a couple of laps—more to wash off the detritus of the day than for exercise. The pool was blood-hot, perfect; no shock upon entry. It is expensive to maintain an Olympic-sized pool at such a tem-perature, but what is wealth for if not to provide such little luxuries?

I slipped into the Jacuzzi with Maureen; she snuggled up to me and offered a sip of her margarita, hooking one leg under mine. "How was your day?" she said.

I sighed in contentment. "Just fine," I said. "Everything is on schedule. It looks as though we have a hit."

"And that means?"

"Millions, my sweet," I said, giving her a kiss. "Millions." She smiled.

The view was spectacular. An inversion trapped smog over San Jose, making the floor of the valley only dimly visible, but the mountains on the other side were clear, above the pollution. Behind us, a door opened; Consuela approached. "Excuse me," she said. "Dinner's ready."

"Thank you," I said, got out of the Jacuzzi, and gave Maureen a hand up. I put on a shirt and sandals while Maureen put on a wrap, and we strolled down a path to the patio.

"What's for dinner?" I asked.

"Rack of lamb," she said.

"Have you picked a wine?"

"Some of that Burgundy you bought," she said.

"The Chambertin-Clos de Bèze?"

"Yes."

"Wonderful," I said.

And it was. Consuela had cooked the rack of lamb on a rotisserie, over the grill, with fresh rosemary from the garden; Michael brought it sizzling to the table, and sliced it into individual chops. There was a mixed green salad with goat cheese and a delicate lime-cumin vinaigrette, and green beans with oregano, all as fresh as only produce from one's own garden can be. The wine was—well, I am not as fluent with adjectives as a true connoisseur, but it was noble, as well it ought to be after so many years in a cellar. As we ate in the warm California air, surrounded by my thousand acres of golden hills—selected so that development would never mar our vista—the stars above came twinkling out, and, below, the lights of San Jose. We talked lazily about a vacation in the Andaman Islands, or possibly in Belize—someplace tropical and off the beaten path.

Desert was fresh melon with kirsch. As it was served, a toe ran up the inside of my calf. I smiled at Maureen as the far hills shone red in the setting sun.

Ah, life was sweet . . .

2

FRIEND$ IN HIGH PLACE$

. . . BEFORE THE ALIENS CAME.

I missed the first broadcast. I rarely watch the TV news; I'm not in a business where I have to think like the common American, and the actual news content of TV news is negligible. I read the *Times*, the *Times*, the *Times*, and the *Times*—New York, LA, of London, and Financial—and *The Economist* for a broader perspective; and for fast-breaking news, there's always Reuters on the Web. In any event, I was working late that evening. About quarter after seven, the western sky turning red through my office window, I got a call from Maureen. "Did you see the news?" she said.

I frowned. "No," I said. "What's up?"

"You'd better turn on CNN," she said.

So I turned on the TV in my office; I used it mainly to screen our commercials. One of the usual blow-dried idiots said something I didn't catch, then they cut to some footage from a bad *Star Trek* episode.

Three robed creatures with gray skin, eyes on stalks like snails, and enormous, pulsating heads stood before a red-lit backdrop. Ethereal music played. "Greetings from the galaxy," said one, gliding forward slightly. "I am Captain Sh'tsitsin. We come in peace from the stars."

Another glided forward. "We have received your radio and television transmissions for many years," it said. "Our Council has now deemed your race to be worthy of admission to the galactic community. We come bearing gifts, and wish to discuss Earth's future role among the civilized races with your world leaders."

"Peace," said the captain.

"Friendship," said the one that had not previously spoken.

"Prosperity," said the third.

"Our current position and vector is—" said the captain, and reeled off a string of figures and terms that meant nothing to me. "Your astronomers may follow our progress through your star system; we shall assume orbit around your planet in approximately three days."

"We apologize for usurping your usual broadcast transmissions," said one of the others, "and will recompense your broadcast authorities and businesses at the prevailing commercial rate for the time we have taken."

"Thank you," said the captain, "and have a pleasant tomorrow."

They disappeared. Our blow-dried friend appeared, with a scientist who hadn't brushed his hair in recent memory. The scientist babbled something about the color of the light indicating that the aliens came from a Class M dwarf star.

"What do you think?" asked Maureen.

"Trite," I said. "And the special effects are lousy."

BUT AS IT TURNED OUT, I WAS WRONG; IT WAS NO HOAX. The astronomers easily spotted a spaceship decelerating atop a fusion flame at the indicated coordinates. Nobody knew quite what to make of it all; the market was up, then down, then up again, as rumor after rumor swept the world. Religious nuts wanted everyone to worship the aliens, or stone them as emissaries of Satan, or some such nonsense; academics portentously debated the likely effect of the aliens' visit.

Since there was virtually no data to rely on, no one had any real idea what was going on—but that didn't stop the TV from displaying hour after hour of talking heads jabbering nonsense.

It was all very interesting, to be sure, but the impact on my business seemed nonexistent, at first. We had a product to release, the preliminary orders were good, we had to work like the dickens to get everything ready for CES. If the aliens caused us any problems, it was in terms of staff time lost: People crowded around portable TVs or radios with each new report.

I called a staff meeting, everyone above the level of director: quite a crowd in the room. "Listen, gentlemen, ladies," I said. "This company is at a vital juncture, as you know. I realize the world as a whole may be at a vital juncture, too, but the amount of staff time being spent on the news is—"

"Sir?" said someone I didn't recognize. He had a phone receiver in one hand.

"Can't it wait?" I said. "This is important." You don't waste thirty employees' time to take a call in the middle of a meeting; not only is it expensive, in terms of man-hours and salary dollars, but it's bad for morale. There isn't a phone call that can't wait.

"It's the president, sir," he said.

The president? But *I* was the president of— Oh.

"Hello?" I said into the phone.

"Yo, dude," said the president. "How's it hanging?"

"Very well, Mr. President," I said. "And how is Jeannette?" We'd been friends when he was a senator from California, and I'd always contributed generously to his campaign fund.

"Happier'n a pig in shit. Loves the whole capital social dealie. I hear surf's up at Laguna Beach," he said mournfully.

I smiled. "Well, the congressional session should be over soon. Then you can take a break."

"Yeah," he said perking up. "Maybe we'll go to Maui. Hey,

listen, Muks. These alien ginks are landing on the front lawn on Tuesday."

"Sir?"

"Hey, wasn't my idea. But at least it makes it easier on security. I think they've been watching too many sci-fi movies; like, it's traditional to land on the White House lawn or something. Anyway, Hapsburg's flying in from Brussels, and Fujaki from Japan . . . whole bunch of world leader-type dudes're gonna be there. I figure we gotta have some high-flying Americans, too. A coupla eggheads, a coupla suits . . . Any chance you can show?"

Hmm. Did I want to meet the aliens? Did I want an opportunity, albeit a remote one, to get my paws on some advanced interstellar technology? Do I look like a blithering idiot? "I'd be delighted and honored, sir," I said.

"Tubular," said the president. "Be there or be square!"

"Yes, sir," I said.

"Later, dude," said the president.

"YOU CAN'T GO," SAID TANISHA, PALMS FLAT ON THE CONference table. "And certainly you can't take David with you." Outside, a harsh noontime sun baked down on the smoggy valley. Inside, it was as chill as ever.

"Granted this is a critical point," I said, "but everything is running smoothly. David, is your presence needed to keep the MDS-316 on track?"

"Nope," he said. "Out of my hands, like I told you." I wanted him with me; he was far likelier than I to pick something useful up from the aliens. And he was thrilled to be going; to meet real, live creatures from another star? What more could a technogeek desire?

"You'll have our units ready for CES?" I asked Hsieh.

"Rollout is a go," he said. "Final preproduction tests are in ultimate assurance mode. All systems A-Okay."

"And our loan with MuniBank is lined up?"

Tanisha looked a little uneasy. "Yes," she said reluctantly. "Then what's the problem?" I said. "Surely MDS can run for a few days without me in situ. It's not like I'll be in Bora-Bora; last I heard, phone and Internet links between here and Washington were pretty good."

So they let me go.

THE PRESIDENT LOOKED TERRIFIC. BUT THEN, THE PRESIdent always looked terrific. He had a crack team of White House cosmetologists to make *sure* he looked terrific. "You look terrific," I said.

"Hey, thanks, *amigo*," he said, punching my shoulder. "Who's the geek?"

David Greenblatt looked extremely uncomfortable in a suit. I'd had to badger him for a good half hour to get him into it. His tie was loose and crooked, his pants showed a good two inches of white athletic sock, and he was obviously sweating heavily. "This is David Greenblatt, our chief technology officer," I said. "I brought him along in case we need to discuss technical issues with our extraterrestrial brethren."

"Yo," said the president. "Howaya?" He shook hands with Greenblatt.

"Copacetic," Greenblatt mumbled, eyes downcast.

It was a brisk spring day on the White House lawn. The gardens were bursting with flowers; a striped awning overhung a podium. Aides and Secret Service men ran about on mysterious missions, chattering desperately into walkie-talkies. Journalists, scientists, businessmen, diplomats, and anyone else with the pull to wangle an invitation milled about confusedly. There were really too many people; the lawn was gradually being churned to mud. Even so, far fewer people were there than wanted to be. Curious faces pressed against the wrought-iron fence that ran the perimeter of the White House lawn.

"Gotta motor, Johnny," the president said, patting my

shoulder. "Gotta press the flesh. Later, dude." He meandered off in the direction of the president of the European Council of Ministers, who was conversing with the Brazilian ambassador.

David and I strolled off toward the deck chairs. It was well that we did, for moments after we took our seats, the PA system crackled to life. "Attention," it said. "Ladies and gentlemen, may I have your attention please? Would you be so kind as to take your places? The Strategic Air Command reports that the alien craft has entered the atmosphere. We expect our visitors to be here momentarily."

Everyone scrambled for a seat. The journalists fiddled with their cameras and lights and microphones. I took a cigar from my breast pocket, and found my pocketknife to slice off the end.

David looked upward as I lit the cigar. I followed his gaze. The crowd had grown silent and the sky was darkening. Above us was . . .

A shape that blotted out the sky.

We had expected the aliens to send down a landing craft; instead, their entire ship, all hundred kilometers of it, was hanging over Washington. The ship was so huge that it was impossible to make out the overall shape; the best I can do is to say that it was a vast, grayish mass, covered with wells and protuberances that might make visual sense if viewed in isolation, but that together seemed chaotic. If the aliens had intended to impress us with the capacities of their technology, they had succeeded.

A small craft, shaped like a teardrop, broke off and spiraled toward the White House lawn. The mother ship lifted orbitward.

As the teardrop descended, the Marine Corps Band broke into the theme from *Star Wars*. Eyes shining, David hummed along. The craft touched down in silence.

There was applause as a hatch slid open. Three of the slug-like aliens glided gradually forward. I had that sense, again, of a bad *Star Trek* episode; their costumes were iridescent silver, their glide serene, their enormous, pulsating heads gave an impression of vast intelligence and wisdom.

The president was at the microphone, his very stance indicating that he had set aside the "surfer dude" he preferred to show his friends in favor of the "august statesman" he presented on TV. Welcome to twenty-first century America; even our presidents aren't presidents; they just play them on TV.

"This is indeed an historic day," the president said, nodding sagely. "Captain Sh'tsitsin, Ambassador X'rksis, it is an honor to welcome you to Earth."

The aliens glided across the grass and up the podium stairs. I saw no legs, but wondered how that snail-like locomotion managed the stairs so easily. One of the creatures glided up to the president and accepted the microphone. "Greetings, Mr. President, humans everywhere!" it droned. "Greetings, and peace to all." The bad sci-fi atmosphere was reinforced by the alien's voice: a flat monotone.

"May I introduce you to Dietrich Hapsburg, president of the European Council of Ministers? Takeo Fujaki, the Japanese foreign minister . . . João Canderao, ambassador of Brazil," said the president.

The aliens bobbed their heads in a curious bow to each dignitary. "Charmed," said Hapsburg with a faint accent, returning their bow. "I do hope you'll visit our continent while you're here; we look forward to speaking with you."

"Greetings," said the alien. "Thank you for your kind invitation. Unfortunately, it will not be possible."

"No?" Hapsburg said.

"Please accept our apologies," said another one. "We chose to make first contact here, in the shade of the American White House, because our studies of your media indicate that this is the appropriate venue. We will be departing for New York in a short time, however."

"*New York?*" said the president with the incredulousness of the native Californian. "Why on Earth would you want to go to *there?*"

"In their beneficence," explained the alien captain, "the wisest minds of the galactic community have decreed that all negotiations with fledgling spacegoing races must be through their planetary government. We may not upset the balance of power."

"Planetary . . . what?" said Fujaki.

"Planetary government," droned the alien. "We understand it is headquartered in New York."

"It . . . is?" said the president.

"In fact," said the second alien, "where is the Secretary-General? We expected him to be here to greet us also."

There was silence for a long moment. Then, Canderao said, "The Secretary-General? You mean—of the United Nations?"

"The United Nations?" shouted Hapsburg, his accent becoming more noticeable with distress. "That meaningless talk shop? That pointless facade? That addle-pated . . ."

"The UN," said the president sadly, shaking his head.

"*Iesu Christe,*" said Hapsburg brokenly.

'God help humanity,' thought I.

I DIDN'T CHECK MY VOICE-MAIL UNTIL I GOT BACK TO THE Hyatt; there was an urgent message from Tanisha Grant for me. I called her in California. "Johnson," she said, "MuniBank is balking on the loan."

"What?" I said. "Whatever for?"

She sighed. "I'm not clear on the reasoning," she said, "and I'm looking for an alternative lender. We may be able to float some bonds on the Euromarket—but cash flow for the next few weeks will be awfully tight."

"Damnation," I said. "Would it help any if I talked to MuniBank?"

"It couldn't hurt," she said. "You know, Johnson, you're betting the company on the MDS-316."

I frowned. "All the sales projections look good," I pointed out. "You know, Tanisha, it's not like we're novices at this game. We may be betting the company, but we know precisely what we're doing, and we're reasonably certain of success."

"I'm not arguing, Johnson," Tanisha said. "I'm just pointing out the downside."

"Yes, yes, of course."

I TOOK THE SHUTTLE TO NEW YORK. IT WAS HELL GETting in from La Guardia; half the streets were blocked off by the police, it seemed, to guard the way for diplomatic motorcades. There was a veritable feeding frenzy of global notables at the United Nations—which, unfortunately, was not far from the MuniBank building. I arrived quite late for my appointment, but MuniBank had the courtesy to meet with me nonetheless.

"MuniBank has always had good relations with you, Mr. Mukerjii," said the white-haired executive, "and we hope to continue doing business with you in the future."

"I'm offering you an opportunity to do business with me now," I said with irritation. "I don't understand your problem. The loan is small by comparison to our existing debt. And our sales projections for the MDS-316 . . ."

The executive sighed and stood up from his massive oaken desk. "Mr. Mukerjii," he said, "may I show you something?"

I stood up also. "Certainly."

He threw a hand around my shoulders and took me to the plate-glass window that ran floor to ceiling at the back of the office. "Look out there," he said. "There, that's the New York Stock Exchange, that building. There's the Federal Reserve.

That's where Credit Suisse/First Boston is. Salomon Brothers. Goldman Sachs. Nomura's American headquarters. Over there . . ." He shaded his eyes and peered off across the river. "Yes, over there, on the Jersey side, you can see the back offices for half the banks in the city. And when it's clear enough, you can see the headquarters of Prudential-Bache, off in Newark.

"These buildings, these edifices, these towers of steel and glass—these are wizards' lairs, Mr. Mukerjii," he said. "Through them flows the lifeblood of the world economy, the capital that determines whether an oil refiner in Indonesia may expand, or a coffee grower in Brazil can sell his crop at a profit. The ley lines run here, Mr. Mukerjii; from all over the world, they converge, via satellite link, fiber-optic cable, microwave communication. That is why we wizards are here, because here is the magic, here flows power we may tap."

He looked at me seriously. "But magic is not science," he said. "It is wild, unpredictable; the wizard who seeks to master it rides a dangerous, capricious mount. Many are the mighty who are cast low; and many are the unworthy who are raised high.

"The essence of our magic is risk—risk and the management of risk. We serve the world by providing capital; and when a venture fails, it is capital that suffers first. Always, we search for predictability: stable cash flows, rising sales. But always, we know, the world is wholly unpredictable; so we spread our risks, hedge our bets. And in times of uncertainty, the standards tighten. In times of uncertainty, we demand a premium for the use of money, for then all investments are uncertain. And we lend less, invest less, for in uncertain times, it is best to have investments that are unlikely to decline in value: cash, government securities, precious metals.

"A new factor has appeared within our crystal balls, Mr. Mukerjii; a new element of risk has sped across our Quotrons.

The aliens are among us, and no one can say what this may mean."

He turned back to his desk and pressed a key on his keyboard with one manicured finger. New images and data spread across the screen. "You hope to refinance the loan with a public offering, do you not?" he said.

"Yes," I said. "We'd have—"

"Your stock is down six points since trading began today," he said.

I blinked. Six points? "Well . . . a temporary—"

"The market as a whole is down nearly twenty percent since contact was first made with the alien craft," he said, and sat down.

"Down today," I pointed out, "up tomorrow."

"The market has been quite volatile," he said, nodding. "That's my point."

"Surely," I said, "if we learn new technology from the aliens, this will redound to the benefit of the world economy."

"Ultimately," he said, shrugging. "But some industries will gain, and others will lose. Some investments will turn out to be disastrous; MuniBank has considerable money tied up in an Argentinean dam project, for instance. If the aliens provide us with the secret of controlled fusion . . . You see, any change, even one for the better, turns commitments made in ignorance of that change into malinvestment. Ultimately, we stand to gain. Proximately, we stand to lose. And the greater the change, the more wrenching the transition."

He peered at me. "Will your company gain? Will your company lose? Abracadabra," he said, waving his hands, then shrugging. "The auguries are uncertain; the heavens hold their peace. We can only make judgments based on available information. And our available information says: Be cautious. Be chary. And Mr. Mukerjii, the debt-to-equity ratio of your company is uncomfortably high—and higher as your stock declines.

"Mr. Mukerjii, you have been an important customer, and we hope you will be again. And you have every right to demand that a highly placed executive explain why we are turning down your request for a loan. But turn it down we must."

I sighed. "I'll simply have to find an alternative source of capital, then," I said.

He rose and offered me his hand. "And we wish you all good luck in finding one."

I WAS IN MY ROOM AT THE PLAZA, GAZING MOROSELY AT the gilded chandelier and talking on the phone to Tanisha Grant. "I've been talking to Credit Suisse about a Eurobond issue," she said, "and it's doable, but the interest rate is awfully high."

"Look, Tanisha," I said, "is our shelf registration still current?"

"Yes," she said. That meant we could issue shares on short notice, without the rigmarole of getting new SEC approval.

"Let's sell equity," I said. "Waiting for the market to rise subsequent to the release of the MDS-316 was a good plan, but the market is so volatile now . . ."

"Uh-huh," she said. "Shall I start on it tomorrow morning?"

"Yes," I said. We exchanged a few further words, then hung up.

I lay there for a while longer; there came a knock at the door. "Room service," I thought—I was waiting for dinner—and went to open the door.

Two gentlemen stood in the hall: one black, one white. They wore identical black suits, black sunglasses, and black fedoras. They both had bulges under their arms. One of them flashed a wallet with some kind of ID. "Mr. Mukerjii?" he said. "I'm Agent Epstein, of the United States Secret Service."

Secret Service? Oh, my God. Data crime. David Greenblatt. Before he came to work for me, he'd been a hacker. He claimed he didn't do that anymore, but there was no way to be certain. And the statute of limitations had surely not expired . . . The Secret Service has authority over violations of computer security. They'd finally caught up with him.

And as his employer, I was at risk, too. Invasion of privacy. Wire fraud. RICO.

Oh, my God.

I slammed the door. "You got a warrant, shove it under the door," I yelled.

"Mr. Mukerjii?" said the door.

I ran to the phone and started dialing my lawyer's number.

"Mr. Mukerjii," said the door, "the president would like to see you."

"What?" I said, receiver in hand.

"You don't have to come if you don't want to," said the door, "but he said it was urgent. We have a military plane waiting, and . . ."

I put the phone down and went back to the door. "Is this a trick?" I said.

"No trick, sir," said the door.

I opened the door.

3

TRANSFORM YOUR SPECIES FOR FUN AND PROFIT

I HAD NO IDEA WHAT KIND OF PLANE WE WERE ON. IT seated twelve; Agents Epstein and Stackpole and I were apparently the only ones aboard, although a pilot was presumably ensconced somewhere. It was amazingly quiet, obviously supersonic.

"Where are we going?" I asked.

Two pairs of sunglasses exchanged glances.

"I'm afraid we can't tell you that, sir," said Agent Stackpole. "Security."

"Well then . . . When will I be back?"

"I can't tell you that, either."

"Um. What does the president want to talk to me about?"

"I can't tell you—"

I waved a hand. "Never mind," I said. "What *can* you tell me?"

Sunglasses looked toward me. Agent Stackpole said, "Braves over Orioles six to two?"

THE BEACH INTERSECTED THE SEA AT A SHALLOW ANGLE. Waves gathered a considerable distance out, rising up and breaking not too far from where we stood. Out there on the tropical ocean, three men surfed in perfect formation, a diagonal line down the surface of the wave. The first and last men wore shoulder holsters and guns. The man in the middle was the president.

I was still in yesterday's business suit and feeling disheveled. I squinted into the morning sun.

The president's board tipped over the top of a wave. When I could see him again, he was belly-down on the board and paddling toward me. Ten feet away, he stood up, grabbed the board in one hand, and began to wade. "Yo, Muks!" he shouted. "What's shakin'?"

His escorts waded up the shore, too, sticking close behind him.

He wore nothing but a tan, a pair of baggy, Hawaiian-print swimming trunks, and a broad grin. He handed his board to Agent Epstein and extended his hand toward me, palm upward. Past experience had taught me that he intended I should slap his palm with my own. Therefore, I performed the requisite act, though such a greeting is not customary with me. The president punched me in the biceps.

"I trust you are well, sir," I said.

"Never better," he said. "C'mon, Muks. We need to jabber." He pointed up the beach to a cluster of palm trees and began strolling that way, bare toes digging into the beach. I trotted to keep up, sand pouring into my expensive Italian shoes.

"So," he said, "we been butting heads with the clowns at the UN. God, they're full of it. They think they're gonna run the world because of this."

"Maybe they will," I said. I was getting hot; I could feel sweat soaking into my jacket.

"No chance," he said. "Anyway . . . The slugs say they're gonna leave in four days. If we want to cut a deal, it's got to be before they skip town. Nyanza—the Secretary-General, right? Mapo Nyanza? He wants to impress 'em with how advanced we are by sending a delegation into orbit; he's flying down to French Guiana with two buddies. The Europeans are gonna launch 'em up.

"We tried to get an American—or at least a European or a goddamn Japanese—onto the flight, but no dice. Nyanza's taking some Arab and a Guatemalan. God help us."

We came to a group of canvas recliners under the palms. The president sat down in one and dug out a large thermos and a set of plastic cups. "Daiquiri?" he said.

"Early in the day," I said, sitting down in another of the seats and emptying out my shoes.

He shrugged and poured himself a drink. "But we persuaded Nyanza to let us put together a group of advisors. Scientists, diplomats, businessmen . . . to brief them before they depart, and for consultation during negotiations. I'd like you on the team. Whaddaya say?"

"The advisors will have no direct contact with the aliens?"

"Yup," said the president. He lay back and sipped his daiquiri.

I sighed. "Mr. President, my company is experiencing some, ah, cash-flow problems at present. I don't think I can spare the time. . . ."

"Look, Muks," he said. "It's only for a few days. And, tell you what. If Nyanza makes a deal, someone's gonna have to look at all the technical stuff the aliens give us. Wouldn't you like first crack at that?"

Hmm. "I'm your man, Mr. President," I said.

I still wish I hadn't; at a critical time for MDS, I let myself get sucked in. Of course, the outcome would almost certainly have been the same regardless.

I WAS BURKINA FASO.

At least, that's what the nameplate in front of me said. The ones in front of the adjoining seats said Benin and Burundi.

We were sitting in one of the chambers at the United Nations. It was laid out like an auditorium, seats facing a desk and podium. In front of me was a telephone, headphones for translation, and two buttons—"yes" or "no," for voting. Not that I got a vote.

I was sorry I had agreed to this charade.

Down at the podium sat Nyanza and his cronies. Up here sat the rest of us. Speaker after speaker went to the microphone and gave his spiel.

A new one was coming up now.

"Secretary-General Nyanza, Ambassadors al-Salim and Roguera. I wish to present the thanks of the Royal Academy of the United Kingdom for your gracious invitation to express some thoughts on the possible scientific benefits of contact with our alien visitors. I congratulate Secretary-General Nyanza, especially, on his farseeing efforts to . . ."

I groaned.

They were all like this. First, shamelessly flatter the politicians. Then, make some plea for a special interest group. Make no effort to say anything important. Say nothing that might conceivably offend anyone.

Meaningless blather. Meaningless *boring* blather. Meaningless time-wasting boring bloody-*bedamned* blather.

I was beginning to feel like flying home and firing a dozen people. One always felt better after applying a pair of boots to backsides that richly deserved a booting. Although, honestly, it was this operation, not MDS, that needed a swift kick in the rear.

It wouldn't ever happen, of course.

I tried to tune them out as I waited for the chance to say my piece, but it was impossible not to catch a phrase or two.

From an elderly diplomat with a faint Polish accent: ". . . The repeated references of the aliens to a 'galactic community' and Earth's fitness to join it leads one to believe that your job will be to negotiate our planet's entrance into this community. These negotiations may be analogous to the negotiations prior to a new country's accession to the United Nations, or to the World Trade Organization. A successful conclusion is devoutly to be desired, so that we may reap the benefits of intercourse with other members of the galactic community. . . ."

From an American in a clerical collar: ". . . the dangers our own civilization has mastered in order to survive to the present day. We must assume, therefore, that the aliens are as far beyond us in ethical and moral development as in technology, and that, therefore, their intentions must be wholly benevolent. This supposition is reinforced by their evident desire to share their scientific and technological knowledge with us. They seem to indicate that some 'price' will be exacted for such knowledge, but it is obvious that the aliens must no longer be motivated by such retrograde and immoral motives as greed or desire for material gain. Instead, this 'price' must be a means of motivating us to take actions for our own good, and we should pay whatever they ask willingly and with enthusiasm. . . ."

At least it was not all sweetness and light. This from a Chinese general: ". . . scouting out our military potential. Beware, Mr. Secretary-General! They hope only to gull us into inaction. Then they will attack. The major powers of the world must rearm, against the inevitable assault from the skies. . . ."

But perhaps the most revealing exchange was this one:

EUROPEAN SCIENTIST:
. . . untold scientific and technological benefit.
SEC-GEN. NYANZA:
Any knowledge obtained by the United Nations will, of course, be controlled by the United Nations.
AMBASSADOR ROGUERA:
For the benefit of all mankind, of course.

AMBASSADOR AL-SALIM *(grinning)*:
We must ensure that the benefits are shared . . . equitably.
(Roguera chortles. Nyanza elbows al-Salim in ribs.)

I sighed.

My turn was coming up.

"Secretary-General, Ambassadors, ladies and gentlemen. I will be brief. It is true, as some have pointed out, that products of an alien evolution must think in ways very different from our own. But it is also true that there are only so many ways for strangers, not bound by emotional or biological or tribal ties, to interact. Either the aliens hope to gain something from us, or not. If not, there is no reason for them to contact us. If so, there are only two ways for them to obtain what they want: by force, or with our consent. The former implies war; the latter, trade.

"It is unlikely that the aliens are intent on war. They have not offered violence, nor have they made any effort to display their military prowess. Yet their technology is sufficiently advanced beyond our own that, were they desirous of conflict, they would surely triumph.

"Instead, since their arrival, the aliens have been at pains to point out, time and again, the benefits their advanced technology can offer us. Obviously, they are baiting the hook; obviously, they hope to make a deal. They are traders.

"This is both a relief and a worry. A relief, because we will not be forced to fight a futile war; a worry, because in the negotiations on which you are about to embark, the aliens hold all the cards.

"We do not know what they can provide us. We have no alternative negotiating partners; no other alien craft are in orbit. We do not know what they wish to obtain, and they have been careful not to tell us in advance of formal negotiations. Moreover, when they do tell us, we will be unable accurately to determine the value of whatever it is they desire.

Consider the case of a savage, on some wild coast, faced with, say, Dutch traders. The Dutch say, 'Look at all these lovely beads and trinkets; will you give us this little island here?' To the savage, it seems a fair trade. And so Manhattan is sold for twenty-four dollars.

"Since we do not have the aliens' technology, we cannot know what resources may be valuable to the possessors of such technology. We cannot, therefore, know what we are giving up when we trade.

"Be wary, gentlemen! Be very wary."

I sat down—to less than thunderous applause.

KOUROU SURE WASN'T HOUSTON.

There was a chameleon standing on the window. Its belly was pale green; the pads on its feet made little circles on the glass, where suction gave it footing.

Out there were palm trees and a trillion insects. Across the bay was Devil's Island—no longer a penal colony, of course.

We were in Kourou, French Guiana. Or as our hosts would have insisted, in the *Departement d'Outre Mer*, an integral part of *la Republique Française*, a member state of the European Union.

We were in *Europe*. Never mind that most of the population was black, the adjoining states were Brazil and Suriname, and the principal export was bananas. This was Europe.

A colony? No, no. Heaven forfend. Europe had no colonies. No, that word was a relic of the bad old days of the twentieth century, when man exploited man and racism was rife. No, Guiana was a full part of the French Republic, with the right to elect delegates both to the National Assembly and the European Parliament, and with all the freedoms pertaining to citizens of the European Union everywhere.

Why should Europe want to hold on to this underdeveloped, impoverished, useless little bit of the world?

The complex around us was the answer. For here was the Kourou Launch Facility, Europe's answer to the Kennedy Space Center. From, here, Ariane rockets and ESA shuttles blasted into orbit, to deliver supplies to Europe's burgeoning commercial enterprises in space. There were launches almost weekly, far more frequently than from Kennedy—because Europe had made a firm commitment to space development, while America had not. A commitment, one might point out, that had cost billions of euros and had yet to pay off; and a commitment, in the light of alien contact, that might prove to be what my advisor at MuniBank would term malinvestment.

Why did the Europeans need the site? Why not launch from Italy, say?

Kourou lies less than 400 miles north of the equator. Because Earth rotates once per day, any point on the equator is moving at 30 kilometers per second; any point at the pole is moving at a speed of zero. All things being equal, therefore, by launching a rocket from the equator, you get 30 kilometers per second for free—making it that much easier to get into orbit.

Kourou is a considerably better launch site, from the point of view of orbital energetics, than the U.S. site at Canaveral or the Japanese site in Okinawa; and far, far better than the Baikonur Cosmodrome.

Men and women hunkered over terminals. Reporters stood in the gallery, videocams on shoulders. On the giant screen at the fore of the room was an image of the ESA shuttle, the *Jacques Monnet*.

"Dix—neuf—huit—" said a voice over the public-address system. Flames began to play about the bottom of the launchpad.

"Quatre—trois—deux—un. . . . Nous avons décollage!"

Nearby, a reporter jabbered into a microphone as a cameraman held a videocam to the reporter's face. "And so the

ESA shuttlecraft *Jacques Monnet* rides skyward on a pillar of flame. So Secretary Mapo Nyanza and his brave colleagues launch themselves into space, bearing the hopes and fears of all humanity, to speak for us to the visitors from the stars. Farewell, Mr. Nyanza! We trust you with our destiny."

I gagged.

WE WERE ON CALL. IF THE SECRETARY-GENERAL WANTED to consult us, we were available. And the aliens, as promised, kept the lines of communication open; there, up on the big screen, was a video image of the UN delegation and several aliens, aboard the alien craft—and beyond them, open space. At present, the delegation was being served refreshments: small cakes, and a liquid in squeeze bulbs. I wondered how their stomachs were adapting to free fall.

Leander Huff and I stood in the Kourou control center in front of a computer terminal. Huff made a point of being at every space spectacular, every major launch and flyby; I didn't know how he'd wangled an invitation to this one, but apparently he had connections.

Behind the Secretary-General, out there in space, a darkish, irregular body loomed—an asteroid.

"Damnation," bellowed Huff. "What a farce." Heads turned at the noise.

"What do you mean?" I said.

He waved his pipe, which the staff had refused to let him light. "Asteroid belt's two, two and a half astronomical units out," he shouted. "Time delay between here and there is a good twenty minutes. Suppose the Secretary-General deigned to consult us. Twenty minutes later, we'd hear his question. Twenty minutes after that, he'd get an answer." He stuck the stem of his pipe in his mouth and sucked furiously.

"Point taken," I said, a little sadly. "Albeit, the Secretary-General does not seem inclined to consult anyone but his own good conscience."

Huff snorted—whether at the notion that the Secretary-General had a conscience, or whether said conscience might be good, I cannot say.

OVOID ROBOTS ZIPPED AWAY ON AIR JETS, TAKING WITH them the boxes that had held the refreshments. Other robots zipped around, vacuuming up the free-floating crumbs that, inevitably, the eaters had allowed to escape.

"As we promised," said one of the aliens, "we will be towing this asteroid—containing more metal than you've mined out of your planet in your species' entire history—to near-Earth orbit. Think of it! All the metal you could possibly desire—as a free extra bonus, yours to keep whether or not you accept our offer!"

"Wonderful," said Ambassador Roguera, eyes shining. He put the straw of the squeeze bulb in his mouth and sucked out another mouthful.

"And," said Ambassador al-Salim, "since space is the common heritage of humankind, who shall control this asteroid?"

"Why, the United Nations, of course," chuckled Nyanza. "In the name of all humanity." He and al-Salim grinned at one another.

"But that's not all you get!" said one of the aliens. "We'll happily provide you with complete libraries of all our scientific and technological knowledge, together with a device to translate into your terrestrial languages. See how easily we tow this asteroid? Think of the things you can do with such power!"

"Yes, you, too, can transform your planet!" said another of the aliens, taking up the spiel. "Put an end to war and strife! End hunger and disease! Settle your surplus population on gorgeous paradise worlds (available at modest additional charge)."

"Think of it!" said a third alien. "The splendored vistas of alien worlds! A universe of energy and dead matter, waiting to be transformed into riches for your people! A wealth of resources to enrich all humanity!"

"New frontiers," said the first alien, "new minds, new experiences. A universe so vast it dwarfs all human aspiration."

"Wonder," supplied another slug. "Awe at creation. The quiet rapture of scientific discovery."

"And all yours," said the first alien, "at one low, low price!"

"Yes, yes!" said Secretary Nyanza. "Think, Rashid, Raoul. Think what it would mean for the United Nations to control access to such technology."

"We would see that deserving countries have access to it," said Roguera severely, "instead of neocolonialist environment-raping bloodsuckers."

"It would mean that at last our organization would be accorded the respect it so richly deserves," murmured al-Salim.

"It would mean," said Nyanza, "that we would control the means by which our world might enrich itself. And—I have observed, in the course of my career, that wealth has a tendency to—ah—*encompass* all those who stand in close proximity."

"Quite so," said al-Salim.

"No, no," said Roguera excitedly. He gesticulated, and his drink bulb went flying across the alien craft, to hit a bulkhead and squirt juice on one of the aliens' silvery robes. The creature wriggled in disgust, but did not comment. "We must have no thought of personal gain," Roguera said. "We must manage the information purely for the benefit of all humanity."

"Yes, yes, of course," said Nyanza. "We would act from only the most selfless of motives. It is wise, my friends," he said, turning to the aliens, "that you chose to deal with the disinterested representatives of all mankind, rather than with selfish and parochial national interests."

"But tell us," said al-Salim, "tell us of this low, low price you wish us to pay."

"It is nothing," said one alien.

"A mere bagatelle," said another.

"The planet Jupiter," said a third.

"And in return," said the first alien, "we offer the stars! Interstellar travel! The miracle of eternal life! Controlled fusion! Unlimited energy! Unlimited resources! An end to want, hatred, warfare, fear! Yes, in just a few decades you, too, can transform your civilization!"

"But this offer is only available for a limited time!" said another of the slugs. "We're on a rather tight schedule, we're afraid. We've got a hot date at 61 Ursae Majoris next week, and have to leave within the next twenty-four hours."

"Jupiter?" said the Secretary-General in some surprise.

Roguera, al-Salim, and Nyanza looked back and forth. Then, the Secretary-General shrugged, and said, "Well, why not? What is it good for?"

"NO! NO! NO!" BELLOWED HUFF, HURLING HIS PIPE AT the screen. It fell well short and bonked a technician on the head.

Huff hustled off and got someone to send Nyanza an urgent message telling him to stop.

Twenty minutes later, the Secretary-General got the message. But by then, it was too late. The Treaty of Ceres was signed.

WORLD OPINION WAS WITH THE SECRETARY-GENERAL. What good was Jupiter? It was too far away, and put out too much radiation for its satellites to be useful. And we got everything the aliens knew in exchange.

That evening, I visited Huff in his room at the barracks near the launch site. He lay on his bed in his underclothes, looking defeated. It was humid and hot; the overhead fan did little more than push the mosquitoes around.

"Why were you so upset?" I said. "Admittedly, Nyanza was

a fool not to bargain. But why do you consider Jupiter such a loss?"

He cranked himself up out of bed and stumbled over to a heavy book that sat among his luggage. "Here," he grunted, heaving it open and pointing to a line of figures. "Here, look at this."

This is what it said:

PLANET	MASS (10**24 kg)
Mercury	0.33022
Venus	4.8690
Earth	5.9742
(Moon)	0.073483
Mars	0.64191
Jupiter	1898.8
Saturn	568.50
Uranus	86.625
Neptune	102.78
Pluto	0.015

"So?" I said.

"So?" he grunted. "So Jupiter is seventy percent of the free mass in the solar system."

I didn't see his point. He must have seen the incomprehension on my face. "Think, man!" he bellowed. "They may have faster-than-light travel, but it can't be cheap. I doubt anyone imports raw materials from other star systems. So all we have to work with in this solar system, all the resources we'll ever be able to use, in the entire history of our species from this moment forward, is out there, in the planets and asteroids and comets we can reach.

"And seventy percent of it is tied up in Jupiter.

"Which we just sold—for the equivalent of the Grolier Encyclopedia on CD-ROM!"

It took a moment to digest that. "But most of it is hydrogen," I pointed out, "and down a steep gravity well, and subject to killing radiation besides."

Huff shrugged contemptuously. "Believe what you will," he said.

4

A $HARP BLOW WITH A 2 BY 4

AH, HOME AT LAST.

Home at the office. The deep leather chair. The smell of crisply conditioned air. The view of the Valley. The computer, the phone, the T1 line, the bottle of single-malt scotch whiskey in the bottom drawer.

After a week of futile effort, it felt good to be back. I was looking forward to clearing out my in-basket, dealing with accumulated e-mail, sitting in on a meeting or two—spending a few days getting back into the swing of things. But such was not to be.

Tanisha Grant was waiting for me in my office. "Back from your Caribbean vacation?" she said nastily. "Have a pleasant time?"

I raised an eyebrow. "French Guiana is not what one would call a tropical paradise," I said, "unless one finds mosquito netting, insect repellent, and eighty percent humidity intoxicatingly romantic. I forbear to mention the luxurious army barracks–style accommodations. Whence this hostility?"

"We've been going to hell in a handbasket," Tanisha said. "Our cash position is close to nonexistent."

I was alarmed. "But the share offering—"

"Failed," she said.

"That's not—"

"Oh, the investment bank gave us a guaranteed price," Tanisha said. "They're stuck with about eighty percent of the offering. Our share price nose-dived on news of the sale; the analysts said it indicated a lack of confidence on the part of management, and—Well. We only raised half of what we expected to raise. Based on expected sales for the MDS-316, Hsieh started retooling the Singapore plant as well as the one in Bangkok, draining our reserves further; I argued against the move, but Fred Sharps voted with him, and David was about as much help as you might expect—"

"What's the bottom line?" I said.

"We barely have enough money to cover this week's payroll," she said.

"What are our options?"

"You tell me. We certainly can't float more stock. We can't sell bonds because the market for junk is dead and we aren't investment grade anymore. We can't get a bank loan. What's left? Should I go out on the sidewalk with a little tin cup and a sign that says, 'I am a homeless Vietnam vet'?"

"Tanisha, Tanisha, Tanisha," I said. "You're supposed to solve these problems, not—"

"Or maybe you should take next week's payroll, fly to Vegas, and bet it all on number thirty-two."

"Tanisha—"

"I spent the last week on the phone lying to suppliers. 'Oh, Ah do beg yo' pardon, Mr. Salesman, suh,' " she said. " 'I just *cain't* think what might have happened to your l'il ol' bill. We all'll cut you a new check just as *soon* as we can.' "

"I'm sorry, Tanisha, but—"

"Christ on a stick, Mukerjii. We've been running this operation like the corner candy store. You can't float the company by sticking it to your suppliers, not for more than maybe a week. And if I wanted to make a career in lying on the phone, I could have started a boiler-room brokerage and made a fortune victimizing widows and orphans."

"But—"

"If we don't come up with some cash by the end of the quarter, it won't be me yelling at you," she said. "It'll be a bankruptcy judge."

"Tanisha, the Consumer Electronics Show is in two months," I said. "Don't worry about it. The MDS-316 will cause a sensation, and we'll write a truckload of orders. With those in hand, we can go to any bank or venture capitalist in the country and get the money we need. Surely you can keep things together for that long."

"I'll do my best, Johnson," she said, shaking her head. "I'll do my best. But you'd better produce some sales, or our collective ass is grass."

WITH THIS MUCH PRESSURE AT WORK, HOME WAS MORE of a relief than ever before. As usual, Maureen met me with a big smile and a bigger drink.

"Hi there, soldier," she whispered in my ear. "Back from the wars?"

And I felt the tightness I always felt when she was in this mood. "Indeed," I said. "How have you been?"

"Lonely," she said, kissing the side of my neck.

Well.

RATHER LATER, WE SNUGGLED IN THE HOT TUB. EVEN with the bright lights of San Jose down in the valley, the stars above were crisp and clear. I told her about our cash-flow problem.

She frowned. "You can't find an alternative to MuniBank?" she said.

I shook my head. "All the banks seem shaken," I said. "And another public offering is clearly not in the cards. Oh, we'll pull through, but the MDS-316 had better sell as well as we've been hoping."

She moved away from me, sidling around the side of the

tub. "Do you . . . do you want to borrow some money?" she said, looking away toward San Jose.

"Eh? Oh, no, no. Nothing like that. Six figures wouldn't do it, anyway. And—I don't think we should risk your money, in any event. If worse comes to worst, and the company goes under, we'll need your money to live on."

"Yes," she said. "We will."

And was there the teeniest stress on the word "we"?

Suddenly, I was a little chill, even in the steaming water of the tub. I knew why I had married Maureen; and I knew why she had married me.

It was not, I mused, frowning a bit and nursing my drink, as if I needed additional motivation to ensure the company's success.

"NEW YORK?" SAID DAVID, BLINKING IN A CONFUSED WAY. "But we've been working on some really nifty VR interface ideas, and—"

"Can't your staff work on it in your absence?" I said.

"Uh—sure. But—why New York?"

"Look here," I said. "I went to French Guiana at the president's behest for one reason, and one reason only: to get first crack at the alien library. It's going to revolutionize the world! If even a tiny iota of what the aliens claimed is true, they've left us the secret of controlled fusion, faster-than-light travel, extended life span . . . And we have first crack. Or anyway, we'll be one of the first groups to take a look at it. We can get a jump on the competition. If we can be the first out the door with a major product exploiting alien technology . . . We have a shot at turning Mukerjii Data Systems into a major industry player. I'm not going to give this up."

So David went to New York.

TIME PASSED.

The market was down. The world was waiting for the

other shoe to drop. The aliens had come and gone and—now what? Scientists were studying the data they'd left us, but nothing revolutionary had yet been reported.

Meanwhile, I danced, like a *gringo* in the hands of *banditos*. ("Dance, *Yanqui!* Dance! *Bang! Bang! Bangbang!* Har har har.") I danced madly to keep the company afloat until the day of CES.

There were a million technical issues to iron out. They were having problems tuning the display lasers; the prototypes had worked fine, but it was another matter scaling up to assembly-line production. One of our suppliers was providing us with too high a rate of defective chips. A Thai general wanted a bribe; if we wanted our Bangkok factory ready on time, it was advisable to give it to him.

And there was the show to prepare for. The display had to be okayed. Advertising copy needed to go out to the trade-show program book. We needed flyers, posters, an electronic press kit, and other promo materials.

And someone had to tap-dance our creditors. After Tanisha lied to them six or eight times, she began to lose a certain degree of credibility. It was my turn to start lying.

I immersed myself in work. There's always a rush around the time of a show. Trade shows are the punctuation of the working year, the times by which you must produce. And a lot was riding on this one. The company's future, perhaps.

So I did little more than notice when Secretary-General Nyanza won the Nobel Peace prize, and when another alien ship—a different group, apparently—arrived in orbit.

At last, CES came around.

The day before we left, Tanisha came into my office, pecked me on the cheek, and whispered in my ear: "Come back with orders—or don't come back."

Charming woman, Tanisha.

Maureen, at least, provided a warmer good-bye.

• • • •

THE SOUK, THE COUNTY FAIR, THE TRADE SHOW—THEY'RE
all the same. An energy runs through them. Here we are to
show our wares, to scout out the competition, to see old
friends and old enemies, to get drunk, and to celebrate ac-
complishments or rail against bitter fate. A trade show is a
high-pressure sales call, a family reunion, and a giant party,
all rolled into one.

I always look forward to trade shows, but this was going to
be a special one. We had the MDS-316; not vaporware, but
the actual machine. We'd even air freighted a few thousand
into our warehouse in Long Beach to fill early orders; the rest
were proceeding from Thailand at a more sedate rate, inside
an Evergreen Lines container ship.

Our booth was a modest one. We had enough space for a
few chairs and a sitting area, product samples, plenty of
lighted panels and full-color displays—but no rotating holo-
grams, no seminude models, no brass bands or audiovisual
presentations or banks of blinking lights.

We didn't need spectacle. What we had was spectacular
enough.

Let me present the MDS-316, the first full-color holographic computer display retailing for under $10,000. No,
ma'am, there's no problem with the strobe rate; as you can
see, the display refreshes faster than the human eye . . . That's
the Huntington gardens, ma'am. In LA. Yes, it's beautiful,
isn't it? No, it requires no special processor. Any standard
microcomputer operating at ten gigahertz or more can . . .
Yes, that's our price. Delivered, yes—anywhere in the U.S.
Overseas, we . . . Ah, in orders of twenty-four units or more,
we can offer a discount of forty—Yes. Thank you. I'm very
glad to hear that. Thirteen gross? Wonderful.

That, at least, is how I anticipated the pitch would go.

But the booth was practically empty. None of the sales-
people could figure out why.

It wasn't until I broke for lunch that I found out. I wandered around the floor until I came across a large, roped-off area. A huge line of customers ran toward it. Inside the area was nothing but bare floor—no chairs, no decoration; nothing. About this bare space wandered a few men and women in business dress; some of them seemed to be talking to open air.

In front of the ropes was a more normal display—if you call a floor-to-ceiling hologram running with an animated sales pitch to be normal.

"What's this?" I asked someone in line.

"Dunno," he said. "This is the aliens' booth. I got in line to see what they got. Buddy of mine raved about it."

"Aliens?" I said. "From that new ship in orbit? I didn't know they were at the show."

"Got in too late to reserve space in the program book," he said. "But they're here."

"Glad to see my staff is on top of developments," I muttered in annoyance, and got in line.

"Welcome to the space age," said a hologram of someone who looked like a young Ronald Reagan. "Your friends from the stars, the crew of the *sht'kl'p* ship *Pedantic*, welcome you! For the first time ever on this planet, we present the sensation of the galaxy: direct corticostimulation. An experience so . . ."

Egad. Worse than a television commercial. Young Ronald blathered on, saying absolutely nothing, until I got to the front of the line.

A young man—a live person—greeted me. I wondered at the complete absence of aliens; later, I learned that the *sht'kl'p* were methane-breathers and had hired a human ground crew. "Hi," he said. "May I have your name? And your company?" He readied a palmtop to write down the information.

Ah—yes. When scouting the competition, you don't want them to know that you *are* the competition. It's better practice to have them believe you're a potential customer. "James

Fenster Meriweather," I said. "Meriweather Electronics." I handed him a business card that said the same. One must be prepared for these eventualities.

"I'm not familiar with your company," he said. "May I ask . . . ?"

"We're a small retail chain," I said. "Six computer stores in Ohio and Kentucky." The card bore the address of a PO box in Louisville.

"Good," he said. "If you will, please walk through the opening in the ropes . . . this way."

I did so.

What . . . ?

I was standing on crystal sands by a sparkling sea. The water was the clear, light blue seen only in ads for Caribbean vacations. The air was lushly warm—but, curiously, not uncomfortably so for a man in full business dress.

Where was the convention hall?

A maiden strolled toward me across the sand. She wore a saffron sari and sandals; one nostril was pierced, and her forehead bore a caste dot. She smiled prettily and said something in Hindi.

"I am sorry," I said. "I'm afraid I'm rusty even in Bengali, and have never learned Hindi. I would prefer to converse in English."

"Certainly, sir," she said. "Am I to your satisfaction?" She turned a profile and sucked in her stomach to display her, ah, features.

The expression on my face must have puzzled her. "I'm sorry," she said. "Is there something wrong? Perhaps—" The alto voice turned to bass. Suddenly, a tanned and rather muscular young man stood before me. "—your sexual preferences vary?"

I blinked. "Ah . . . No," I said. "I am heterosexual. But what has that got to do with . . . ?"

The Hindu girl was back. "We prefer to make our customers as—comfortable as possible," she said, smiling with the tip of her tongue between her lips.

"I see," I said. "And what precisely is it that you are selling?"

She offered me her arm, and we began to stroll down the beach. "Why, this," she said. "All this. And this."

Suddenly, we stood on the Ginza in Tokyo. It was night; multicolored neon shone chaotically through the rain. She was Japanese, and wore a designer raincoat.

"And this," she said. Now she was red-skinned—a deep maroon, not the color of Native American—and clad in something with beads that hid very little. We stood on a wide desert, a bit like Arizona, before a canyon so vast that the Grand Canyon would be lost in its depths. Nearby, a six-limbed, green-scaled animal the size of a horse cropped on purple vegetation.

"Where are we?" I said.

"The image is of Mars," she said. "With some . . . artistic license. But where are we? Inside a convention center in Houston, of course. Where would you like to be?"

I considered, then said, "Versailles." And there we were, with the glittering mirrors and the parquet floor. She wore an elaborate silk gown and gloves that came to her biceps; her blond hair was piled at least two feet high. A ship model floated among the curls. The caste dot had drifted down her face and was now a beauty mark on one cheek.

"You see?" she said.

"I do see," I said. "The illusion is perfect. And the display rate is astonishing."

"And hear," she said. Suddenly, a bewigged orchestra was before us, playing something Mozartean. "And smell," she said, and I could sense the perfume she wore. "And feel," she said, pulling me into an embrace. "And taste," she whispered, her tongue intruding into my mouth.

"Yes, yes," I said, pulling away, realizing that I must be

standing on a bare floor somewhere, kissing air to the bemusement of passersby. "But what would happen if I sat
down on one of those illusory chairs by the wall?"

"You would feel the presence of a chair," she said, "but,
unbeknownst to you, your body would fall to the ground. We
are engaged in direct cortical stimulation. We can either sup-
plement the evidence of your own senses—for instance, as
you walk about here, you feel the true ground beneath your
feet, and I am steering you to prevent you from crossing the
ropes or bumping into another customer—or we can replace
that evidence entirely. We are doing so with the sense of
sight; you see Versailles, not the convention hall. We could
superimpose the images"—and there was the hall, and Versailles, simultaneously—"or not," she said, and Houston went
away.

"Fantastic," I said. "Virtual reality."

"With," she agreed, "any physical interface—no helmet,
no implant into the brain. And complete sensory support.
And the ability to generate complete illusions upon the user's
command."

"Without what computers is it compatible?"

"Computers of terrestrial manufacture are incapable of exploiting the VR-1 to anything like its fullest extent," she said.
"Consequently, we are selling the processor and display unit
as a single device. You can connect the processor to any terrestrial LAN or display device, if you like; it will deduce the
appropriate communications protocol. And since the processor alone is approximately six trillion times as powerful as a
Cray supercomputer, a single unit can provide for the processing needs of any human company."

"What?" I said.

"Welcome to the wonders of interstellar technology," she
said, smiling. She had a nice dimple.

"But this—this means the end of our entire computer industry," I protested.

She shrugged. "Perhaps," she said. "But consider the boon to computer users. And we are offering retailers a very generous discount rate. How many units do you think Meriweather Electronics can sell?"

"What—what's the suggested retail price?" I asked.

"Just under ten thousand bucks."

In shock, I mumbled something. I barely had the presence of mind to avoid ordering a shipment then and there. I stumbled back toward our booth, forgetting about lunch and my grumbling stomach.

The VR-1 might mean the end of our entire computer industry. It *certainly* meant the end of the MDS-316. Who needs animated hologsams when you have complete illusion?

Disaster. Unparalleled disaster. Not only had we no orders, we'd invested millions in useless inventory.

There was only one hope, one tiny, forlorn hope: that David Greenblatt had found something useful.

"Hiya, boss," said David morosely over the phone. "Can I come home yet?"

"David," I said. "We've got a major problem." And I told him about the aliens and their virtual-reality machine.

"Neato!" he said. "When can I get a look at one?"

"Forget that!" I yelled at him. "You're our only hope! You've got to find something in that technical data! And you aren't coming back to California until you do!"

"But boss," he whined, "we're getting nowhere. There's just reams of this stuff. Getting a grip on it is gonna take years. . . ."

"David," I said, "listen to me. MDS is declaring bankruptcy."

"What? Ohmigod. I'm out of a job?"

"No, you idiot. Declaring bankruptcy just means you don't have to pay your bills—for a while. We'll still be in business. But you've got to come up with something, and quick, or the bankruptcy court will close us down."

"Roger," said Greenblatt. "Wilco."

5

$77.42

"WHAT'S NEXT ON THE DOCKET?" SAID THE JUDGE, TAKing his glasses off and pinching the bridge of his nose.

My mouthpiece got up. "If it please the court," he said, "there is the bankruptcy of Mukerjii Data Systems, Ltd., incorporated in the state of California and—"

"This is a Chapter Eleven filing?" said the judge.

"Yes, sir. I have here—"

"Counselor, I'm sorry to cut you short," said the judge, "but in these unhappy economic conditions the bankruptcy courts are overloaded. If we can get to the heart of the matter, I'd appreciate—"

"Yes, Your Honor," said my lawyer. "I don't believe we need to take up much of your time. This is a fairly standard Chapter Eleven filing. MDS has experienced adverse cash flow as a consequence of the introduction of alien technology in its main area of business, and is seeking protection from its creditors, among whom are Monsoon Microsystems, Evergreen Lines, and MuniBank—"

"They've all had time to review your filing and are in agreement with your recovery plan?"

"Er . . . all except MuniBank, Your Honor."

"Very well. Is a representative of MuniBank here?"

Another Brooks Brothers-and-vest stood up. "I have the

honor of representing MuniBank, Your Honor. We have a motion to transform this to a Chapter Seven filing." I winced; Chapter Seven meant liquidation, rather than continuation under current management.

The judge sighed. "Give me the gist, please," he said.

"Um, yes, Your Honor," said the MuniBank lawyer. "Mukerjii Data System owes my client approximately twenty-three million dollars at the present time, making us their single largest creditor. MDS is in the business of manufacturing display and sound systems for microcomputers, a business which our research indicates is likely to experience dramatic change as a consequence of—"

"Counselor, when I say gist, I mean gist."

"Er—yes, Your Honor. Very well. The gist is that they've got about as much chance of pulling their company out of the hole as a hound dog has of screwing a fence post. We say, close 'em down and sell 'em off before more money goes down the tubes."

"Objection!" said my lawyer.

"This isn't a trial, it's a hearing, Counselor," said the judge. He turned to the MuniBank lawyer. "In other words," he said, "you recommend liquidation."

"That's correct, Your Honor."

The judge sighed. "In that case," he said, "I suppose I shall actually have to read all this damned paperwork. Will we need to hold an additional hearing, or will both parties accept my subsequent judgment?"

"Er—subject to the right to file for an extension or make additional filings should circumstances change . . ."

"Yes, yes, of course."

"MuniBank would be happy with that," said Brooks Brothers.

"And MDS?" said the judge.

My lawyer looked at me. I nodded wearily. We needed the

protection of Chapter Eleven, and soon, or our creditors would start seizing our assets.

"We agree," said my lawyer.

The judge banged his gavel. "Right, then," he said. "Next."

I DROVE INTO THE OFFICE PARKING LOT AND WHEELED the Jag toward my reserved space. I got out; the hot sun was a shock after conditioned air. I locked up and slammed the door.

Normally, the lot is pretty deserted during working hours; but, oddly, a crowd stood between me and the office building. I wandered over to see what was up.

A bunch of the engineers were there, standing in front of a red convertible. ". . . zero to the speed of sound in sixty seconds," one of them was saying, to oohs and ahs.

What . . . ?

I looked more closely. What was that nameplate on the hood? Was it . . . No, not Toyota. Not Mazda. Not BMW, Maserati, or even Ford.

I couldn't read the damn thing. It was in some alien squiggle.

The "car," if one might term it such, floated a good two feet off the ground. Hovercraft? Antigrav? I couldn't say.

"What's the top speed?" said one of the engineers.

"Mach six," said the owner proudly.

"What about sonic booms?" asked another geek.

"There aren't any," said the owner. "Antisound generators cancel out the noise. I could buzz you at supersonic speeds, and all you'd hear would be a sound like a bee."

The geeks were impressed. So was I.

"How much does it sell for?" I asked.

"Thirty thousand dollars," the owner said.

Yoiks.

MDS was not the only company likely to go under.

Although—something Huff had said came back to me. Could it really be economically viable to ship whole automobiles across interstellar distances?

"Where's it made?" I asked.

The owner turned to me, blinking in surprise as he recognized his ultimate boss. He pointed to a decal in the window.

Below the alien squiggle was an English translation: "Made with pride on Callisto."

"Callisto?" I said.

"One of the moons of Jupiter," supplied an engineer.

Perhaps Huff had been right about Jupiter after all.

I MET DAVID AT THE AIRPORT. AS WE HUSTLED DOWN THE corridor toward baggage claim, I asked him what he'd found.

"Bupkis," he said sadly, searching through his pockets for his baggage-claim stubs.

"Right," I said with irritation. "Back to New York for you."

"But boss," he whined, "it's hopeless. There's just nothing we can use. Not without years of work."

"Why not?" I said.

We came to the baggage carousel. "Look," David said, "suppose I was to give copies of the *Encyclopaedia Britannica* and the *Rubber Book* to an Aztec. Now, this Aztec is a specialist in obsidian knives. He makes some of the best darn obsidian knives in all of Mazatlán. And here is the wisdom of the future, the sum total of its scientific and technical knowledge. Great! It's gotta be able to tell him how to make some really spiffy obsidian knives, right?" He broke off, digging hands frantically into pockets. Where were those claim stubs?

I reached over and dug my fingers into the plastic protector in David's pocket. Sure enough, there were his stubs. "But he can't read English," I prompted.

"Thanks," David said, taking the stubs. "No, forget about the language problem. The aliens provided translation. Say we give the Aztec all this stuff in Azteckian. Or whatever. He can read it, sure enough, but there isn't much about obsidian knives in there.

"If he's really, really smart, he'll puzzle out that they apparently don't use obsidian for much in the future. He may even figure out that they make knives out of metal. But he knows gold doesn't work too well. What other kinds of metal are there?" His head was swinging back and forth now, following various bits of luggage around the carousel. He focused on one bag and, preparing to grab it, stuffed his claim stubs in his rear pants pocket.

"There's steel," I said. "Most knives are made out of steel."

"Sure," he said, yanking a duffel bag off the carousel. "The *Britannica* talks about steel. But what is it? It's made out of iron. What's that? A kind of metal. How do you make it? Well, you smelt the iron ore in a blast furnace . . . But what is iron ore? What's a blast furnace? What's *smelting*, for Quetzalcoatl's sake?"

He grabbed another bag.

"Are they that far ahead of us?" I asked.

He nodded. "Look, from everything we know, the rate of growth of scientific knowledge is exponential. Try projecting that ahead a century or two—and they've been starfarers for thousands of years. To even begin to do something useful with what they know, we have to build the tools to build the tools . . . It'll take decades just to figure out where to start." He grabbed a third bag, picked up all three, and headed for the exit. Then, he stopped, dropped the bags, and began searching through his pockets, a look of panic on his face.

I sighed. "Your rear pants pocket," I said.

He blinked, and reached for the pocket. The stubs were there. "Thanks," he said.

"The least of your worries," I said sadly.

He stuffed the stubs in his mouth and picked up the three bags. "Mmmph?" he said through the stubs. We came to the exit; with some distaste, the guard took the stubs from David's mouth and went to check the tags on the bags.

"Your main worry," I said, "is your job."

He looked stricken. "Huh? Boss? What do you—"

"Oh, I'm not firing you," I said wearily. "But we're up shit creek, I'm badly afraid."

I HAD A SHEAF OF PAPER ON MY DESK: A PRINTOUT OF THE names of all the employees of Mukerjii Data Systems. I was going down the list with a red pen, checking the ones to fire: this one. And that one. And I never liked him. Who was this? If I didn't know her name, she couldn't be too vital, right? Fire her, too. And that one. And that one. . . .

The phone rang. Damn. I picked it up. "Grant!" screamed a male voice. "You bitch! Three hundred thousand bucks isn't your goddamn water bill! I want payment and I want—"

I hung up and sighed. Obviously, he'd wanted Tanisha Grant and had got the wrong extension. I went back to the list. That one. And that one . . .

Tanisha walked in just as the phone rang again. I waved to acknowledge her presence, and picked up the phone. "Hello, Mukerjii here," I said absentmindedly.

"You," said a voice that sounded like its owner ate gravel for breakfast. "Good. Rather have da boss than da flunky. Dis is Morty. Morty Caparula, remember me, Mukerjii?"

I did, unfortunately. CalWest Commercial. They owned this office building. The rent was three months in arrears. "Er . . . How do you do, Mr. Caparula?"

Tanisha smiled at me and winked.

"Not so hot," Caparula said. "I got a royal pain in da garbonzo. Da name of dis pain is Mukerjii. *Capisce?*"

"I'm afraid . . ."

"Now some people, when dey got a pain in da garbonzo,

dey take two Tylenol. But me, I come from, heh, from a good family. Y'unnerstand, Mr. Mukerjii?"

"Ah . . ."

"We deal wit' pain a little different," Caparula said. "We tough it out. Wit' red-hot tweezers, sometimes."

"Ahem," I said. "Ah . . . We're currently working on a re-capitalization plan, and I . . ."

"Two days," Caparula said, and hung up. I did likewise.

"Ah, good old Morty Caparula," said Tanisha. "What a sweetheart."

"How did he get through to me?" I asked.

"I programmed my phone to forward all calls to your desk," Tanisha said.

"What? Why did you do that?"

She shrugged. "Somebody's got to take those calls," she said. "And it ain't gonna be me. Good-bye, Johnson." She held out a hand.

"Good-bye? But Tanisha, I need you now more than ever. When we reorganize, we'll—"

She let her hand drop and snorted. "Dream on, Mukerjii," she said. "It's over."

"Come on, Tanisha," I said. "You know bankruptcy isn't the end. It's just a way to get protection from your creditors . . ."

She shook her head wearily. "I've gone down with companies before, Johnson," she said a little sadly, "and I know when one is beyond all hope. This is the end of the line. Bye. Have a nice life."

And she turned and walked out the door.

The phone rang. I hesitated then picked it up.

"Listen to me, you silly slut!" screamed a voice.

"Pistolera Pizza," I said. "Especial today on anchovy, free weeth large pie. You have order, *si?*"

There was silence on the line for a moment. Then a voice muttered, "Sorry. Wrong number." There was a click.

I picked up the list again. That one and that one and him
and her . . .

I WALKED DOWN THE HALLWAY TOWARD DAVID'S OFFICE,
passing empty cubicles. The ceiling lights were off; no point
in keeping them lit, with so few employees remaining. Outside, the sun shone through the drab orange of photochemical
smog.

Down at the front desk, I could hear the phone ringing.
There wasn't any secretary to answer it. I ducked into a cu-
bicle and took the call.

"Hello?" I said cautiously. I didn't want another damned
creditor.

"Hello, may I have Mr. Mukerjii, please?" said a voice.

Still cautious, I said, "Mr. Mukerjii is unavailable at present. May I take a message?"

The voice harrumphed. "Very well," it said with some irritation. "This is Omar Captious, of Captious, Invidious,
Conniving & Cruik." Ah. My lawyer. "Tell him that Judge
Meander has ruled on the bankruptcy filing—and in favor of
the MuniBank motion to make it a Chapter Seven."

Oy.

"Is that all?" I said sadly.

"Yes," snapped Captious. "If Mukerjii wants me, he has
my number."

Well. That was it. The court would appoint a liquidator,
and in a matter of days, we'd be out of business.

I stared out the window at the smog for a moment. There
was an odd, electronic noise from down the hall: "Zzzzz-
ZDOOM. ZzzzzDOOM. ZzzzzBRAKAKAK. Ta-dump-da-
dah!"

I walked through David's doorway. Little alien ships descended toward a plain. Missiles leapt to intercept. David
whacked feverishly at the keyboard.

"Greenblatt!" I said. He jumped, hit the keyboard—and

the graphics disappeared. Text rolled upward across the screen.

"Uh . . . Hi, boss," he said.

"What was that?" I asked.

He looked sheepish. "Just a game," he said.

I sighed. "I thought you were trying to get into the UN database from here," I said.

"I got in," he said. "They haven't updated security since I was in New York."

"Oh, good," I said. "You've got the alien library on-line?"

"Yup," he said. "I've got the computer performing an automated search. Plenty of processing power left over to run a little game."

"Okay, okay, David, I'm not criticizing."

"It's not going to work, you know," he said.

"Why not?" I said. "I accept your conclusion that we can't adopt alien technology whole cloth, that it's too far advanced beyond our own. But shouldn't their historical records be able to tell us what the next step after our own technology is? Why can't we improve incrementally?"

He sighed. "Look," he said. "Do you know what a spinning jenny is?"

I drew a blank. "No," I said.

"There's a whole history of the development of spinning technology in the seventeenth and eighteenth centuries," David said. "There were dozens, hundreds of different machines, different makers; tiny, incremental, gradual improvements. A lot of the history we can track from patent records. But a lot is lost. Each improvement in the jenny was an important development to people of the day, as important as the development of a new microprocessor, or a new generation of DRAMs today. But—who knows or cares now? It's all ancient history. And not very interesting history, at that. People would rather read about wars and revolutions than the development of a new way to twist thread.

"You want me to search for alien records about the development of holographic display technology, I'll do it. But I don't expect to find anything useful. It's too long ago, for them, and too minor, and too unimportant."

He shrugged, and picked his nose.

Morosely, I contemplated things for a while: life, existence, business, the exigencies of nature. My multimillion-dollar business, my manifold employees, my leading-edge technology; it had all boiled down to this, lines of text zipping up the screen of a computer, a hopeless search for something that wasn't there.

David went back to his game, and I sat there for, oh, I don't know, an hour or two.

And then there was a noise in the hall. There shouldn't have been; no one else should have been on our floor. I went to take a look.

A man was walking toward the freight elevator, carrying a computer, cables drifting behind him. He was a big man, biceps the size of Kaiser rolls, black, wearing dirty jeans and a grimy tank top.

How had he gotten in?

"Hey!" I shouted. "You! Where are you going with that?"

He turned to me and shielded his torso with the computer. "You leave me alone, man!" he shouted, backing off. "You just leave me alone!" I saw that his shoulders and arms were solid muscle. He had a three-day growth of beard. He was sweating.

Another huge man appeared. He was white, with a scraggly beard and the large belly you see in overmuscled men—solid muscle, every pound of it. He had a swastika tattooed on his left biceps, along with the words, "Ride Hard and Die Free." He scuttled around a corner, dived behind a partition, and crouched, letting only his head appear above the partition. "No violence!" he shouted. "No violence. Keep it calm. Rashid, stay out of sight. Jesus, be ready to go for help."

I was rather bewildered. There I stood, in a hand-tailored Hong Kong suit, a pudgy, middle-aged Bengali-American; and these hulking monsters were, to all appearances, deathly afraid of me.

"I don't see no gun," said the black man.

"Don't mean nothing," said the fellow with the beard. "He could have a dozen buddies around the corner."

"I say," I said. "This is absurd. What the devil are you doing here?"

My friend with the beard stood up and came rather hesitantly toward me. He pulled a piece of paper out of his black-leather vest. "Acme Office Supplies," he said. "Got authorization from the court-appointed liquidator." He handed me the paper.

He was right; it was a letter from some VP at MuniBank, authorizing Acme to enter the premises of MDS and carry off anything and everything for immediate sale. I sighed. "How'd you get in here?" I asked. Reassured by our peaceful exchange, the black man disappeared with the computer. Elsewhere on the floor, I could hear noises as the other Acme men began to disassemble the office.

"Got the keys from the landlord," said the man with the beard, evidently the foreman. "CalWest something. You owe them, too." He was studying me carefully. "Some guys go nuts when we show up," he said. "I been shot at three times in the last year. You behave, you got me? No violence."

I raised an eyebrow. "My good sir," I said, somewhat indignantly, "I am a complete stranger to the practice of violence. I am a businessman, not a—a terrorist."

"Gotcha," he said, with apparent relief.

"I had assumed that I'd have a couple of days before you people arrived," I said.

"Nah," said the foreman. "Too many guys try to sell off the stuff before we show up."

"Ah," I said. Now why hadn't I thought of that? If I'd

started unloading equipment when I began firing people, I could probably have pocketed mid–six figures by the time the bankruptcy went through. . . .

Well. No point in worrying about spilled milk. I sighed. "All right," I said, turning to go. "I'll be in room 102."

"Yeah?" said the foreman, interested. "What's in room 102?"

There was a pinging noise. Then, David Greenblatt yelled, "Boss! Hey, take a look at this!"

I trotted to David's office, my friend with the beard lumbering along behind me. David gesticulated excitedly at the screen. "Hey, I think we got something," he said.

The foreman's eyes lit up. David had top-of-the-line equipment. The machine on his desk was worth ten of those sitting in the cubicles outside. "Jesus!" he yelled. "Get in here. We got a primo box here."

I stared at the screen. "What is it, David?" I said.

"It's an imaging algorithm," he said. "Gosh! I bet we could get ten times the holographic resolution of the MDS-316 at the same processor speed with this. And . . ."

Jesus, an Hispanic with a large mustache and larger muscles, showed up at the door. "I take?" said Jesus.

"Yeah," said the foreman. Jesus pulled the plug and starting yanking cables out of the back of David's machine.

David's screen flickered and died. His mouth formed a perfect "O." His eyes grew to the size of eggs behind his glasses.

Jesus picked up the computer and tucked it under one arm.

"You . . ." David said. "You . . ."

The foreman shrugged. "It ain't your machine no longer, buddy."

With scream of pure, unadulterated rage, David leapt from his chair.

"Hey! Hey!" yelled the foreman. "No viol—"

David sank his teeth into Jesus' arm. Jesus gave a howl of pain and jerked in reaction.

David flew out the door, through the partitions of three cubicles, and came to rest against a desk. His glasses were cracked.

"He bite me! He bite me!" shouted Jesus.

"And I'll bite you again!" screamed David. Shirttail untucked, glasses hanging half over his face, he sprang to his feet and charged Jesus.

Clutching his injured arm, Jesus fled in terror.

David's computer lay on the floor. The plastic casing was cracked. I winced, wondering what the hard drive looked like now.

The foreman had a length of lumber in his hands. He was advancing toward me. "No violence," he shouted, smashing the stick into the doorframe so hard he dented the metal of the frame. I backed off, swallowing.

"No, no, absolutely not," I said.

"If you don't want violence," the foreman yelled, "get the fuck out of here."

Right. Some people have a peculiar notion of pacifism.

I FOUND DAVID IN THE PARKING LOT. HE WAS LEANING against his ancient Ford Escort. There was blood on his shirt; he had his chin skyward, his neck bent back, trying to stop his nose from bleeding.

"Are you all right?" I asked him.

"Yed," he said. "I'b oday."

"What about Jesus?"

"Wed do da hospidal. For his bide."

I sighed. "David," I said, "I'm sorry it had to end like this."

"Be doo," he said.

I noticed that my parking space was empty. There was an instant of sheer panic. "Where's my Jag?" I said.

"Reebo man god id."

"Repo man? It was repossessed? While you were standing here?"

"Yed," he said.

"But I'm current on the car payments," I protested.

He shrugged. "He said you were monds behide."

"Months . . . That can't be," I said. It couldn't be true. The car payments didn't come out of the corporate account; they came out of my own personal checking account, which had never been in any danger of bankruptcy. It was a joint checking account; Maureen paid all the bills, and she was always conscientious about it.

I didn't understand it at all; and this last bit of frustration was not what I needed.

"What a day," I said.

"Dell be aboud id," said David.

I USED THE LAST OF MY CASH TO HIRE A LIMO TO TAKE ME out to the house.

"Maureen!" I yelled as I strode up the steps.

I opened the front door with my keys. Where were the servants? "Michael! Consuela!"

Silence. The only sounds were my footsteps on the parquet floor and the quiet tinkle of the foyer fountain.

There was a note on the table in the living room, in Maureen's writing: "Play DVD."

And sure enough, a disc was loaded and ready to go.

"Darling," said Maureen, there on the TV screen. She wore a spandex top, a short skirt, and sunglasses—California tart. My gonads ached for her; my heart was ice. "I know you will be saying I betrayed you. But that is not true, not really true.

"A contract is a contract, my love," she said. "And though our contract was never in writing, we both knew what it said: that, marrying you, I would never need to worry about money.

"It is not I who broke this contract."

She appeared to hesitate, perhaps wondering how to say what came next without saying something incriminating. "It was sweet of you to give me your power of attorney," she said, "but it was, perhaps, unwise. The house has been sold . . ." I groaned. ". . . and the new owners are arriving to take possession tomorrow. The Maplesons, a lovely couple; you won't like them, I think. I'm afraid you'll need to vacate by 10 A.M.

"And so, I bid you farewell, my darling. I am sure that you shall fare well; for whatever obstacles you face, you are an intelligent and vigorous man. I wish you well, and, though you may not believe me at this juncture, all happiness to be.

"And as for me, you need not worry," she said, and smiled faintly. "I am a survivor, you see."

And then she reached forward and touched something off-camera. The image flickered away.

And I was left with a screenful of static.

I STARED AT THE STATIC FOR AT LEAST A MINUTE. THEN, with a shock, I wondered what else she'd done.

I went to the safe in the study; there were bearer bonds in there, ten thousand in Swiss francs, several ounces of gold—in case of emergencies.

Gone.

I ran to the library, to check on my collection of Elizabethan manuscripts. . . .

Gone.

The garage, where I kept the '23 Rolls, the Mustang, and the Miata. . . .

Gone.

The Monet. . . .

Gone.

Even my clothes. . . .

Gone, save for the socks and underwear.

Groaning, I poured myself a hefty scotch and sank into the armchair.

And then another thought struck me, and I went to the computer, booted it up, and signed on to the net. I called up the records for our joint checking account. . . .

She *hadn't* paid the finance charges on the Jag in three months. Nor any other bill she thought she could evade.

And the account was closed. The last check, for the remaining balance, she'd written to herself. And it had cleared days ago.

The money market account was closed, too. And my Keogh. And the brokerage account. And Credit Suisse denied any knowledge of my numbered account.

She had, I realized in dawning horror, taken everything— *literally* everything.

All I had left in the world was the change in my pocket.

I counted it: seventeen dollars and forty-two cents.

Seventeen dollars and forty-two cents.

6

DOWN AND OUT
IN OAKLAND AND $AN JO$E

I AWOKE TOO EARLY: BLEARY-EYED, DEHYDRATED, AND IN pain. I'd downed most of a fifth the previous night. Probably foolish, but why not? Who knew when next I'd be able to afford a bottle of decent scotch?

I swallowed a gallon or two of water, then stood apathetically in a scalding shower before drying myself and, somewhat distastefully, donning the same soiled suit I had worn the night before.

The first order of business was to find a job. Depressing thought, but there it was: I was no longer my own master. Still, without some source of income, the gods only knew where I'd wind up. It shouldn't be so hard; hadn't I been CEO? There ought to be companies that would kill for someone with my experience.

Who to call first? Hmm. What was that fellow's name? Mark something. Didn't recall the last, but the company was Atomic Era Ventures, a start-up to develop hundred-atom-domain data-storage technology. An exciting technology, real potential there, and they'd gotten eight figures from some venture firm; they could use me, and the money should be good. The phone number was on my computer, so I let it dial.

"We're sorry, but Atomic Era is no longer in business. For

more information, contact Josiah Grinch at Vulture Funds, 201-175—"

Damn. Vulture Funds must have yanked the plug. They'd probably been figuring the same thing as my friend at MuniBank. Who knew what data-storage technology the aliens had? Probably wrote notes in quantum chaos or some damn thing.

Next. DataStan Peripherals. Stan Hernandez and I had had our differences, but . . . I got his voice-mail. Where could he call me back? I couldn't count on being here once the Maplesons arrived; the phone in my car was gone with the Jag; my cellular was dead, since Maureen hadn't paid the bill . . . Gad. I gave him the number at home. Maybe I could finagle something.

In desperation, I called Sukhreet Dalaji at Taj Imports. She was my only relative in the States, second or third cousin, something like that. Taj imported mostly textiles, anything they could buy cheap around the Indian Ocean for sale in North America. Not a business I knew much about, but family is family, and I needed *some*thing. She was in, thank God.

"Johnson," she said. "How are you, old friend?"

"I have seen better days, Sukhreet," I said. "MDS is in liquidation, and I'm looking for a position. May I ask if Taj is looking for people at present?"

Silence for a moment. "I think not, Johnson. As it happens, I've just been laid off."

"What? Oh, Sukhreet! I am sorry."

"Our sales are down thirty percent in the last quarter," she said. "The economy is going to hell, and with the dollar plummeting the way it is . . ."

"Yes, yes. I quite understand."

The problem with Sukhreet is loquaciousness. She wanted to catch up on old friends; even being as abrupt as was possible without active rudeness, it took me fifteen minutes to get her off the phone.

Calls four, five, and six: voice-mail, secretaries, disconnected phone.

There never was a call the seventh. The Maplesons arrived.

THE MAPLESONS LOOKED LIKE AMERICAN GOTHIC IN A time warp. The old man was dried-up, prunelike, Adam's apple sticking out like a dorsal fin above a gaudy Hawaiian-print shirt. You could roast marshmallows over his tan; he looked like the Marlboro Man in his seventies. His wife was blond, early twenties, absolutely ravishing; she ran a gimlet eye over my house, a faint acquisitive smile on her face. Second wife, or maybe fifteenth.

"You the gardener?" Mapleson *l'homme* said upon my appearance.

I drew myself up. "Certainly not," said I. "Johnson Mukerjii, at your service."

Mapleson grunted. "Well," he said, "get your black ass out of my house."

"I beg your pardon?" I said, somewhat taken aback. It had been some time since I had experienced such open discrimination. It was quite annoying, especially since this twit had no right to such pretension: I am a Balliol man myself, while Mapleson had probably attended Indiana University or some such dreary place, if indeed he boasted a university education at all.

"I don't know who the hell you are," Mapleson said, "but if you aren't off the grounds in five minutes, I'll have you run off."

"This, sir," I said, "is my property, and I shall have no more of this nonsense."

He peered at me. "Crap," he said. "Bought it from Maureen D'Angelo." My wife's maiden name. "Closed two weeks ago."

"Maureen Mukerjii is my wife," I said. "And if she sold this property to you, she was in violation of her fiduciary responsibilities, and such sale is null and void."

Mapleson seemed genuinely shocked—not, I think, at my claim to own the place, but at the notion that Maureen D'Angelo, a woman he had met and perhaps knew socially, might care to consort with a Paki. Not that Bengal is in Pakistan, you understand, but "Paki" seems to have become the catchall racial slur for people from the subcontinent, save in Britain, where "nigger" is applied indiscriminately to Asians as well as Caribbean blacks.

Mapleson *la femme* was eyeing us speculatively now, perhaps wondering where this all was leading. Her husband rocked back on his heels, taking the news like a punching bag taking a blow. "I have a deed," he said slowly, "and I intend to take possession. If you have any complaint, your lawyers can talk to my lawyers. Now scat."

"Do me the great good honor of removing yourself from the premises," I said, "or I shall be forced to call the security firm." Might as well put up a good front, and the ARMED RESPONSE placards were still in place at the front gate, albeit Maureen hadn't paid that bill, either.

"Albrecht!" shouted Mapleson. I had been turning to reenter the house, but paused to see what response this call would bring. I was not required to wait long, for soon there was the squelch of wheelchair tires over the gravel of a garden path. Albrecht, for such, I surmised, was the name of the wheelchair's occupant, was a fit, brawny young man; tanned, blond-haired, well muscled, garbed in a tank top, shorts, and Birkenstock sandals. Save for the disability that left him confined to wheeled transport, one might have taken him for any random beach bum, with only this distinction: the muscles of his upper arms would have given a bodybuilder credit.

"Get rid of this putz," Mapleson told the young man.

"Sir?" said Albrecht, clearly a little startled. One hand flipped open a compartment in the arm of the chair and pulled forth a compact and, by all appearances, rather deadly little automatic. It was my turn to be startled.

With some irritation, the old man said, "Put that away, you idiot. Just get him off the grounds."

"Ah," said Albrecht, wheeled closer to me and, quite unexpectedly, seized me and pulled me facedown onto his lap.

"Unhand me!" I said, and struggled to rise.

Albrecht made no reply. One-handed, he held me down, while the other hand went to a wheel to turn us about. It was embarrassing, that even one-handed a cripple could keep me from freeing myself. He flicked a switch; apparently, an electric motor went to work, for we were soon flying down my driveway at considerable speed. In desperation, I made a grab for his genitals, a low move, but under the circumstances, I considered, a reasonable one. He slammed my temple into his chair, saying, "Naughty, naughty." Stars spun, and, my vision unfocused, I desisted from further resistance. In any event, we by then appeared to be traveling at least twenty miles an hour, not a speed at which I would care to be thrown from such a conveyance.

Albrecht applied brakes as we neared the gate. He moved through it at a slow pace, halted, slung me into the shoulder of the road, wheeled around, passed through the gate again, and shut and locked it.

Still somewhat dazed, I arose, brushing dust and gravel from the seat of my pants, and stared at Albrecht through my own cast-iron bars.

Albrecht smiled gaily, spun about, threw up a hand and a cheery, "*Auf Wiedersehen,*" and sped back up my driveway.

"It certainly," I mused, "gives new meaning to 'physically challenged.' "

NO ONE CARED TO PICK UP A HITCHHIKER IN A SUIT, AND the sun was hot. It took several hours for me to get to town, and by then I was sweat-stained, dusty, and footsore. I spent some of my last few coins on a soda and sucked it thirstily down, then found a pay phone and resumed my calls. To my surprise, I got through at DataStan Peripherals, and Stan Hernandez, though chuckling gleefully at my plight, agreed to interview me that afternoon.

Luckily, a bus route went out toward the DataStan offices, albeit with the usual desultory frequency of California public transport, that is, once in a blue moon. It got me there in time, however.

I entered the lobby and strode toward the elevator bank. A uniformed hand grabbed my arm.

"Where you going, buddy?" said the security guard.

"Release me, sir," I said.

"No bums in here," he said. "You beat it, now, unless you want maybe a vagrancy rap."

I drew myself up, and said, "Sir, I have an appointment."

Clutching me distrustfully, he dragged me over to the desk, where they called up to the DataStan offices and verified that I did, in fact, have an appointment.

Riding up in the elevator, a little shaken, I surveyed myself in the mirrored walls. No wonder the guard had intercepted me: that walk in the hot sun had done me no good. My suit was as rumpled as if I had worn it for weeks, with prominent, dark half-moons of sweat under either armpit. Albrecht's blow had left me a large purple bruise on one side of the face. But the worst discovery was yet to come; when I approached the receptionist, she visibly flinched. I understood at once that hours in the sun had done nothing for my personal odor.

But I did have that appointment with Hernandez, and I got my interview. Hernandez's secretary told me to go on in, so I opened the door—

SPRITZ. Water in my face. It thrummed against my suit jacket. I wiped my eyes. Stan Hernandez was holding a seltzer bottle and grinning like a maniac.

"Hah!" he said. "Gotcha that time, huh, Johnny?"

"You sure did," I said. "Hah-hah."

"No hard feelings," he said, extending a hand. "Put 'er there."

I took his hand and—

BZZRT. A shock ran up my arm. I was unable to control a grimace of annoyance. A joy-buzzer, goddamn it. What an asshole.

Hernandez was chortling. "Heh, heh," I said through gritted teeth, doing my best to smile.

"You look like something the cat dragged in," said Hernandez. "Here, take a load off." He motioned me toward a chair—

THWPPPPPPPP. A whoopie cushion. Good Rama almighty, would it never end? Sure, Hernandez had always been a practical joker. But wasn't this a little much? He was doubled over, hugging his stomach, gasping and wheezing with laughter. I sat there with a fatuous smile on my face, fuming within. I needed this job. I'd put up with a lot to get it.

Hernandez got ahold of himself and sat behind the desk. "So, Johnny, I hear you've been having some trouble. Cigar?" He held out a cigar to me, taking one himself.

"Thanks," I said. It was going to explode. I knew it was going to explode. Hernandez would love it when it exploded. He wanted to humiliate me; fine. I could play this game, so long as a job was at its end.

He leaned over to light my cigar. "Bankrupt, ain't you?" He seemed quite happy with the thought.

"Yes, yes," I said, as Hernandez leaned back and lit his own stogie. "Listen, Stan, I know we've had past differences, but I want you to know I've always admired your business acumen. I feel I can contribute much to—"

Stan Hernandez's smile widened, and he let me babble while he slowly exhaled smoke into the office air. "This is rich," he said. "You must really be desperate to come to me, Johnny. What about your mansion? Your wife's income? Losing MDS shouldn't have wiped you out."

"Ah, yes," I said. "See here, Stan, I'm willing to do just about—"

"There's no job for you here," Hernandez said, smiling. "I just wanted to see you crawl."

BOOM. Damn cigar blew. I had somehow forgotten about it; nearly had a heart attack. Hernandez cackled nastily, whipped out the seltzer bottle again, and spritzed me in the face. At least it put out the last of the cigar's flame.

I have said I am a stranger to the practice of violence and, in the usual way, that is true. However, at that moment, I was, I am forced to admit, overcome with such an excess of rage that, I fear, I went so far as to spring to my feet, hurl myself across Hernandez's desk, and attempt to throttle the living daylights out of him.

"Guards! Guards!" he shouted, cringing away in fear. I had him on the floor; he was turning red.

At this juncture, I felt a sharp blow to the base of the skull. My vision blanked for a moment; the next I recall, I was being hustled down a corridor by two security guards. They were theoretically unarmed; that is, they bore neither guns nor clubs. They did, however, carry enormous metal flashlights, each charged with at least a half dozen D-cells. As I began to struggle and protest, I received a sharp blow to the stomach from one of these flashlights. "Shaddup," a guard advised me, and, wishing to avoid further contusions, I took his advice to heart.

I was hurled out the freight entrance into the parking lot with such force that I fell, painfully skinning my palms in the process. The door was slammed and bolted behind me, and I found myself once more in the hot Californian sun, without transport in the land of cars, money in the land of wealth, a bath in the land of vanity.

• • •

I WALKED UNHAPPILY DOWN THE HIGHWAY, DOWN THE line of glittering office buildings, all of equal height, as if some law of nature cut down any that rose too high. Each was surrounded by a phalanx of cars, gleaming in the California light; within, suited men and women in dresses chatted in hallways, sipped coffee, studied phosphor tubes, clattered at keyboards. On the road itself, a constant flow of vehicles sped, each enclosing its occupant in a protective, air-conditioned cocoon, conveying them to offices, homes, shopping malls—all the glittering, well-kempt buildings of middle-class life. These folk felt this sun only as they scuttled from office to car, from car to home, or purposefully, at the beach, to obtain a healthy glow. It was a separate world, inches away from the one I now occupied, but as distant as Mars, as close and as far as an alternate reality where California was part of Mexico, or Emperor Norton's descendants ruled.

One might enter these buildings, hoping to obtain an interview; but one would be ejected by guards, as too disreputable to have any legitimate business there. No, the only hope was the phone; the phone gave no hint of appearance and could intrude on anyone's business at any moment of the day, hence might be used to gain an appointment.

I found a gas station with a pay phone, entered the booth, and surveyed the contents of my pockets. I was down to a tad over ten dollars; it would not last long, not a half-dollar call at a time. With increasing desperation, I dialed.

The exercise was in vain. Voice-mail and secretaries conspired to keep me from most of the people who might hire; economic uncertainty kept me from the rest. There were no jobs to be found in Silicon Valley for love or money, not in these times, and I had little money and less love to offer.

By nightfall, I was sitting on the floor of the phone booth in a state of complete despair.

A cop car pulled into the gas station, perhaps to refuel. I sighed, got up, and approached it.

"Good evening," I said. "I am a vagrant, in some distress. Could you gentlemen perhaps conduct me to a shelter?"

And so they did.

OH, BLISS! A SHOWER. THERE WERE NOT, HOWEVER, stalls; the showerheads lined the walls of a large, tiled room where stagnant puddles lay, undoubtedly rife with athlete's foot and less determinable diseases. A dozen unattractive men of various shapes and colors showered about me, but despite this, I luxuriated in the warm water, closing my eyes and abandoning myself to the steady flow.

"Outa my shower, tubby," grunted a voice like that of a two-pack-a-day smoker. I opened my eyes to behold a large, uncircumcised Hispanic man with a lip twisted by a deep scar. "Knife fight," I thought; "As you wish," I said, and left for the dressing room, where I had left my suit.

I had replaced my shirt with one from a pile of castoffs from the shelter supply, but despite its state, would not discard my suit. It had cost me a thousand pounds; it was my last link with normal life, and I would not part with it.

I got in the cafeteria line. It was several minutes before I reached the food counter. Behind it, a squat, indifferent woman in a hairnet presided over a steam tray of bluish slabs swimming in gray liquid. "What is that?" I asked.

"Meat," she said.

"Yes," I replied, "but I am interested in its provenance."

"Ya want it or not?"

"Could I ask what *kind* of meat?"

"Sirloin tips," she said.

"And what, pray tell, are they?"

"Look, buddy, ya want it or not?"

"Please."

She scooped some out and slammed it onto a chipped plate, which she smashed onto my tray.

Next was a deep, circular pot filled with a grayish liquid indistinguishable from the gravy around my "sirloin tips." A hairy-armed Hispanic man in an apron stood over it with an enormous ladle.

"And what culinary delight do you have in store?" I inquired.

"*Yanqui* bean," he grunted, from which I divined that *gringos* had somehow made it into his pot. I declined, but accepted a thin gruel from the next server, something she claimed was "mashed 'taters." Last was a dollop of something resembling olive-drab library paste rolled into small balls— putatively peas.

To cleanse the palate between courses, we had a delightful, expressive little apple juice, redolent of the steel cans from which it had been drawn.

I never got to my dessert—something resembling dog's vomit, which the *chefs de cuisine* maintained to be apple crisp—for as I was choking down the mystery meat, my scarfaced friend from the showers leaned over my table, and rasped, "Give me your money or I keel you." He showed me a large and quite lethal knife, shielding it from everyone else with his body.

I looked about the huge shelter. There were a couple of cops, way over at the other end, but there was no doubt that my charming acquaintance could have my intestines on the floor before they could get anywhere near my table.

"My good sir," quoth I, "if I had any money, do you suppose I would be eating this offal?"

"You see dat one?" he said, pointing to our right. I looked down the aisle to the next table over, where an elderly black man sat, scarfing Yankee bean as if it were ambrosia. His arm ended at the elbow. He looked up, and met our eyes; his own widened in fright, and he immediately stood up and slunk away, leaving his meal half-uneaten.

"I cut off his arm," said Scarface, with satisfaction. "I cut you off, too. Turn your pockets inside out."

Scarface chortled in glee at my wallet; I had little enough cash, but he seized my credit cards and driver's license with alacrity. I forbore to point out that the credit cards were canceled; he probably wouldn't care.

"You try to cheat me," he said. "You stay here tonight, I stab you, okay? You sleep on street. Then you know what good for you, do what I say from now on."

He walked away.

'Gods,' I thought, 'I no longer have so much as ID.'

FROM COMFORT TO CATASTROPHE IN SCANT HOURS. I trusted Scarface's veracity so, upon concluding my repast, I made my way from the shelter and down a deserted street. I was not far from what passes for downtown San Jose, so went to a park where, in better times, I had sat on a bench and eaten a take-out lunch after a business meeting in one of the surrounding office buildings. I was not the only one there; derelicts and junkies were draped over most of the benches. I was hard put to find a place to sit. An occasional cop car drove slowly past, but we were not harassed. I presume this was because there were no citizens around, no one but us bums; the office buildings emptied out by seven, and there were no residences in the area.

I sat gloomily on the bench, tired but not yet nodding, listening to the tinkle of a little fountain, where several of my compatriots were washing. A small man with a week's growth of beard and unclean clothes sat down by me, clutching a brown paper bag.

"New here?" he said.

"Yes," I replied, somewhat despondent.

He grunted, and took a swig. "Name's Spejak," he said. "Useta be a CAD/CAM designer. You?"

I looked at him; his face was lined with grime and care, but he was not old. "What happened to CAD/CAM?" I asked.

"Nobody's designing much of anything," he mourned. "Everyone's looking to alien tech. And anyway, they got artificial intelligences can do it better."

I nodded, and told him of my company.

"Uh-huh," he said. "Lot of that going around." And he offered me a swig.

"Night Train," he said.

"Ah," I replied, downing a noxious gulp. "Yes, I recall it; a fruity little Concord, pressed only from the grapes grown on the wrong side of the railroad track. The August vintage, isn't it? Or perhaps the September."

Spejak chuckled. "Not exactly a primo chardonnay," he said, "I'll give you that."

7

$TRANGE DAY$

"WHAT DO YOU THINK?" DEIRDRE ASKED. SHE WAS A HAG-gard, middle-aged woman, graying hair in a rat's nest, clad, like most of us, in ill-fitting government-issue fatigues.

There were six large cases of Campbell's tomato soup. There were twelve smaller cases, labeled in Thai. The Thai cans were quite small; the labels, which I could not read, bore a picture of a fish. The tops of the cans were stamped, "not fit for human consumption."

"It's cat food," I protested.

"It's tuna fish," she said.

"But it says—"

"They claim people can eat it," she said. "It's just the greas-ier flesh of the fish, with some organs and ground bones. Nothing hazardous about it, it just doesn't meet FDA stan-dards."

"Gah," I said.

"I'm sorry," Deirdre said wearily. "It's the best I can do today. The city's budget for the month is already spent, Fa-ther Gonzalez can't help, and—"

"Deirdre," I said, "I know you've done your best. I just don't see how I can make this edible."

She began to say something, but her voice was drowned out by thunder.

We looked out, over the bay, toward San Francisco. The five o'clock rocket was taking off, its flight path across the water toward the Oakland side. The contrail gleamed in the afternoon sun—just steam, I knew, reaction mass; the power came from fusion engines. Aircars, too, flitted across the sky, rush hour already beginning. Alien technology, of course; the world was changing with amazing speed.

After the rocket's thunder died away, Deirdre said, "If anyone can make it taste good, you can, Johnson." And she left.

I sighed, and began to potter about my kitchen. The work space was sheltered by plastic garbage bags, stapled to posts; my "stove" was a fire, burning driftwood and random scrap, over which I could suspend a pot or a pan. Chez Panisse it was not. But someone had to cook for the shantytown.

It lay all about me: boards culled from construction scrap, green corrugated plastic sheets, rusty tin sheeting, all nailed, baled, and stapled together—rickety structures, but they kept off the sun and rain. Deirdre, thank heaven, had organized a latrine; I shuddered to think what the place would be like otherwise. Still, the settlement had a permanent smell, of fires burning, people too long unbathed, the dust of our unpaved "streets." People were already beginning to drift "home"—some from casual labor, most from a day of hopeless browsing through other people's garbage, or panhandling, or smearing greasy rags across the windshields of cars. They would be hungry, and I had to find some way of making cat food taste good. Or at least edible.

It was my role, here in Sludgetown, so named for the consistency of the bay water in which we bathed. I was the *chef de cuisine*, if one may use so grand a term. I had volunteered for the task when it became obvious that I was not cut out to be a panhandler. Even in castoffs and used clothing, I appeared too prosperous to earn much pelf; I had the girth of a successful burgher, the orotund Oxbridge tones that even Americans associate with class and wealth. "I say, my good man, if you will forgive the temerity, I find myself in financial straits just at present. The donation of a quarter or two would not go unappreciated." It just doesn't work, you see.

I had always been something of a gourmet cook, and the slop prepared by my predecessor had been completely inedible. I had gently suggested that I might assist her, and she had eventually been happy to cede the role to me entirely. It was almost enjoyable; I never knew what Deirdre might be able to beg, buy, or steal, and so the challenge varied wildly from day to day. This one, though, looked virtually impossible.

Wait; I had a twenty-five-pound bag of macaroni, did I not? Wasn't there an Italian pasta dish . . . ? Yes, *pasta al tonno*, that was it, a tomato sauce with canned tuna in place of meat. If I boiled down the tomato soup a bit . . . Did I still have any of that oregano? Yes, yes, several ounces; excellent.

I rubbed my hands and set to work.

I WAS READY BY SIX-THIRTY. THE TRAFFIC WAS ALREADY thinning out, not too many aircars flitting out over the bay. Even the ground traffic on the highway to our east was declining. Since the crash, of course, rush hour hadn't been nearly as bad. Half as many jobs, half the traffic. An ill wind, and so on.

"What's for grub?" asked Spejak, peering into my pot. He was the first acquaintance I'd made after becoming a bum; we'd drifted up toward Oakland together. He was pretty useless, all told; spent his days reading paperbacks and his nights swilling cheap vodka. I didn't know where he got the money for that, nor much cared.

"*Thon pour chat, avec une sauce tomate,*" I said.

"Sounds good," he said. "Something I want to show you later."

I grunted, and ladled some of the cat food onto his macaroni. Anything sounds good in French.

The line inched along. They came with dull faces and chipped crockery, mess kits, even planks washed in the bay; we had no utensils to spare. Someone I hadn't seen before came up holding a battered tin plate; a white man with a scraggly, unkempt beard, lined face, filthy overcoat, and dirty sneakers. He studied me suspiciously, then peered in the pot. "You one of them?" he demanded.

"One of what?" I asked, a little taken aback. "A tuna?"

He leaned forward, and whispered, "The Jews."

The Jews? "No," I said, blinking.

"Peace," he said, apparently mollified, and accepted a plate of food.

There were more behind him. The line was long, longer every day, longer as unemployment relentlessly rose. The government had given up on unemployment compensation; there wasn't the money, there were too many unemployed. I didn't know how we could keep on feeding them all if the numbers kept growing.

Yet somehow, I reflected as I dished out slop, somehow I felt almost at peace. I had been driven all my life; there had always been meetings, deadlines, calls to make, a schedule to keep. You don't build a business by rocking on the porch and sipping lemonade. But I had been building something, something worthwhile, something of lasting value; jobs, opportunities, products to help people, economic growth, personal wealth. People had depended on me, there had always been something to do. . . . And then, with shocking abruptness, it had ended. No one needed me; there was nothing that needed to get done. For six months, I had lived in a daze: apathetic, slow-moving, taking each day as it came.

'It must be,' I thought, 'how most people lived their whole lives.'

Manuel came up, with an ancient piece of cracked Fiestaware and a copy of the *Wall Street Journal*. Smiling, he gave the newspaper to me; I gravely thanked him, and dished out his food. *"Gracias,"* he said, and left to find a place to sit.

Manuel was one of the few shantytown dwellers who held down a job. He was an illegal, cleaning offices for less than the minimum wage. He lived here to save on expenses; the bulk of his income went back home, to some village in south Mexico, where it allowed his wife and children to escape even more abject poverty. It was hard to imagine, I thought; hard to imagine poverty more grinding than this.

He knew I liked to read the *Journal*; whenever he found a copy in the garbage, he'd retrieve it for me. One of the perquisites of being the cook: Everyone wants to keep on your good side.

I glanced at the left-column headline before folding the paper and putting it away until dinner was over: Fed Chairman Calls Crash "Greatest Business Bust Since Fall of Rome."

ANOTHER PERQUISITE OF BEING COOK IS THAT SOMEONE else cleans the pots. But one of the drawbacks is that you know what's in them. I did not look forward to bolting back cat food. The *Journal* was just the ticket; reading it, I'd be less aware of what I was eating.

So I went to sit in front of my own hovel, spread out the paper, and read by the streetlights that line Route 80.

Dow Jones Industrial Average: still clunking around in low double digits. Unemployment: just shy of 50%—twenty points higher than during the Great Depression. "The greatest business bust since the fall of Rome" might be hyperbole, but not by much.

MuniBank had filed for bankruptcy, I saw; I smiled.

They had been right, I mused while studying the NASDAQ listings to see which of my competitors had gone under of late. But the problem was even more severe than MuniBank had reckoned. Half of the planet's investment since the time of the pyramids was "malinvestment"; we had a thousand years of alien technology to absorb at once. We were like Asia, America, and Africa faced by European explorers. Our own society was crumbling, and gods only knew what we needed to do to survive. At best, we'd be like Japan or China, and eventually adapt; at worse, like the Aztecs or Incas, we'd be obliterated.

Finished with food and *Journal*, I put the paper away, then went to wash my plate in the bay. Spejak had wanted to see me.

SPEJAK'S SHACK WAS MADE OF PLASTIC SHEETING, LASHED to posts; it wouldn't last a heavy rainstorm or a strong wind, but such things were rare here. He had a bottle of something in hand and rocked violently back and forth in a rickety rocking chair by the dim freeway lights. The joints of the chair needed gluing, and it creaked loudly. He was jerking his head in sharp nods and muttering angrily.

"Spejak," I said. He kept on rocking, creakily back and forth. Mutter, mutter. It was easy to see why he couldn't hold down a job.

"Spejak!" I said, a little louder; he stopped rocking and seemed to see me for the first time. He took a swig of whatever was in his bottle. "Mukerjii," he said at last, a little hoarsely. "Have some swill." He extended the bottle toward me.

"No thanks," I said. "You said you had something to show me."

"Mmph?" He looked blank for a moment. Then, his eyes cleared. He set his bottle down, stood up, and wandered unsteadily into his dwelling.

I followed; Spejak lit a kerosene lamp. I frowned; the whole shantytown was a firetrap, really, and Spejak's hovel was worse than most. The walls were lined with paperbacks, stacked from floor to ceiling, set on cinder blocks to avoid contact with the dirt. I hated to think what might happen if, in a drunken stupor, he were to knock his lamp over.

Spejak was an avid sci-fi reader; where he got the books I had no idea, nor how he could afford them. I picked up one idly, and saw it had no cover: a stripped book. Some bookstore had returned the cover for credit from the publisher, and had sold it or given it to Spejak. Quite illegal, that.

He was burrowing into a pile of newspapers and magazines nearly as tall as he, tossing bits of paper heedlessly. "Here it is!" he said triumphantly, holding up a dog-eared, months-old copy of *Publishers Weekly*. The cover depicted Leander Huff, pipe in hand, in his tweeds, standing before a nondescript sci-fi landscape with words in an alien script at top and bottom. "You said you knew Huff, didn't you?" he asked.

"Well, yes," I replied.

"I thought you might be interested," he said. More to be polite than anything else, I accepted the magazine and sat down to read it. Spejak went to fetch his bottle of swill and returned.

It was quite interesting, actually. Per the cover story, Huff had sold interstellar rights to his books to several different alien species, making him one of the few terrestrial authors to find an offworld audience. The story reported one sale for $30 million. 'Astounding,' thought I. 'These aliens must have money to burn.'

"Why Huff?" I wondered.

"You mean, why does his stuff play in Pi Pisces, when practically no other writer gets published out there?" Spejak shrugged. "Huff used to specialize in *Terra uber alles* stories."

I must have looked blank.

"Stories where humanity always proves superior to the aliens it meets," he says. "From the German national anthem, *Deutschland uber . . .*"

"Yes, yes," I said. "But I still don't understand. Why should pink elephants with brains, or whatever—why should they want to read a story that portrays monkeylike primitives as supermen?"

"They probably think it's hilarious," chuckled Spejak.

"Of course." I chuckled, too. "Huff will hate that. He'll take the money, of course, but he'll hate the idea that a bunch of bug-eyed monsters are sniggering behind his back."

I looked at the cover of PW anew. It did appear that Huff bore an expression of faint annoyance.

DINNER OF THE FOLLOWING DAY. TRIPE FLORENTINE. Deirdre could often beg the less salable innards from meat packers; I didn't know where the spinach had come from, but it was wilted and unattractive. Perfectly edible, though, and brief cooking rendered it more appetizing.

When I finished doling out the food, I went to the open area where most people ate and sat on a fallen telephone pole. Deirdre was with Manuel, forcing him to eat; he was ashen, red-eyed, obviously in shock. My friend the Jew-hater sat not far away, masticating tripe like a cow chewing cud. It is fairly rubbery stuff.

"What's wrong with Manuel?" I asked.

"He got fired today," she said.

"Oh, dear," I said. "Manuel! What happened?"

"Robot," he looked at me tearfully. "Robot do cleaning, now. They say it cheaper."

Odd; housework had proven quite resistant to automation. Hard to prevent the vacuum cleaner from vacuuming the cat, you see; it was a more complex AI problem than one would, a priori, have thought. As far as I knew, no one had been close to solving the problem. "Who made the robot?" I asked.

Manuel spat. "Aliens," he said.

Ah.

Jew-hater rocketed to his feet. "The Jews!" he shouted. "The Jews from the stars! Poisoning us with their lies! Taking our jobs away! Stabbing humanity in the back! The Jews are behind it, I say!"

He had our undivided attention.

He paced back and forth, gesticulating, the lights of San Francisco behind him. "Read the Bible! Joshua's fiery chariot, remember? It wasn't just Israel their god gave them, the whole Earth was their promised land!" He suddenly whirled, then looked intently around at the circle, pointing at each of us in turn. "Do you know why they circumcise their young?"

No one cared to venture a suggestion.

"They don't!" he screamed, pointing overhead. "That's how they grow naturally! Because they aren't human at all! They're *aliens, too!*"

"Oh, come off it," I said.

"For thousands of years, since they first arrived on Earth, they've been cut off from their allies in the void. They've had to scheme against us, tighten their iron grip step by nefarious step. Read the *Protocols!* But now, they can crush us beneath their heel, destroy us, now they are reinforced by the slobbering monsters from the stars, now the day of Armageddon is nigh!" His audience was listening in bemusement, but he didn't seem to be winning much sympathy.

"They're taking us over!" he shouted. "Isn't it obvious? It's all around you."

"The Jews?" I asked.

"The Jews, the aliens, they're stealing our jobs! Destroying our economy! Soon, they'll send in the death squads, and it will be the end for mankind! We have to smash them, cut them off! Kill all the vermin and turn our back on the stars, until we're strong enough to stand on our own. Drive them off Earth, kill them all! It's the only way!"

"You're crazy," I said. "There's no conspiracy. Times are tough, true, but we have to adapt—"

"Adapt?" he said, turning on me in fury. "Adapt to what? Eating slop? Living like swine? Pretty soon, there won't be *any* jobs. And then, we'll all starve! That's just what the

Christ-killers want! They've always cheated us, and now they're cheating us out of our world!"

"What cheat?" I said. "The aliens are just selling us goods we want to buy. If that hurts our economy, well, that's too bad; they don't *mean* to hurt us."

"It's a conspiracy," he insisted, "and here's the proof. They destroy our industry, buy up our planet, but have you ever heard of anyone selling *them* anything?"

To my astonishment, I saw that several people were actually nodding. In hard times, people will latch on to any explanation, I suppose. And it's traditional, isn't it? Something goes wrong, blame the Jews.

He paced toward me, fire in his eye, finger stabbing in my direction. "You're one of them, aren't you," he said. "Jew!"

"Ridiculous," I said. "I'm East Indian, not—"

He grabbed my arm and shouted, "If you aren't one of them, get down on your knees, get down on your knees with me and pray to Jesus, to Jesus Christ, I say, pray to Jesus to save our beloved Mother Earth from the Christ-killers from the Void!" He was on his knees by this time, yanking me down to join him on the ground. I wrenched my arm free.

"If I were to pray to anyone," I said coldly, "it would be to Krishna, I suppose. Although, in point of fact, I have been an atheist since the age of eight."

Egad, the world was getting strange. I stalked back to my shack.

I SAT ON MY BEDROLL AND WONDERED. THE LUNATIC HAD a point; had no one sold anything to the aliens? Wait; of course. Leander Huff had, obviously. But no one else?

That couldn't be true; we were buying aircars, suborbital rockets, household robots, who knew what else from the BEMs. What were we paying them with? Certainly not dollars, nor yet euros; what use was some stupid local currency, valuable only on its planet of origin, to an interstellar voyager? We must be selling *something*, to earn hard interstellar currency to pay for our imports.

That's an inflexible rule of economics; you have to earn what you pay for. A trade deficit can't go on forever. Over the long term, imports equal exports—with, to be sure, some other factors included, like fluctuating currencies, and earnings on overseas investment, repatriated profits . . .

I pored over yellowing *Wall Street Journals* and found what I was looking for. Here, Anglo-American had sold a few million in gems to an alien ship. There, one of the Russian industrial combines had sold some titanium. Ah, here was an interesting one; a trio of junketing alien tourists had gone to Christie's and bought everything in sight for three times the expected price. Interviewed, they said they had done it on a lark.

A lark? Two hundred millions bucks, on a whim?

So we were selling something. But pitifully little. Artwork, occasional raw materials.

Hmm. Here was something odd; astronomers observing Jupiter had noticed two plumes of gas emanating from the planet, and settling down into a ring about it. Spokesaliens had no comment, except to say that this was "normal industrial development." I wondered—

"Johnson?" came a voice—Deirdre's. "Can I come in?"

"Of course, my dear," I said, and held back the flap of fabric that served as my door. She had Manuel in tow.

"You have to talk to him," she said.

"Is it true?" he asked me despairingly.

"Is what true?" I said, motioning them in and sitting them down on stools. I resumed my seat on my blanket.

"That you're a Jew."

"No, Manuel," I said, "but what would it matter if I were?"

Manuel mumbled something to himself. "Maybe it is true," he said at last.

"What that lunatic said?"

He spread his hands. "No one says anything that makes any sense," he said miserably. "Maybe . . ." He shrugged hopelessly.

I blinked at him. It was all so obvious . . . But how could I possibly explain it to an illiterate peasant with shaky English?

"We are the Aztecs," I said. "The aliens are the Spaniards."

His eyes grew hard. "Then they *will* destroy us."

"No, no," I said. I sighed, and tried again. "Their technology, their—their tools are far better than ours. They have guns, horses—"

"They want our gold!" said Manuel.

"No, no, no, forget the Aztecs! Forget I brought it up. It's more like the Chinese."

Manuel looked at me uncomprehendingly. What did he know about the Chinese?

"Look. Why is Mexico backward?"

"The *gringos*," he said. "They stole half our country, bought up our *patrimonia*—"

I shook my head. "No, no! When Salinas opened Mexico up to free trade, the economy picked up and . . ."

Another blank look of incomprehension; the rapid development of Mexico had left many *campesinos* behind, apparently his village included.

"Is it the Jews, I am thinking," he said. "The priests, they were always down on the Jews. There must be a reason."

But I wasn't listening; I was thinking. Mexico had been backward because it was an insular economy, but when they saw how Asia had developed, exporting to earn the hard currency to buy the machine tools and know-how to export more, to—

Of course! I shot to my feet. "Exports—ouch!" I had hit my head on the plywood ceiling.

Deirdre and Manuel stared at me as if I were mad.

"That's the answer," I said, rubbing my head and grinning

like a fool. "Exports! We need to make stupid little tacky pieces of garbage for export! Like Taiwan! Earn the hard currency to modernize, little paper folding umbrellas, and pencils in fruity tropical colors!" I was dancing about the shack, now, shouting. "Kistchy knickknacks and plastic souvenirs! Joy buzzers, latex vomit, plastic flowers that squirt! Pink plush teddy bears, fuzzy dice, dolls with enormous eyes! 'Made in Japan,' 'Made in Taiwan,' and now"—I gestured grandly "—'Made on Earth.'"

Deirdre was watching me, smiling, her head on one side, as if I were quite as alien a creature as any she had seen on TV or the pages of a magazine.

"I think," muttered Manuel, "I think it is the Jews."

IT WAS LATE AT NIGHT. I WAS SITTING IN SPEJAK'S HOVEL, my back to a wall of stripped paperbacks; he and I had both consumed a substantial bit of his white lightning. Deirdre sat on Spejak's bedroll, grinning. We plotted the economic conquest of the galaxy.

"That's why my company failed," I babbled. "We can't compete with the aliens on high tech—their tech is far higher than ours. And we can't develop our indigenous technology fast enough; we'd need to build the tools to build the tools— far easier to buy the tools from the BEMs. But to do that, we need hard interstellar currency. . . ."

"You're nuts," said Spejak. "What makes you think the aliens want to buy latex vomit?"

"If they did," said Deirdre, "wouldn't someone be selling it to them?"

"Bah," I said. "Nonsense. That's the theory of perfect markets; 'if there's an excess profit to be made, competition enters until profits disappear.' An old joke: An economics professor and one of his graduate students are walking down the street, and they see a twenty-dollar bill on the sidewalk. The student starts to stoop to pick it up, but the professor says, 'Don't bother.' The student says, 'Why not?' The professor says, 'If it were really there, someone would already have picked it up.' "

"You really think they'll buy latex vomit? And paper umbrellas?"

I mulled over that, somewhat fuzzily; Spejak's swill had done nothing for my higher mental functions. "No," I said reluctantly, "you're quite right. There must be equivalent pieces of trash that the aliens *would* buy, but they are specific to their own culture. I need to know more about their culture before I can figure out what to sell."

"Market research," said Spejak. "How're you going to do that?"

Good point. Depressing one. How was I going to get into the interstellar market starting as a bum in a shantytown on the verge of Route 80?

"You've had some exposure to the aliens," Deirdre said, "haven't you, Johnson? Didn't you tell me you were in French Guiana when the Secretary-General went into orbit?"

"Yes," I said absently, "and at the White House when the aliens landed." What good did that do me? Maybe I could sell them Mylar clothing, or something; styles out of bad *Star Trek* episodes.

"Think back," said Deirdre. "Didn't they use anything we might be able to make, cheaper and less well? The alien equivalent of a cigarette lighter, or a mechanical pencil? A wristwatch, a . . ."

"Drink bulb," I said. "In zero gee, the aliens served the UN delegation refreshments in squeeze bulbs."

Hmm. "That Guatemalan," I mused. "What was his name? Roguera. He was part of the delegation that went into orbit. He gestured a little too violently with his bulb; it spun off across space, hit a bulkhead, and squirted juice on one of the aliens."

"Embarrassing," said Deirdre.

"I can see it might be a problem," said Spejak, taking a hefty swig of rotgut. "I mean, how do you put your drink down in zero gee? If you just leave it lying around, it'll drift off with random air currents. You'd have to hold on to it all the time."

"Inconvenient," I said. "What if you had a little gizmo with a suction cup on one end, and a clip to hold the neck of a standard-size squeeze bulb on the other?"

Spejak rose and unsteadily rummaged through his papers, Deirdre and I looking on in some bemusement. He found a sheet of paper that was blank on one side and the stub of a blue pencil. "Something like this," he said, and began to sketch me side and frontal views.

"I thought engineers couldn't draw schematics anymore," I said, watching him work. It was amazing that so drunk a fellow could draw so straight a line.

"That was before pen-based computers," he muttered, "when everything was done with mice. After they came in, we had to relearn drawing. Here."

I studied it. "It looks doable."

"Should be able to find a plastics shop in Tijuana to make it," Spejak said.

"Are you guys serious?" said Deirdre.

Well. "Why not?" I said. "It beats eating cat food."

"Where are you going to get capital?" said Deirdre.

I shrugged. "What do you want for the design?" I asked Spejak.

He turned up his hands. "Just give me a small equity stake," he said.

At which point, we heard the mob.

SHOUTS AND BELLOWS, CRASHES AND BANGS. DEIRDRE and I dashed out of Spejak's plastic shack; Spejak, I think, passed out. We followed the sounds—toward my residence.

Jew-hater was there; so was Manuel, and a half dozen other unstable sorts. My hovel was already burning.

"There he is!" shouted the lunatic. "Got you now, Jewboy!"

"What is all this nonsense!" shouted Deirdre. "Fire! Fire! Wake up, everyone, we've got to put this thing out! Manuel, what the hell do you think you're doing; you know better than this."

Deirdre began to organize a bucket brigade; she knew as well as I what a fire could do to Sludgetown.

As for me, I was sprinting as fast as I was able toward Route 80, my friend and his converts in hot pursuit.

8

THE WINTER OF LOVE

THUS IT WAS THAT, IN THE SPRING OF 20——, DURING THE
depths of the Crash, I found myself penniless and destitute
by the verge of Route 80, along the bay just north of Oakland,
pursued by persons with a strong desire to do me murder. It
was late at night, and I far from sober; moreover, I am a
complete stranger to the practice of physical violence, so that
my only recourse was headlong flight. Alas, some forty-two
years, the latter twenty of them involving the consumption
of superb food and excellent wines, had rendered me less than
a fine physical specimen: The individuals in question were
mere steps behind me. One, in particular, waved a piece of
lumber through which several rusty nails protruded, screaming "Jew bastard" at me.

An aging Silhouette van screeched to a halt in front of me.
A thin-faced grandmother with flowers in her hair threw open
the side door, and shouted "Get in!"

I got. The van sped into motion, hurling me into one of
the seats even as the door slammed shut. Through the rear
window, I could see the lunatic and his pals, capering angrily
as we sped away.

There was a curious, sweet scent in the air. It took me a
moment to place it: marijuana. From the music box in the
dashboard sounded grating electronic music. I was unable to

determine its provenance, albeit it was clearly the product of an earlier decade. Later, I was to learn it was Jefferson Airplane.

The driver was an old geezer, wearing a tie-dyed shirt, jeans, and beads. He squinted into the headlights of the cars across the median, smoking an enormous spliff.

The exertion, the van's violent motion, the rotgut I had consumed with Spejak, and the omnipresent smell were doing nothing for my internal serenity. "Beg pardon," I said, hitting the DOWN button on the window control, then leaned out and vomited all over the side of the vehicle.

"Peace, man," said the driver serenely.

"HAVE A TOKE," GRANDPA OFFERED.

"Huhn . . . Huhn . . . BLOOOORT," I replied.

"It's good for nausea," grandma claimed. "They used to prescribe it for chemo patients and like that."

"Chort. Cough. Urgh."

"Fascists won't even let 'em do that, anymore," grandpa said, swerving into another lane to pass a tractor-trailer on the right side. We were doing at least ninety.

"I'm Moonshadow," grandma claimed. "This is Eagle. He's my old man."

I was gradually regaining control over my digestive system. "Charmed," I said. "Johnson Mukerjii, at your service."

Grandma looked at me a little narrowly, then reluctantly said, "Or you can call us Pat and Jerry, if you like."

I was at a bit of a loss. Pat, or Moonshadow, wore a fringed suede shirt, a loose, patterned cotton skirt, and sandals; her wrinkled arms bore rough-cut turquoise jewelry. Camellia blossoms were stuck in her thin gray hair—so thin that her scalp was visible in places. Jerry, or Eagle, wore a tie-dyed T-shirt, V-necked to display scraggly, gray chest hair. A beer belly flopped over dirty jeans; he was apparently barefoot. Behind thick, wire-rimmed glasses, dope-reddened eyes gleamed maniacally below a shiny pate. One hand gripped the steering wheel, while the other held his joint.

"What's his name, babe?" he bellowed.

"Eagle's a little deaf," Moonshadow told me. She turned to him, cupped her mouth, and shouted. "Johnson Mukerjii, sugar pot."

Eagle flashed me an arthritic crook-fingered V, and said, "Peace."

Not quite sure of the culturally appropriate response, I muttered, *"L'chaim."*

"What did those fascists want with you, anyway?" Moonshadow asked.

It was hard to know how far Jew-baiter would have gone, but—"I suspect they would have done their level best to kill me," I said.

Moonshadow looked a little shocked. Eagle, who had apparently caught most of that, bellowed, "Fucking fascists are everywhere."

"Now, dear," said Moonshadow, "you used to vote Republican."

Eagle looked faintly shamefaced, and muttered something inaudibly.

"It's a good thing we picked you up, then," Moonshadow said. "We're going to Big Sur, but we can let you off anywhere between here and Santa Cruz if you want."

I considered this. Where did I want to go? If I was serious about this export idea, I needed capital. That would be hard to find, in this economic climate.

What about Huff? He was rolling in it, was he not? And I had a connection. . . .

Far-fetched, but what the hell. Huff, as I recalled, lived in Costa Mesa. Big Sur was at least in the right direction.

Eagle slowed down to match speed with a BMW. There were two older men in the car, perhaps in their sixties; they were neatly dressed and looked fairly prosperous, but were

obviously not too wealthy, or they'd be driving an aircar by
now. Eagle beeped his horn, and the man in the right-hand
seat of the BMW, perhaps thinking his headlights weren't
working, rolled down his window to talk with Eagle.

"Tune in! Turn on! Drop out!" Eagle screeched over the
wind of our motion, and tossed a joint neatly across the gap
between the two cars and into the man's lap.

To my astonishment, the old man broke into a grin, flashed a
peace sign, and as we sped away, I could see him lighting up.

They could take me to Big Sur. But did I really want to be
in the same vehicle as these lunatics?

We were doing ninety again. If the cops pulled us over—
Christ on a stick, who knew what kind of dope they had in
the van?

Oh, well. Beggars can't be choosers.

"I am bound for Orange County, actually," I said. "I would
be happy to accompany you as far as Big Sur, if you find my
presence pleasing."

"Groovy," said Moonshadow.

"All right," said Eagle.

"If grass isn't your thing, we have some poppers," Moonshadow said.

"And don't forget the 'shrooms," said Eagle.

"Errrrm," I replied.

I FELL ASLEEP SHORTLY THEREAFTER, STRETCHED OUT ON
the middle row of seats. I awoke sometime in the middle
of the night; the van was parked, there was no sound save for
the distant susurrus of breaking waves—and faint moans of
pain.

Moonshadow was doubled up in her seat, arms wrapped
about midriff, facial wrinkles reinforced by a grimace of ag-
ony. She rocked back and forth.

Eagle had awoken as well, but failed to note my wakefulness. Sleepily, he opened the glove compartment, scrabbled around in it, and drew forth some pills. He put them in Moonshadow's mouth, and she swallowed them dry.

After a while longer, she quieted, then gradually drifted away into sleep.

I studied her anew; she was painfully thin, her complexion gray. And that thin hair atop her head; the consequence of chemotherapy? I wondered. . . .

After a pass, I, too, slept again.

WHEN I NEXT WOKE, MY HOST AND HOSTESS WERE ASLEEP in their bucket seats. I had a headache and was slightly dry—the consequence, no doubt, of my binge with Spejak. I searched through the untidy mess of supplies at the rear of the van, but all I could find to drink was what appeared to be home-brewed ale. Well, hair of the dog, and so forth; and while additional alcohol would dehydrate me over the long term, it would rehydrate me over the short, and I could hope to find something else to drink in the medium.

We were parked along the verge of the Pacific Coast Highway. It was dawn, or a little thereafter. Out there were wisps of clouds, waves sparkling in the sun, gulls wheeling in the morning air. Before us, a cliff fell away to jagged rocks where breakers crashed. I think perhaps I caught sight of a seal or two, slipping through the waters. Sea lions, rather; seals are eastern.

Flanking our van were other parked vehicles. There was a Mercedes, painted with psychedelic flowers; an aging Ford Taurus with a Grateful Dead bumper sticker; and a decrepit electric Infiniti, with tie-dyed drapes over the windows. I wondered how they planned to recharge, out here in the middle of nowhere, until I saw the cracked solar panels spread out along the shoulder.

I got out and walked along the road for a while, enjoying the morning air. Along the way, I passed a crone levering herself painfully along with a walker. She wore a caftan, love beads, and a pair of glasses on a string about her neck. She eyed me suspiciously, then quavered, "Love."

I have, in the course of my career, had to adapt to the business customs of a great many cultures. Never let it be said that Johnson Mukerjii is impolite when it is in his power to respond in the correct and customary fashion. "Peace," I said, flashing her a V.

She scrabbled for her glasses, put them on, and peered at me, suspicion not entirely gone from her gaze. "How old are you, dearie?" she demanded.

I blinked. "Forty-two," I responded.

"Oh," she said, smiling. "That's all right then. Never trust anyone under thirty."

"Err—right on," I said.

We passed, I at a stroll, she at her painful crawl.

WHEN I RETURNED TO THE VAN, EAGLE HAD THE DRIVER'S door open and was sitting with his knees facing outward. He placed a number of small, white pills under his tongue. "Heart medicine," he explained, noting my glance. On his lap was a copy of *Rolling Stone*, which he had tilted at an angle; in it lay a considerable quantity of a crushed weed that I took to be cannabis. He was brushing it up the slope of the magazine with an index card. Round seeds fell down the slope, off his lap, and onto the highway shoulder.

"Ah—if you have heart problems, is it wise to smoke so much marijuana?"

Eagle chuckled, and in the overloud voice of the partially deaf, shouted, "Hope I die before I get old."

"Begging your pardon," I said, sitting down on a rock, "but you do not strike me as the proverbial spring chicken."

"Young in spirit," Eagle claimed. "I'm seventy-five if I am a day. Listen, son, if you're going to wreck your body with drugs, might as well do it when you don't have too many ycars to lose. Anyhow, I don't aim to wind up a vegetable in a home somewhere."

Moonshadow was rousing. "How do you feel about that?" I asked her.

She smiled. "We'll go together," she said. "The Goddess will provide." She hauled an ancient Coleman stove out of the mess at the rear of the van while Eagle lit the first spliff of the day. "How does a macrobiotic tofu omelette sound?" she said.

Loathsome. "Wonderful," I said.

SOON WE WERE ON THE ROAD AGAIN, HEADING FOR BIG Sur. Eagle stuck a disk in the music player, cranking the sound up much too loud. I looked at the box from which the disk had come: *Mick Jagger at Caesar's Palace*. Soon, the creaking, familiar voice came forth, belting out the hits of seven decades.

Highway 1 twists and turns about. At every place where the shoulder widened, there were aging ground cars: Audis, Saabs, Lexi, Acurae. About them were elderly women and men, lying in the sun, listening to music, doing drugs, spontaneously dancing.

Moonshadow took some photographs out of the glove compartment and showed them to me. "This is our daughter, Liza," she said, shouting over Jagger. Liza looked impeccably groomed, the sort of business-suited young woman I'd readily have hired in a previous incarnation.

"You must be very proud," I murmured.

"Establishment bitch," Eagle boomed.

"Now, dear," said Moonshadow. "That's our daughter." She turned to me, and said, "She's still employed." I couldn't tell whether her tone was mournful or proud. It was something of an accomplishment, to be sure, with the unemployment rate approaching 50%.

I looked out the window, wondering at this senile activity

along the Coast Road. Certainly the economic crash was
throwing up odd movements, as had the Great Depression;
yet this one struck me as inexplicable. Moonshadow must
have seen puzzlement on my face.

"You don't grok it, do you?" she said, smiling blissfully.
"It's the Winter of Love."

"We're Dropped-out Again," said Eagle. He reached over
and gave Moonshadow's knee a pat.

"What a drag it is to get old," Mick sang.

"WE LOST EVERYTHING," SAID MOONSHADOW.

"When the aliens came," Eagle explained. "In the Crash.
Have you ever had a mortgage?"

Had I ever. "Indeed," I said.

"Then you know what it's like," Eagle shouted over the
music. "We'd been hippies, you know? But life goes on."

"We got caught up in the materialism thing," said Moonshadow.

"Split-level ranch in Marin County," shouted Eagle. "Mu-
tual funds. I was in MIS for Bank of America."

"I was an account executive for Nomura," said Moonshadow.

"Shit, we were the revolution! Never came. Wound up just
like our goddamned parents. Social-climbing bullshit. Too
many things. 'Just say no.' Pfaugh." He began to cough violently, the cough of a longtime smoker. The van wandered
about the road until he got control.

"Voting Republican," said Moonshadow. Eagle winced, but
she patted his shoulder to take the sting out.

"Then, the Crash. The stock portfolio was worth nothing.
The pension plan went under. Social security isn't worth shit.
The banks foreclosed on the house."

"Thank heaven, Liza was out of college by then," Moonshadow said. "She can take care of herself."

"The only good thing out of those years," Eagle complained. "Too many years."

"We found ourselves with nothing but the van," Moonshadow said. "We'd already paid off the loan."

"Took the Mercedes, though," said Eagle. "Good riddance."

"And we found—you know?—we didn't miss it."

"Nope," said Eagle. "No responsibilities, no debts, nothing. Bust, and free."

"Just like we used to be," said Moonshadow.

"We heard about a Phish concert, and what the hell—we went. And you know, it's happening all over."

"The Winter of Love," said Moonshadow.

"We're Flower Geezers now," said Eagle contentedly. "Never been happier."

I was bemused. "But the drugs," I said. "Aren't the police rather harsher than they used to be?"

Eagle gave a braying laugh. "Than in the sixties? Nosirree. Anyhow, who's gonna bust someone's grandpa for smoking a little weed? And what else are you gonna do at seventy-five but groove in the sunshine?"

NEAR BIG SUR, WE TURNED OFF THE ROAD AND DROVE through redwood-shaded dimness. And then, abruptly, we were in full sunshine again, the forest behind us, squinting into the unaccustomed light. To the side of the road was a meadow, grasses and wildflowers delimited by rocky cliff. Dozens of vehicles were already parked there, evidently belonging to Flower Geezers. We parked and disembarked. Eagle had a little difficulty leaving the driver's seat—arthritis, I believe. I lent him an arm.

"Eagle and Moonshadow are here!" quavered an old man, one of those already present.

"All right!" came a voice.

"Peace!" said another.

"It's about time we got this party started, man!"

SOMEONE HAD SET UP AN AWNING, SEWN OF VIBRANTLY colored patches; beneath it were card tables bearing a cornucopia of food. Beer, most of it home-brew, was available. No music boxes were in evidence, but several people were playing instruments to attentive groups: guitars, lutes, a flute-and-harp duet. There were acres of long, unkempt gray hair, scraggly beards beneath bald pates, peasant dresses, wrinkles, and tie-dyes. The aroma of marijuana was everywhere, as were glassy eyes and blissful, vacant smiles. In the space of a dozen steps, I was offered hash brownies, Quaaludes, and the opportunity to gain carnal knowledge of a woman who could not have been less than eighty.

The beer was good, the food at least palatable. There are vegetarians who claim to be gourmets, but it is difficult to dine well on beans, organic brown rice, and tofu. Meat adds flavor as well as body.

The assemblage seemed to be enjoying themselves greatly, grooving, as it were, in the lambent California sunshine, here amid the beauty of the wild Pacific coast. I was faintly uneasy, as I often am at parties where I know virtually no one; they talked among themselves of events that might have happened yesterday, and might have happened sixty years ago, greeting each other with glad cries and a curled-finger handshake I am not sure I can duplicate. Still, between the beer and a contact high from the omnipresent smoke, I attained a certain plateau of bemused composure.

My hosts had mentioned a ride only to Big Sur; surely, amid this company, I could find someone to take me to points farther south? I did my best to make small talk in the hopes of finding a connection, but my unfamiliarity with the culture made it difficult.

Near the cliff, a man and two women were working over a

bamboo-and-plastic structure I identified as a hang glider. "Beauty, ain't she?" the man said as I approached.

"Indeed," I said. "Do you intend to fly her today?"

The workers exchanged glances. "Not me," he said cheerfully.

TOWARD THE LATE AFTERNOON, I WAS FEELING NO PAIN. I had more or less given up my attempt to find a ride and was simply enjoying the day myself. I sensed a change in mood in the crowd; they were more sober, and there was a definite drift in the direction of the glider.

By the time I got there, there was a spatter of applause; it appeared that Eagle and Moonshadow had made some kind of brief speech. They moved among the other Geezers, exchanging hugs and kisses; more than one eye, I saw, was wet. Eagle approached me and, unexpectedly, hugged me, too. "Here," he said gruffly. "You'll need these." Into my hand, he dropped the keys to the van. I was too surprised to respond before he turned away.

"I feel the acid beginning to kick in," said Moonshadow.

"It's time, then," said Eagle. With the assistance of the people who'd assembled the hang glider, they strapped into the bamboo frame. I had not previously noticed that there were two triangles below the glider's body; it was a two-person craft.

"There'll be an updraft over the cliff, the breeze off the ocean turning vertical," one of the women told Eagle. "And over the hills behind us, too; they should be hot from the afternoon sun."

"Gotcha," said Eagle, nodding. He turned toward Moonshadow. "Let's go, hon."

Others lifted the wingtips as Eagle and Moonshadow stood up, bearing the bulk of the glider's weight. They trotted forward and flung themselves off the cliff.

They swooped off, over the ocean; the glide ratio was sur-

prisingly good, for such a basically primitive device. After a
moment, they angled it into a climb. They were rising, rising;
it took a moment before I realized that the glider was moving
toward us as well as gaining height. This was no *trompe l'oeil*;
the breeze was moving faster than they, actually pushing
them back toward us, toward the cliff face, though the glider
was pointed directly away.

We watched as they sailed above us, perhaps forty feet over
our heads. Eagle spoke to Moonshadow, something I could
not hear at the distance. They leaned into a bank, turned,
and angled off toward the hills.

It was late, the sun hanging over the Pacific, yellow orb
beginning to be tinged with orange. The black-plastic bird
circled over the golden hills for lengthy minutes. About me,
the crowd was as rapt as I, watching them climb, spiraling
upward, upward and high. . . .

At last, they broke free. The glider swooped out again, a
shallow dive directly west, over the vast Pacific. It was hard
for me to look at the craft, for from our vantage, it was now
too close for comfort to the sun, the reddening sun. Away
and slowly down it drifted, far above the waves, its visible
aspect diminishing as it soared into the west.

Someone took my hand. I saw that everyone was linking
hands, and staring west, across the ocean, toward the setting
sun. There were wet eyes, and still I did not see why.

I peered at the glider again. There was an intake of breath
about me—

Two small shapes tumbled down, toward the water so far
below.

I never saw a splash.

The glider soared on, unattended, for a moment or two,
before it banked, crumpled, and tumbled toward the ocean
itself.

"Beautiful," whispered the crone to my right in the human
chain.

"But . . . why . . ." I stuttered.

"Didn't you know?" she said. "Moonshadow had inoperable cancer."

"What about Eagle?"

"Dicky heart," she said, turning away. "He might have lasted a few years, but . . . it was what he wanted."

IT WAS A LONG, LONELY DRIVE, TO COSTA MESA, ALONE in someone else's van.

OUTFOXING THE DE$ERT FOX

ROUND ABOUT PISMO BEACH, I WAS RUNNING OUT OF fuel, but luckily managed to pick up a hitchhiker who wanted to get to LA and was willing to pay for gas in exchange for the ride. Still, by the time I reached Costa Mesa, I had not bathed in several days; moreover, my army-surplus fatigues were not the appropriate costume in which to pitch an investment opportunity. I needed cash.

I had the Silhouette. Unfortunately, Eagle and Moonshadow had neglected to drive me to the nearest DMV site in order to formally put the van in my name before committing suicide, so I had no documentation. It was not too difficult to find an unscrupulous dealer who would take it off my hands for about a quarter its Blue Book value. The sum was exiguous, but I managed to stretch it to satisfy my immediate needs. Upon impulse, I got the dealer to throw in a free ride to the nearest Motel 6.

There, I took a room for one night, mainly to use the shower. Having groomed, I persuaded the desk manager, who went off shift at noon, to drive me to the South Coast Plaza mall in exchange for a small pourboire. There, I located a Sears and bought a suit on sale.

The experience was humiliating. I had resigned myself to dining on cat food, but the act of donning a suit from Sears, no less, was somehow the culmination of my degradation. To think that I had sunk so low.

It sufficed, however. It was a suit. It had a matching jacket and pants. There was a tie. I was attired as a businessmen, no matter how unsophisticated and ill-bred a businessman I might appear to be.

I was ready to go. There was lacking only one necessity: the address of the man I intended to hit up for money.

He was not in the telephone book, to be sure.

HOW TO FIND HIS ADDRESS? HIS PUBLISHERS WOULD know, of course. But from here to New York was a long-distance call. Every pay phone in the mall accepted credit and debit cards; and I had benefit of neither. I did still have a considerable quantity of cash.

It took some searching to locate a phone antiquated enough to retain a slot for coins. Alas, none of the banks in the mall boasted a human teller, and none of the ATMs was equipped to issue coins. I finally persuaded a vendor at one of the newsstands to give me fifty bucks worth of dollar coins in exchange for fifty-five dollars in paper.

Then, I dialed New York information, got the phone number of Tor Books, Leander Huff's publishers, fed in the requisite number of coins, and called them up.

"Hiya, babe," I told the receptionist, affecting my best British-turned-Angeleno accent, "gimme editorial will you, there's a doll."

"Hey, this is Jonas Swale with Hypermedia Productions. I need the phone and address of Leander Huff, one of your authors."

"Ah—you know, sir," said the voice on the phone, "it's not our policy to reveal the addresses of our authors. If you want to write him care of Tor, we'll happily—"

"No can do, no can do, babe. I've got a slot to fill on the *Written Word*, eight to nine Eastern Standard Time, Internet

Hypermedia. We can deliver an audience share of between 1.4 and 2.7, depending on competition and prepublicity. We want Huff, and I need to talk to him *muy pronto*, dig?"

"Ah—just a minute. Here it is—213-015-9989."

"Brilliant, thanks a mill. And the address?"

"Um, Mesa Grande Avenue, uh, the number is—"

And then a recorded voiced chimed in. "Please deposit fifteen dollars for an additional three minutes."

"Hey," said New York. "What is this? What was your name again?"

"The street number?" I said, desperately feeding the phone.

"What do you need the address for, anyway?" said New York suspiciously.

"Good point," I said, and hung up.

OF COURSE, THE ADDRESS WAS PRECISELY WHAT I needed. At least I had the street but, as a quick glance at a map in a nearby bookstore proved, Mesa Grande was quite long. Sighing, I used my last coin to call a cab to take me to one end of the street. I could, I supposed, walk up and down the length of it, peering at mailboxes until I found the right house.

I need not have worried. Touring up the street, I noticed that before one house stood a gaggle of aliens—six in all. Three were serpentine, boasting rows of legs; one manipulated some mechanical object in its pincers. Two were vaguely humanoid, with kangaroo-like tails, unclad; one of them bore a copy of a book. And the last rolled along in a wheeled contraption that resembled an iron lung—presumably it was not an oxygen-breather.

I told the driver to halt, paid him off, and stepped out of the cab. By the curb, three aircars were parked. I was interested to see that the interiors were fitted quite differently from ones I had seen before. Instead of the usual seats, one held elongated saddles; one was fitted with knee pads and stomach supports; and one had something that resembled nothing so much as a docking port. I perceived that the aliens had driven them there.

By the time I returned my attention to the house, Huff was at the open door. He was dressed in a terry-cloth bathrobe—at two in the afternoon, I may point out—and cradled a shotgun in his arms. "I don't give autographs, goddammit!" he shouted. "You're invading my privacy! Get off my goddamn lawn!"

"But Thor," wheezed one of the millipedes, "we hath come many light-yearth to meet famouth Earth author. Thurely it ith not too mutch to athk—"

Huff pumped the shotgun, pointed it overhead, and discharged it. I reflexively ducked. No doubt, lead shot was now gently sprinkling someone's barbeque, or ripping small holes in someone's vinyl swimming pool. It was not behavior I would have expected of the man.

Nor, apparently, the aliens. They recoiled from Huff, and as he bellowed, "Get away from me, you slobbering, bug-eyed monsters!" they came alternately teetering, bounding, and careening down the lawn to their cars.

Iron Lung and the Roos took off, but the Millipedes, apparently stouter in character, merely took shelter behind their vehicle, shouting. "But Thor! But Thor!" in plaintive, flutelike tones.

Huff's head reappeared from an upper-story window, along with the barrel of a rifle. "Die, alien scum!" he screamed, and plinked at the aircar. I was thankful he had traded in his shotgun, as I was sufficiently close to the aliens that, at this range, I would probably have been sprayed with lead myself if he had not. Nonetheless, discretion being the better part of valor, I flung myself half across a little Japanese rock garden, doing rather severe injury to a pretty little bonsai. Where in hell were the local cops? Or had I received an entirely incorrect view of American suburban life from the situation comedies?

The aliens were making faint chirring noises now, elbowing each other in the thorax with several legs simultaneously. They babbled at each other in a fluting alien tongue, then entered their vehicle and sped away.

I got the distinct impression that they thought Huff was hilarious. Had they been goading the Terran Supremacist precisely to elicit this response?

I picked myself up and did the best to get the dust off my suit, then gingerly approached Huff's door and rang the bell.

Almost instantly, it was flung open. There stood Huff, red-faced, tendons straining in his neck in rage, bathrobe half-open, a pistol with a bore the size of a golf ball clenched in both hands and pointed directly toward my forehead.

"WHAT DOES IT TAKE—" he screamed.

"Would this be a bad time to call?" I asked.

He peered around the side of the gun. "Oh," he said. "Sorry." He lowered the gun and stood there, blinking at me several times.

"I suppose it would be fruitless to ask how you are, Dr. Huff," I said. "The answer seems evident. I have a business matter I wish to discuss with you; if another time would be more convenient . . ."

An expression of dismay passed across Huff's face as he realized that he had successfully driven off his admirers only to have them replaced with a salesman of some sort. "Got one already," he said, attempting to slam the door. Luckily, I had the foresight to insinuate my foot between door and jamb in the expectation of just such a maneuver; or perhaps "luckily" is not the correct word, in view of the bruise I suffered to my instep.

"We are, in fact, acquainted," I pointed out. "Johnson Mukerjii, formerly of MDS."

Huff peered at me anew, half turned, his loaded gun still

in one hand. "Mukerjii," he said. "Yes, I remember. Holographic displays. Out of business, aren't you?"

"Yes, but I'm starting a new venture and . . ."

"Oh, hell," said Huff, "I'm not going to get any work done anyway. Want a drink?"

"Nothing," I said in some relief, "would please me more."

THE LIVING ROOM WAS EXQUISITE, DECORATED WITH A Victorian sensibility that, I suspected, Huff did not possess. Even bought at auction, the pieces in the room would easily have cost high five figures. At the sideboard, Huff located a bottle of Macallan 25—his preferred tipple, as I recalled—and poured us both a generous four fingers. I took ice; he, a purist, did not.

"*Prosit*," he said, and downed two fingers in a single gulp, enough to put the fire in anyone's belly. "Life is hell."

I was sipping mine more slowly. "Not with a scotch before one, surely."

"You don't know what it's like," said Huff, landing heavily in a chair, knobby knees poking up from the bathrobe. He looked uncomfortable; Victorian furniture is not designed for comfort. "The world's going to hell, I can't write, and the goddamn aliens keep offering me money."

"We should all have such problems," I offered.

He snarled. "Lot you know about it." He sat upright, glared at me with haggard eyes; he had evidently not been getting much sleep. "They're laughing behind my back," he said in a hoarse whisper. "I know they are, the googly-eyed swine."

I saw no profit in pursuing this avenue of conversation, not if I wanted to avoid further violence. "And how is—" From nowhere, my memory dredged up a name—"How is Mildred?"

"Fine," said Huff morosely, slouching back against the uncomfortable horsehair backrest of his chair. "She's in Sedona. Said she'd come back when I was livable." He rose and poured himself another glass of scotch. He was, I saw, weaving.

"And what of you?" he asked. "How have things been?"

"Ah, a little rough, since MDS went under," I temporized, "but all in all, I've been, ah, handling it well."

"Fine, fine," said Huff, clearly not listening. A thought had struck him. "Say, do you play games?"

I blinked. "Games? Chess? Go?"

"Wargames," he said.

Er. Well, anything to ingratiate oneself with a backer.

HE SAT ME DOWN AT THE CONSOLE. IT WAS RECOGNIZA-bly a computer, albeit I'd never seen the nameplate before; alien manufacture, Huff assured me. The display was wraparound holographic, the interface direct mind-to-machine. Huff set a bucket of ice and a bottle of scotch down by me. "Since you're a novice, we'll give you a bit of a handicap," he said. "Let's see; I have it. You'll be Montgomery; I'll take Rommel."

"That's a handicap?" I said weakly.

"Yes, yes," he said. "Alamein. You've a ten-to-one superiority in tanks, double the men, a virtually infinite supply of materiel. I'm at the limit of my logistical tether. Even a nincompoop like Montgomery was able to trounce a genius like Rommel." He grinned wolfishly. "We'll see if you can do as well." He disappeared.

"General?" said a young man in desert tan. "I've been assigned to be your adjutant. Shall I take you on a tour of the lines? HQ thought it would be helpful to see the situation firsthand."

Behind him was a military Land Rover; and in the distance, the vast Sahara.

Well. In for a penny, in for a pound.

I FOUND IT RATHER TEDIOUS, ACTUALLY. SUPPLIES, SUP-plies, supplies, organization charts, little wooden blocks pushed around on a table. Staff meetings. And so forth. Still, it beat going up to the front lines and getting shot at, even in simulacrum.

IN TEN HOURS, I WAS DROOPING WITH FATIGUE, MY SHIRT was soaked with sweat, the bottle was empty, and the 8th Army was routing toward Alexandria. Oh, well.

But then, I am, as a general rule, a complete stranger to—
Ah. I've said that before, have I?

I WAS AFRAID THAT HUFF MIGHT HAVE TAKEN MY FEEBLE opposition amiss; no doubt, I had not been much of a challenge. To the contrary, he seemed exhilarated; I took him to be the sort of chap who likes winning and detests defeat, regardless of the conditions under which either transpires.

If he had been weaving before, he was virtually glowing now. He threw a companionable arm about my shoulders, and said, "Good game, Johnny." We staggered together into the living room, where he unwisely poured us each another drink. I forbore to mention that I was starving.

"Say," he said, virtually collapsing onto a chaise longue that did not appear as if it could bear the impact. "Din't you come here on bus—bus—bidness?"

"Indeed, Dr. Huff," I said, my own speech not entirely as distinct as it normally is.

"Les, Les," he said. "Call me Les."

"Certainly," I said. And I told him of my idea. Oh, not the philosophical basis, the need to earn hard currency; merely the notion of the Drink Valet, the usefulness in null gee.

When I finished, I feared he had lost the thread; his eyes were glazed, and his head was nodding.

"How—how mush?" he said.

"How much?"

"How mush money you need?"

"Ah, a couple of hundred thousand should do for starters," I said.

He lurched to his feet, stumbled into the study, and came back with a checkbook. He wrote out a check, in a shaky hand, for two hundred thousand, and passed out, the checkbook falling from his hands.

I picked up the checkbook and disbelievingly studied the check.

MANY A BUSINESS HAS BEEN LAUNCHED ON THE BASIS OF A swift scribble on paper. Probably more than we know, in truth, have been launched on the basis of drunken approval.

My shaking hands held the capital I desired; yet I knew Huff. He would never have done this, sober, without a contract, no *quid pro quo* established; and were he to sober up, it was easy enough to stop the check.

I sat, drunk myself, yet tense with the will to action, on Huff's Bokhara carpet, and furiously thought.

A check drawn on a California bank will clear in one day, in California. Would it not? I prayed it would, even for one the size of this.

It was five o'clock in the morning, when Huff passed out. I had not eaten in eighteen hours, nor slept in twenty-four. Nonetheless, first things came first. I searched Huff's pockets and found the keys to his car, then stretched him out more comfortably on the chaise longue and draped a blanket over his form. Then I took his aircar and drove it—in ground mode, I feared to experiment with its more advanced capacities—to the nearest Bank of America. I was waiting at the doors when they opened at eight; I opened an account and deposited the check. I asked them if I could make some phone calls; they, happy to have a new account of such dimensions, gladly agreed. After a call to directory inquiries, I phoned a Banamex branch in Tijuana and opened an account

there. Then, I left instructions at the Bank of America to wire
90% of the money to my Banamex account as soon as the
check cleared.

How long, I innocently inquired, would that be?

One full business day, they said.

All glory be to electronic funds transfer! All hail the wisdom of the Federal Reserve, and the sage benevolence of the
bank regulators of the Golden State! One business day to
clear; and why should it not be so? Did Huff not have the
funds? Did I not have ID?

One full business day. As it was Tuesday morning, that
meant the check would clear as of Wednesday close of business, 3 P.M.

I found a McD's, gorged on several helpings of their foul
fast-food treyf, drove Huff's car back to Huff's house, parked
it, and replaced the keys in his pocket.

It was now 9:30 A.M. I collapsed on a nearby couch.

At approximately two on Tuesday afternoon, I awoke when
a hungover Huff blundered into my couch, holding his head
in his hands. I was somewhat under the weather myself, but
immediately arose.

"Good God, man," I said cheerily. "You look like what the
cat dragged in. Hair of the dog, that's what you need. That,
a gallon of water, and a heavy dose of ibuprofen."

"Oh shut up," moaned Huff, but happily accepted my min-
istrations.

By three, he was tipsy again. I got a TV dinner into him
(and one into me), and proposed a rematch. This time, I, as
the Japanese, was sadly trounced by the British defenders of
Singapore.

"Didn't you notice the defensive guns only face toward the
sea?" Huff said gleefully. "Nesh time, you can invade Polan'.
Only way you might win."

"Ah, well, old man," I acknowledged, "you did have me
outfoxed there, I fear."

He collapsed again at 4 A.M., Wednesday morning. I slept as well; at two that afternoon, I awoke. I studied Huff's loudly snoring form, then decided to take the risk of leaving him alone for an hour. I did, however, take the precaution of cutting the phone line to his house before departing.

At the bank, I verified that the check had cleared and the money had been wired to Banamex. I closed out the account, taking several thousand in cash, and the rest in the form of a cashier's check.

Then, I took a limo to John Wayne International, to book a flight for Tijuana.

And as we baked in honking traffic on Macarthur, en route to the airport, I sat in air-conditioned comfort reflecting on the day.

Two hundred thousand: a pittance. Once, my mortgage alone had cost me so much in a year. But it was a hard-won pittance, and it gave me a shot at something more.

There would be the IRS, of course; the bank would report any transaction so large. And there would be the SEC; Huff had foolishly failed to negotiate any recompense for his funds, but in gratitude, I decided, I would give him 2% of my company for fully funding the firm. The SEC would be involved the moment I issued him shares. And there would be the DEA; any funds transfer that size to Mexico would interest them.

But as far as I could tell, I had as yet done nothing actually against the law. Well, cutting Huff's phone line, to be sure. And he might argue fraud. But based on his story, what DA would prosecute?

And I'd be in Mexico, of course. Ah, sunny Mexico, where life and law are cheap.

10

AD A$TRA, 20% OFF LOWE$T TICKETED PRICE

DID I SAY SUNNY?

They call it Tio Diego, now, a vast metropolis rivaling LA, sprawling across the border on both sides. But the Free Trade Agreement of the Americas has not succeeded in abolishing the border entirely.

Goods, raw materials, and workers pass smoothly back and forth. But the workers do not stay; subcutaneous chips chirp at them when it is time to return home, and if they do not, *Immigraçion* is not far behind.

On that side, the sky is clear; on this, a constant murk of smog. On that side, fat Anglos slurp margaritas while watching *campesinos* tend their verdant lawns; on this, skinny children clamber over steaming refuse at the dump, searching for a fragment of aluminum or steel they may sell for the price of a crust of bread. On that side, bland suburban comfort; on this, penury and squalor.

One city, two worlds, San Diego and Tijuana.

One city, two jurisdictions, thank the stars.

INCORPORATING IN MEXICO IS A NIGHTMARE. THE STATES can learn a thing or two from the bureaucrats of the *Republica Federal*. But Pater grew up in Mombai. I know how to deal with bureaucracy. A well-placed penny or two can do wonders. Well, not pennies; New Dollars, nice crisp multi-color Booker T. Washingtons. The Mexicans have yet to begin to trust home-grown pesos. My greatest start-up expense was bribery.

I incorporated as Mukerjii Interstellar, Ltda. In retrospect, the name was foolish, for two reasons. First, it was unreasonably optimistic; I wasn't to make an offworld sale for some time. Second, a simple web search for "Mukerjii" would give Huff—rather, his attorneys—information I'd really rather they didn't have.

Still, in a matter of a week, I had fistful of newly minted share certificates, an office on Calle Ocho, and a telecoms line. I had Spejak's schematics. What I didn't have was a product.

I pulled out the phone book and started looking under *Plastica*. Dozens of companies were listed; it was hard to know which were good, which lousy, which crooked, which straight; that's one of the advantages of working in a field, you get to know the score. But I was starting up in a business I knew nothing about; high-tech Valley is a long way from low-tech import-export. But you have to begin somewhere.

I noticed with a start that one firm—Plastica Cruz, SA—was in the same building as my new office. That, I realized, was the cause of the noxious smell from the sixth floor. I smelled it every time I took the elevator.

It was an industrial loft building. Most of the floors held small manufacturers or warehouse space; some, like mine, had been subdivided into cheap offices. I rang for the elevator and waited for it to appear with elephantine slowness. I took it down to *seis*.

The internal door opened; the external grate did not. It had been locked. Beyond, the office lights were off. This did not look promising—but a buzzer was set by the grate, so I pushed it, and yelled "¡Hola! ¿Hay alquien aqui?"

"¡Un momento!" came a reply, so I waited while someone

on another floor rang furiously for the elevator.

Presently, a gaunt, sallow, fortyish fellow in jeans and, of all things, a faded Strangers in Paradise T-shirt appeared with an enormous ring of keys and unlocked the grate. He had a full head of gray-spotted hair, flying every which way about bushy brows, and several days growth of stubble. "*Buenas tardes,*" he said enthusiastically, grinning madly. "*Me llamo Mauro. ¿En qué puedo servirle, amigo?*"

I stepped into the office—unpainted wallboard, bare wires where light fixtures had once been—and said, "*Solo hablo Español un poco.* Do you speak English?"

"Sure!" said Mauro. "Everybody in Tio Diego speaks English, have to, to do business."

"You don't seem to be doing much business."

Mauro gave a carefree shrug, motioning me to follow him. "No business to do," he said happily. "Economy is for shit. Had to lay everyone off. Want to buy a plastics company?"

He led the way into a large loft space: bales and canisters of supplies against the walls, six or eight machines scattered across the grimy floor. The only thing I recognized was a plastics extruder. I assumed the other machines performed other processes—casting, curing, whatever. I don't know much about plastics manufacture. Mauro sat on a creaky office chair by a beaten-up metal desk, leaned back on the swivel. With an extravagant sweep of an arm, he motioned me toward the scarred wooden chair nearby. "Take a load off, *amigo,*" he said. "*Mi casa es su casa.*" A liter bottle of cheap mezcal, uncapped, stood next to a battered old computer that hadn't had its case cleaned in years; he rummaged in a desk drawer, found two dirty jelly jars, set them on the table, and poured us each four fingers. I gingerly took the glass, which he proffered with a flourish; I was reasonably certain he'd been drinking from the bottle before I arrived, and the glass was none too clean.

"You seem like an awfully happy fellow, for a bankrupt," I said.

Mauro grinned at me, tossing back a half inch of liquor. "Not bankrupt yet," he said. "Tomorrow, maybe. Unless you're business."

"I might be," I said, somewhat tentatively, "but you know, this"—I gestured at the silent machinery about us—"does not exactly inspire me with confidence in your ability to deliver."

Mauro made a gesture—hands spread, something that might mean, "So?", except he did it so expansively and violently it was hard to be sure. "I know how to operate every machine on this floor," he said. "If it's a small job, no problem. If it's a bigger job, I can find people *muy pronto.*"

"You can hire your people back?" I asked.

He snorted at me. "You think they find work someplace else?" He shrugged. "Besides, they like working with Mauro. *Salud.*" He downed his mezcal, poured more, slammed the bottle back down.

Somewhat doubtfully, I handed him Spejak's schematics.

Mauro leaned forward to take them, chair creaking, and studied them for a moment. "Three molds," he said. "Vinyl cup, PVC for the shaft. I recommend high-density poly for the clip; give you a little flexibility. How many you want?"

"Actually," I said, "I only want a couple of hundred for samples, but I may need several thousand. . . ."

Mauro flipped a hand through the air, coming close to knocking over the mezcal. "No, no, no, my friend," he said. "Completely uneconomical. The molds, they set you back ten grand—we're talking dollars, of course. A couple hundred units? For a few thousand dollars more, I give you ten thousand units. Assembled. Even then, your unit cost is over a dollar each. For thirty thousand dollars, I give you a hundred thousand units, your unit cost is thirty cents. You see?"

"Yes," I said slowly. "I see. But I can't imagine what I'd do with a hundred thousand. Unless this really takes off."

"What's it for?" he asked.

So I told him.

By the time I was done, he was doubled up in his seat laughing; his glass wavered unsteadily, mezcal slopping onto the grimy floor. Glumly, I sipped the harsh tequila while I waited for him to regain control.

Mauro wiped his tears and took another slug of mezcal.

"And my wife calls *me* an impractical dreamer," he said. "I don't know if I can offer you thirty days on this. I think it's a good idea to ask for cash up front from lunatics."

I was a bit peeved. "Me a lunatic?" I said. "I'm not sitting here hooting and hollering as I go out of business."

Mauro grinned. "Sure," he said. "But I tell you what. Let's say this silly idea works. You buy molds and a few hundred from me. Little green men love it, you want another hundred thou. Guess what? I'm out of business."

I blinked. "But . . ."

"Twelve thousand from you; my cost of goods is maybe eleven. I work on such a tight margin because I know three guys down the street do the same, everybody needs business, and there isn't any. A thousand dollars keeps Evita and me in groceries, rent on the office paid, for maybe a month. You come back in a month to order more, there's a padlock on the door."

"I see," I said. "What if I get the molds from you? That way, if you do go under, I can take them to somebody who still is in business."

"Okay," Mauro said, nodding. "I charge you a little more for the molds. And you know what? If you find somebody still in business, let me know. Maybe I can get a job. But good luck. Whole town's going to shit."

"You're saying the plastics industry around here is disappearing?"

"Like a case of Dos Equis on a Saturday night."

This was a hitch. My plan hinged on the ability to scale up production quickly if I started selling. It depended on the existence of spare capacity—which, I had assumed, would be no problem in the midst of a depression. But if everyone went out of business first . . .

"Were you serious about selling your business?" I said slowly.

Mauro laughed. "Assume the debt and give me another ten grand, and it's yours."

I frowned. "What's your debt?"

"Hundred thou," he said, and dived into his drink.

"I think not," I said. I couldn't afford to take on that much debt. "What's the machinery worth?"

Mauro looked around. "Maybe ten thousand used," he said.

"Right," I said. "Here's the deal. I pay Cruz Plastica, SA, fifteen thousand dollars for the assets of the firm: machinery, lease on this space, the name. Cruz Plastica declares bankruptcy. The creditors get to fight over the fifteen K. I hire you at twenty thousand a year to run my manufacturing division, and give you two percent of my company, so maybe you get rich if I do."

Mauro looked bemused for a moment. "Guarantee my salary for a year?" he said.

"Certainly."

Mauro sprang up and slapped my back, hard enough that I spilled my mezcal. "You got a deal, *jefe.*"

And so I acquired my first subsidiary. My business empire was burgeoning by leaps and bounds.

Of course, I had yet to make a dollar in sales.

THE NEXT DAY, I SAT IN MY OFFICE, TIE OFF AND SHIRT unbuttoned: I am rarely so slovenly, but it was close to 35 degrees—centigrade, of course—and I had no air-conditioning. I had spent the morning watching Mauro work, but he chased me out of his office, claiming I made him nervous. So I spent most of the morning on the phone. I got through to Omar Captious at Captious, Invidious, Conniving & Cruik remarkably quickly.

"Mukerjii," he said, rather nastily, "you owe us three hundred and fifty thousand dollars. Where the hell are you? Hiding from creditors?"

"By no means, Mr. Captious," I said. "And as it happens, I owe you nothing. The debt was owed by Mukerjii Display Systems, a company now in liquidation, alas."

Captious snorted. "A debt is a debt," he said. "Do you intend to honor it?"

"Talk to bankruptcy court," I said. "In the meantime, I have started a new venture, and am in need of legal counsel."

"Goddamn it, Mukerjii, what makes you think we'll take you on after you stick us with three hundred thou in bad debt?"

"Because, sir, you need the work. In these troubled times, I doubt there's much legal work except in the bankruptcy courts."

There was silence on the other end of the phone for a moment. "That's for sure. Do you know what the payout for full partners was last quarter here? I'd jump to another firm in a moment, if anyone else was doing any better."

"I have a device I need patented," I said. "In all the major markets. Trademark, some customs stuff. Nothing major, but billable work."

"Okay," said Captious. "Only I think you'd better pay us a retainer up front, given your past payment history. Say fifty thousand."

I chortled. "In a pig's eye," I said. "Five, maybe."

We settled on ten.

After I hung up, I sat back in my chair and began to think about packaging. Plastic, of course; I owned a plastics company, after all. But there'd need to be some kind of printed cardboard insert with promotional copy. I'd have to find a copywriter, and someone to do the graphics. Shouldn't be too hard. I began to take notes on my laptop.

As I did, I heard the elevator groaning to a halt on my floor. The door creaked open; a Federale in an infrequently laundered uniform stood inside with a bundle of papers.

"*¿Es se llama Johnson Mukerjii?*" he asked.

This was unlikely to be good news; but then, this is Mexico, and I had the pelf to bribe him if necessary. "*Sí, señor,*" I said. "*Yo soy el.*"

"*Esto usted,*" he said, and tossed the papers onto my desk. He watched while I scanned the first line, which was, as it happened, in English: "Dr. Leander Huff, Ph.D., v. Mr. Johnson Mukerjii and Mukerjii Interstellar, Ltda."

They were court papers. The court of jurisdiction was in Santa Ana, California, though my address was in Mexico. I eyed the cop askance; he had no business delivering legal papers from an American court. Then I noticed that he wore no gun; he was off duty, I assumed. He must be moonlighting.

Well, it wasn't his fault. I sighed, said, "*Gracias, señor,*" and gave him a few pesos because it seemed expected.

As he left, I considered the implications; I had few attachable assets in the States. Everything I owned had been lost in the crash—or to Maureen. Everything Mukerjii Interstellar owned was in Mexico . . . although I supposed it might be possible to attach our invoices with U.S. retailers.

But—there were only three places in the world I could go to sell my merchandise: Cape Canaveral, Kourou in French Guiana, and Tyuratam, the Russian launch site. Those were the three locations the United Nations had specified where alien craft might land, and the three likeliest places to sell my gizmo.

The airfare to Cape Canaveral—or rather, to Orlando, the closest major airport—was the cheapest of the three. I had planned to go there first. But I might be legally served in the States, or even arrested, if Huff had also filed criminal charges.

I contemplated trying Kourou first, but I was reluctant. It was part of the European Union; it was easier to ship goods from Mexico to the *Estados Unidos*. And hell, I was trying to invest Huff's money wisely, even if I had gotten it by, um, extralegal means. Besides which, I'd been to Kourou. I didn't *like* it. Filthy bug-encrusted place.

I dialed Captious again. "Omar," I said. "I'd better bump your retainer a bit. I have another problem."

I EXPLAINED THE SITUATION TO MAURO, WHO STOOD over a hot machine, wiping sweat on his shirtsleeve. "No problem," he said. "I take you to Kevin."

KEVIN LIVED ON THE AVENIDA PEQUEÑA IN AN OLD-fashioned apartment building with air-conditioning, thank goodness; clearly a prestigious address. He was American, which I had expected; I had not expected a trim, graying black man, wearing Dockers, loafers without socks, and an Izod shirt, listening to Billie Holliday while exchanging rapid-fire Spanish with Mauro. Clearly, providing would-be immigrants with false identification was a profitable business.

"You're not exactly my usual customer," he told me, "but I can get you a U.S. passport in two days."

"No," I said. "I don't want to be American. I want a Mexican passport."

He blinked at me. "Nobody wants to be Mexican," he said. "Not even the Mexicans."

"I do," I said. "With a Mexican passport, some fake business cards, and a sample case, I can enter and leave the U.S. without any problems, so long as my name comes up clean at Customs."

He shook his head. "You're nuts," he said. "A U.S. passport will take you almost anywhere."

"Nevertheless," I said. I had my reasons; if Huff had filed criminal charges, it was more than likely my face would be in Customs's computer files. And when I passed through customs, a warrant might pop up—if I went through as an American. As a Mexican, they'd scan me against the files for terrorists and drug smugglers, but probably not against U.S. citizens with outstanding warrants. I figured it was a better bet.

Kevin looked contemplatively at the stuffed armadillo on his bookcase for a moment. "It shouldn't be too tough," he said. "The Mexicans are pretty lax. But I've never had to do it before."

"It will," I said with a sigh, "cost extra, I suppose."

Kevin smiled. "Doesn't everything?"

Still, he was as good as his word. In two days, I was Señor Tadeo Rajiputano, vice president of sales for Ortiz Rubio Maquiladores, Ltda.—with a passport, a driver's license, and business cards to match. I liked the surname; Hispanicized East Indian. A nice touch.

THERE WAS NO PROBLEM GETTING TO ORLANDO. I bought tickets out of San Diego at an office in Tijuana; Immigration delayed me only momentarily when I drove across the border to get to the airport.

In Orlando, I rented an aircar on impulse; I had yet to drive one in more than ground mode. The rental agent assured me it was no problem, the controls quite simple, and so it seemed; a lever in place of a gearshift controlled rate of ascent or descent, wheel and pedals performed their customary functions. The vehicle could apparently hover without any problem; I had no idea what technology was involved, nor what fuel it consumed—there did not seem to be a place to put in gas. I had to rent it under my actual name, as Mr. Rajiputano had no credit cards, an omission I vowed to correct as soon as feasible.

Traffic between Orlando and Cape Canaveral was heavy; there were nine lanes each way, arranged three by three; that is, aircars flew above me as well as to the sides. The lanes were marked off by objects that looked like long yellow balloons, the kind that you use when twisting balloon sculptures for kids' birthday parties. They seemed to hold position despite the breeze as well as the backwash from the passing vehicles.

SPEED LIMIT: MACH .9 read a sign as I swooped up the cloverleaf and merged into traffic. I stayed firmly in the lower right lane, apparently the slowest of the nine, as I had no desire to get anywhere near Mach .9. Seventy-five, eighty had been fine by me; going close to the speed of sound in something that didn't look too different from my old Jag did not appeal.

Coming in, I had a nice view of the Cape Kennedy complex: Merritt Island, where the space center is actually located; the elbow of Cape Canaveral beyond it, and the open Atlantic in the distance; the swamps, still a nature sanctuary, the tranquillity of their birds and alligators broken by the roar of spacecraft landing and taking off. The old shuttle gantry was gone, replaced by one of a dozen flat concrete pads, scarred with the exhaust of spacecraft, surrounded by Quonset huts, scattered with service and emergency vehicles. As I drove, I saw an alien craft the size of an ocean liner—it looked like nothing so much as four enormous blue soap bubbles arranged in a tetrahedron—descend toward one pad, slowing as it dropped without any evidence of rocket exhaust.

The enormous cube of the Vehicular Assembly Building, where the old Apollos and shuttles had once been assembled, still stood; but it was dwarfed, now, by NASA Mall.

• • •

IT WAS WHY I WAS HERE, OF COURSE. BUT I WAS FLABBER-
gasted at its size. It was built in the shape of a wagon
wheel—or a space station; a circular central region connected
by vast spokes to an outer toroid. Between the spokes were
open-air gardens, amusement parks, water rides, and the
NASA museum, chronicling the glories of America's space-
faring past—now seeming charmingly antiquated and rather
tacky in the light of alien contact. A light rail ran to and from
the landing fields—as well as the enormous parking garage
where I was now headed.

The light rail trip was uneventful, although I found the
automated voice announcements ("Now arriving at parking
E" in six human languages and three alien tongues) rather
annoying.

We were disgorged at the rim of the mall, where it joined
one of the spokes. A huge teak reception desk ran for at least
forty yards. Beyond, I could see a Tiffany's, a Bloomies, a
Brazilian gem store—and what looked like an authentic tropical rain forest, complete with macaws and spider monkeys.

I looked down the three corridors—the sides of the torus,
curving away to right and left; the spoke extending beyond
the reception desk toward the hub. There were six levels, with
null-gee tubes and, for the less adventurous, escalators and
elevators connecting them. Where the devil was I to begin?

I was greeted by the Marlboro Man in a NASA uniform.
That's what he looked like, at any event: tanned, seamed,
leathery skin, extremely trim. He could have been a test pilot.
"It is big, isn't it, sir?" he said.

"An understatement," I muttered.

"NASA Mall is the largest mall in the solar system," he
said cheerfully, "six times as large as the Mall of America. Yet
the central part of it, the Hub, was thrown up in a mere three
weeks by NASA engineers—demonstrating the same inge-

nuity and know-how that put men on the moon."

I blinked. "Beg pardon?"

"Yes, sir," he said, "when Congress cut our funding to the bone—they didn't see much point in funding smelly rocketships, what with antigrav and faster-than-light travel—NASA responded to the challenge."

"By going into retail," I said.

The Marlboro Man winced, looking briefly disgruntled, before the professional smile reasserted itself. "If you like, sir. People from every continent and innumerable star systems shop here; we're one of the nation's largest earners of hard alien currency."

"You're a glorified duty-free outlet."

The professional smile faltered again. "Yeah, well," said Mr. Marlboro. "You do what you have to, to get by."

I looked at him a little more closely. "It must rankle."

"Six years at Georgia Tech and four in the Navy Air Force, and for what? To greet a bunch of tourists, bug-eyed monsters, and spinsters in blue-polyester pant suits?" He looked as if he were sucking a lemon.

"So why not quit?" I asked.

"And do what? With this economy? Beats starvation."

"I suppose," I said.

He pulled himself together, and the smile, now somewhat strained, returned. "And how may I help you, sir?"

"I could use a map," I said.

"Certainly, sir," he said despairingly, finding one behind the counter and handing it to me. "Have a nice day."

I STUDIED THE MAP. EVERY MAJOR DEPARTMENT-STORE chain in the country, and a fair number from outside, had an outlet here. Wal-Mart, Bloomies, Sears, Nordstroms; Harrods, Gum, Miyamoto. But the list went on and on; not only the normal mall bait outlets, but art galleries, auction houses, antique stores. Bloomies was close, so I wandered into it and tried to talk to the housewares manager, but he wouldn't see me.

Figures; chains buy centrally. I'd have to try through headquarters.

What did that leave? Independent retailers. There ought to be enough here.

I passed by a place called Earth Objet, and wandered in on impulse. It had everything: Balinese sculpture, those Russian wood dolls that open up to reveal more dolls, Louis XIV furniture. The prices were insane. Three hundred dollars for a small Balinese carving of a fish? You could buy it for forty in California, or two bucks in Indonesia.

I had figured on a retail price of five bucks for the Mukerjii Drink Valet, as the packaging termed my gadget; that was a high markup over manufacturing, actually. Mentally, I ratcheted the price up to ten bucks. If everyone else was profiteering, who was I to buck the trend?

Earth Objet wasn't interested, but then, I hadn't expected them to be.

Nor was Kmart, Star Express, Sol System Outfitters, the A&P, Crustaceans R Us . . . I wandered down spoke and around rim, up and down the null-gee tubes, hitting everything that looked remotely plausible.

Six hours later, I sat on a blue-plastic bench, my back to a fountain, shoes off, massaging my feet, feeling very depressed. I had yet to make a sale. I watched as a gaggle of arthropods in Hawaiian shirts passed; the shirts had been tailored for creatures with eight limbs. I'd seen them in Crustaceans R Us. Only about one in ten of the mall's customers seemed to be alien, but they were the only ones buying. Certainly, I wouldn't buy anything, at these prices.

I revised that conclusion; I was starving. Across the hall was a place called Frank's Convenience Store. It had Barbies and a stack of Coke in the window. Signs said REAL EARTH

FOOD! and something in an alien squiggle. I sighed. Real Earth Food was what I needed. I put my shoes back on and wearily went in.

Real Earth Food meant chili dogs and microwave burritos. I wasn't *that* hungry. The place was basically an off-brand 7-Eleven; I wandered down the aisle for toilet articles, looking interestedly at the merchandise; a lot of it was alien, with alien packaging. There was one item like an ice pick with a toothbrush at the end; I had no idea what it was for. Nor the blue egg in plastic, with pictures of what looked like lice on the packaging. But I got the idea; they sold grooming aids and cosmetics and snacks, stuff you might want to pick up before getting back on your starship and heading for Epsilon Eridani. Or whatever.

I took a look at the ice-pick brush. The price tag said it cost $20; I couldn't read the dot pattern on the packaging, but it was obviously not of terrestrial manufacture. Hey, I could make that. In bulk, for probably under forty cents. I wondered what the market for it was, how to reach it; God knows. But I was right, I told myself; we *could* compete with the aliens, if only for shoddy goods, if only because our labor was pathetically cheap by comparison with theirs.

What the hell. I found a shopgirl—sorry, Sales Associate— and asked for the manager.

The manager was a chubby white guy with a shaven head, a bad sunburn, and a permanent scowl. He wore a little plastic sign that said "Hi! I'm Eric."

"How do you do, sir," I said, shaking his hand and opening my sample case on the counter. "I represent Mukerjii Interstellar, and have an item that I think you'll find of interest. You see, travel in zero gee has its problems; you can't drink from a cup, for instance, because . . ."

"Yeah, yeah," said Eric. "We got Coke in squeeze bulbs."

"Ah! Clever marketers, the chaps from Atlanta," I said.

At this juncture, a creature looking remarkably like a bipedal cockroach interrupted us; I tried to avoid flinching at the sight of its four forelimbs, the constantly moving antennae. It emitted a series of chips and buzzes, and a small blue object about its neck said, "Excuse me, do you have thorax wax?"

"Aisle six," said Eric. The box translated this into chirps and buzzes.

"Of course," I continued, "while squeeze bulbs keep your drink from spraying all over the ship, another problem arises; you can't put your drink down, or the squeeze bulb will drift away." The blue box continued translating my words; and the roach, who had turned toward aisle six, looked back.

"So?"

"Let me demonstrate. You see, you simply clip the neck of the squeeze bulb so"—I had a sample bulb, for just such purpose—"and then affix it to any convenient bulkhead, using this suction cup."

"Nah," said Eric dubiously. "First thing, suction cups ain't gonna work in zero gee. Secondly, this is a high-class store, here. We feature first-rate merchandise from across the planet and beyond. I just can't imagine our clientele bein' interested in a tacky little plastic gadget that don't even work. . . ."

"May I see?" said the cockroach's blue box. I handed the Drink Valet to him, and he experimentally stuck it to the side of the counter. Luckily, it held; the squeeze bulb was empty. It would have fallen if the bulb were full; the suction cup wasn't designed to hold much up against the force of gravity.

"Of course suction works in zero gee," I said. "It depends on air pressure, not gravity."

"How {click buzz}!" said the roach; I assume the blue box had trouble translating the phrase. "How much is it?"

"Our suggested standard retail price is ten dollars," I said.

"Your what?"

"It costs ten bucks."

The roach was motionless for a moment, save for its continually questing antennae. "I have changed all my money already," it said. "Would you accept 1/144th of a *gozashstandu*?"

Eric's jaw dropped.

I was nonplussed. A twelfth of a twelfth of—what? "Certainly," I said weakly.

The roach opened a pouch, and withdrew a small plastic square, which it handed me. The square was imprinted with a hologram of a roach wearing some kind of crimson garment. I handed him a fresh Drink Valet, in the original packaging.

"My eggs quiver at your kindness," said the roach.

"Uh . . . You're welcome," I responded.

The roach turned to look for aisle six.

Eric withdrew a handkerchief from his apron, and wiped his brow. "I'll take a dozen gross," he croaked.

LATER, I FOUND A BANK, AND TO MY DELIGHT LEARNED that 1/144th of a *gozashstandu* was worth just under $50 American.

11

MITIGATING FACTORS

BUOYED BY MY FIRST SALE, I MANAGED TO WRITE ORDERS for close to ten thousand units over the next several days; I merely waited to time my pitch when an alien was nearby. This didn't always work, but often enough the alien was interested; the Mukerjii Drink Valet was a novelty. I was extremely thankful I'd had the foresight to print iconographic instructions on the packaging; no English, nor any other terrestrial language, was required to figure out how to use the Drink Valet.

I flew back to San Diego a happy man, and told Mauro to gear up production. I subscribed to Phelon's Retail Guide on the net to get contact information on retail buyers, and started calling the chains. I may not be the best salesman on the planet, but I believed in my product and its potential. I soon had a good three hundred thousand dollars in orders.

Cash flow was going to be tight. We had to buy raw plastic. I had to pay the printer. We had to take on some of Mauro's laid-off employees, to assemble the Drink Valets. I hired a secretary to handle some scut work. And we were offering sixty-day dating; had to. Would you want to deal with a fly-by-night operation from Tijuana unless you could ensure that the merchandise was in your own warehouse and as advertised before cutting a check?

Meaning: We had bills to pay now. We'd get the money later. And no way, without a track record, I could get a bank loan. Still, I had enough: about $40,000 left in the Banamex account. My burn rate was about $8,000 a week. I could probably skate by. Barely. If I dined on burritos and slept in the office.

Still, I was a happy man. Until the Feds showed up.

I WAS ON THE PHONE WITH A BUYER FROM SEARS WHEN the Federales came crashing in through the window. Three of them, with assault rifles. They must have come up the fire escape. "¡Policia! ¡Manos en su cabeza!" screamed one. My secretary promptly laced purple nails atop her head, mashing her extravagant hair. She didn't seem perturbed in the slightest.

"Listen, Gladys, something's come up, can I call you later?" I said into the phone.

"¡Manos en su cabeza, o tu estas un hombre muerte!" bellowed the cop. I cradled the receiver in my shoulder and put my hands on my head.

"Sure," said Gladys. "I'll be out until . . ."

I never did get to hear when; one of the cops yanked my chair from the desk, dumped me onto the floor, and placed the barrel of his gun against the back of my neck. Another gently hung up the phone.

"¿En qué puedo servirles, señores?" I asked. I wasn't too perturbed. This wasn't Colombia. They wouldn't kill me out of hand, nor kidnap me. Torture me to get me to confess to something, yes; but Mexico is reasonably civilized, as such things go.

"Cállese, asshole," said the cop. Another one said, "Dése prisa" into a walkie-talkie.

That was it, apparently. They stood there, not saying much, me on the floor, my secretary chewing gum with her hands on her head. This lasted for a couple of minutes. I heard the elevator grinding, the grate opening. There were footsteps. A pair of black oxfords stopped in front of my eyes. Tassels.

"Johnson Mukerjii," said a voice. "I have a warrant for your arrest. You have the right to remain silent. If you choose . . ."

I dared a look upward. It was my old friend Agent Epstein of the Secret Service. Same black suit, white shirt, narrow tie, same Ray-Bans.

"This is Mexico," I said. "You can't arrest me."

Agent Epstein bent over.

"Sorry, sir, I can." He shoved a piece of paper under my nose. "Here's the extradition paper." Shuffle, shuffle. "And here's the warrant."

"Okay," I said. "I'm not armed, and I'll go peacefully."

"Sorry about that," he said a little apologetically. "But with data crime, well, you know, a keystroke can delete valuable evidence. You can get up, if you stay away from your computer."

The gun barrel against my neck went away. I got gingerly up; there was dust all down the front of my suit. I patted at it ineffectually.

"Data crime?"

"You're under arrest for wire fraud," he said.

Ah. Huff *had* filed criminal charges.

THEY TOOK ME OVER THE BORDER IN A LIMO, CUFFED BE-tween Agents Epstein and Stackpole. I asked them how our friend the president was, but in their usual terse-lipped way, all they would offer was a comment on the weather and a prediction as to the outcome of the coming evening's NBA game.

I was booked in San Diego, fingerprinted, and shoved in a cell with a gawky white teenage boy with a buzz cut. He seemed a little disappointed to see me. "Like, what are you in for?" he asked.

"Wire fraud," I told him. "International data crime. RICO."

He brightened up. "Cool!" he said. "Do you, like, hack?"

"No," I said with some irritation. "And why are you in a federal facility, for God's sake?" I couldn't imagine what a suburban California teener could have done that qualified as a federal crime.

He blushed. "C-conspiracy to kill a bald eagle," he stammered.

"What?"

"It's a felony," he said, half-defensively, half-proudly. "Killing a bald eagle is a felony, and conspiracy to commit a federal felony is—"

"A felony also. I know. Why do you want to kill a bald eagle?"

"Well, I don't! That would be, like, mean, you know? But Jake double-dared me, so I posted something on the Usenet about how we could kill one, and . . ."

"Spare me," I said, sitting on the bunk and trying to get some of the dust off my knees. Would the feds pay my drycleaning bill?

"Are you gonna, like, make me your personal slave in the big house, and, and like that?" said the kid.

"You've been watching too many movies," I told him. I stood up, went to the bars, and yelled, "I wish to call my lawyer!"

"CHRIST, MUKERJII," SAID CAPTIOUS, "I HAVEN'T TRIED A criminal case in twenty years." He seemed a little appalled.

"Well find someone who has!" I snarled. "There's schmutz on my suit! I have to call Gladys back! And I'm stuck in a cell with Richie Cunningham!"

"Oh, settle down," he said. "I'll find you a lawyer."

•   •   •

HE DID. DICK COHEN WAS FORTYSOMETHING; WHAT WAS left of his hair was worn long, pasted over a bare pate. His suit was appalling, the tie even more so—it appeared to be a salmon, hanging by the tail from his neck. He met me in a bare concrete room with two folding chairs and a metal desk. They locked us in.

"So Omar Captious called me. You're Johnson Mukerjii, right?" he said.

"Correct," I said.

"You enjoying life? Wire fraud doing okay by you?"

I blinked. "Counselor," I said, "perhaps it would be more appropriate if you began by assuming my innocence."

He chortled. "Right, right, pull the other. I don't give a crap; everyone's entitled to a defender, that's what's great about the American legal system. Can you pay your bills, is what I want to know."

"I believe so," I said.

"Excellent!" he said. "I've read the complaint, you don't have to fill me in on your alibi until later, the first thing is to get you out of stir, right?"

"We are as of one mind, Mr. Cohen."

"Glad to hear it. They claim you stole two hundred thou, wired it over the border. What's your record like?"

"My record?"

"Come on, don't play dumb with me. When's your most recent arrest?"

"I have never been arrested on any prior occasion," I said. "I am even up-to-date on my parking tickets."

"Really?" said Cohen, obviously impressed. "Well, well. Bail shouldn't be too bad, then. We can probably keep it under fifty thousand."

I paled. "Good, good," I said weakly.

COHEN WAS OPTIMISTIC. THE DA WENT ON AND ON about how I had defrauded a "great American author" (please!) and had skipped over the border; he claimed bail must be set high to ensure I showed up for the trial. Cohen argued my lack of any previous record and my stability. The judge set bail at $60,000.

I didn't have it, of course.

"WHAT DO YOU MEAN YOU DON'T HAVE IT?" SAID COHEN. "You got two hundred thou out of Huff, fer chrissakes."

"Richard, bear with me. This is going to be complicated. I am going to need your full attention; I need you to transmit clear instructions to Mauro at the plant, and to Captious."

"Shove it," he said. "I'm outta here. Deadbeats can rely on public defenders."

"I'm trying to get you paid, Richard."

"You're trying my patience is what you're trying."

"Richard, please. I do not have sixty thousand in cash. I have about forty thousand. Which I cannot touch, as it covers the business's expenses through September. The business has three hundred thousand in receivables. The money is owed by reputable firms. It can be factored."

"It can be what?"

I sighed. Lawyers have their place, but negotiating financial transactions via a lawyer is almost always a bad idea. I had no choice, alas.

"You'll need to take notes," I said.

Cohen got out a lined yellow legal pad and a fountain pen.

"Get Mauro to give you access to the server. Print out copies of the receivables from Sears, Frank's Convenience Store, and Sapients On the Go. Fax them to Omar Captious. Tell Omar to call MuniBank's small-business-finance department, in New York. Omar wants to factor these receivables. Make sure you have the phrase. Yes?"

"Factor the receivables."

"Very good. Tell Omar he may *not* accept a discount in excess of twenty percent. And lower is better, obviously."

"Obviously," said Cohen. "Obvious to any twelve-year-old. Unfortunately, I'm not a twelve-year-old."

I do miss having a competent CFO.

"I am giving you a hundred thousand dollars in receivables," I said, trying to speak clearly. "MuniBank will give you at least eighty thousand for them. They then collect from the retailers when the debt is due. We get money now, at a cost. They make a profit—twenty thousand dollars of profit, pretty damned sweet for lending eighty thousand for two months. They also assume the risk of bad debt, of course; and while Sears is a minimal risk, the others are greater."

"Got it," said Cohen, capping his pen. "So all I have to do is collect the paper from Mauro? Omar does the rest?"

"Yes," I said, sighing. "I misdoubt Omar's capacity to perform the transaction with any panache, but less than I misdoubt yours."

Cohen snorted. "You'd be surprised what I've had to do to get paid by clients."

TWO DAYS LATER, CAPTIOUS AND COHEN SHOWED UP with glad smiles to spring to me.

"I could only get sixty thousand bucks out of the bastards at MuniBank," said Captious, more aggrievedly than apologetically.

This rather soured my joy at being liberated. "That's because you treated them like bastards," I told him, taking my wallet and watch back from a cop. "Lawyers treat everyone like the enemy. You have no idea how to negotiate."

Captious didn't like that. But then, the twit had just cost me $40,000, not to mention his exorbitant *per diem*.

But at least I made bail.

12

BUT I$ IT ART?

SAMENESS IS THE CURSE OF GLOBALIZATION. THE BAI-
konur Cosmodrome was just another mall. I could have been
in Orlando or São Paulo or Taipei. McDonald's, Bloomies,
Sony. The only difference was that the signs bore Cyrillic
characters instead of Roman. And, of course, that the humans
around me were speaking Russian and Khazar. And local
styles involved wider shoulders for men's suits and higher
hems for women than back home.

The Russian launch site was at Tyuratam—actually in Kazakhstan, but the Russians had retained a lease on the site
even after the collapse of the old Soviet Union. And, as at
Canaveral and Kourou, a mall had sprung up to sell to alien
visitors. I had hit the Isle de Diable Mall in Kourou two weeks
previously. Baikonur was the third and final stop of my world
tour; the last major spaceport, the last potential market for
my Drink Valet.

I had just finished a chat with the local 7-Eleven franchisee
and was walking to my next appointment when a place called
Native Earth Handicrafts caught my eye. Actually, it was the
Monet in the window that caught my eye. That, and its price
tag: 500 gozashstandu. A tad under $25 million American.

Admittedly, I had been out of things for a while, down and
out amid the bums. The *other* bums. But the world was in

the throes of a depression. A Monet might legitimately fetch a million or two at auction, but this was absurd . . .

Next to the Monet was a painting of a tiger on black velvet. Its price tag said 20 *gosh*—$1 million American. It was credited to "Sergei."

Okay, look. This is a standard sales technique. Show them what they really want and can't afford, then show them something they can afford, in the hope they'll jump for it. But there has to be some sort of plausible relationship between the two. The alternative to the 36-inch flatscreen HDTV has to be a 17-inch conventional color TV, not a page torn from a magazine and pasted onto a mirror. Anyone with the brains God gave a biscuit would know the black-velvet thing was worth forty bucks, tops, and that only if you didn't mind being laughed at by houseguests.

A thing with a face like a weedwhacker strolled out the door with an oil painting of a sad clown under his arm.

Okay, I told myself. So I was wrong. The aliens didn't have the sense God gave a biscuit.

I wandered in. Cezannes, hotel art seascapes, Renoirs, pastel drawings of Paris streets, Picassos, oils of small children with puppies. Statuary, too: Calder mobiles, lawn gnomes, versions of the Laocoön that looked as if they were genuinely two thousand years old, cigar-store Indians.

These were *handicrafts?* They were, I realized; from the aliens' perspective, stone carved with metal tools and pigments smeared on flat pieces of cloth were probably far too primitive to be considered art. Handicrafts, possibly.

While wandering the store, agog, I came across the manager, who was talking to a customer. The manager was a woman in her seventies, with hair dyed jet-black, a black-lace dress displaying too much décolletage, excessive perfume, and the taut face of the multiply lifted. An unlit cigarette was held in a long ivory holder. Her customer was a large, googly-eyed gentleman with multiple tentacles.

"Sorry, sweetie," the store manager said, "but our return policy is that all sales are final."

The alien said something that sounded like a mournful saxophone. The manager seemed to comprehend him, though I did not.

"No, sugar," she said. "I did *not* tell you it was a Gainsborough. I said it was a free copy *after* Gainsborough, *possibly* by one of the master's students. The World Trade Center, New York, is not a typical subject for the great English portraitist."

A woman after my own heart, clearly.

The exchange did not last much longer; soon, the customer lumbered disconsolately off with his worthless canvas under his arm. The manager turned to me with a smile.

"Good afternoon, sweetie," she said. "And how can I help you?" She lit her cigarette with a large platinum lighter, the kind that makes a satisfying, metallic "clunk" when you flick it open.

"I'm afraid I'm at a bit of a loss," I said.

"Yes?"

"All this . . . do they actually buy this . . . stuff? At these prices?"

She practically purred at me. "Oh, my yes. You have to understand the perspective."

"I'm afraid I don't," I said.

She tilted her head and took a drag from her cigarette, putting the holder to her lips and pointing it to the side and upward. Like something out of a twenties silent flick.

"Have you ever vacationed abroad?" she said, holding the cigarette aloft, smoke curling from her lips. "Suppose you go to Hong Kong, dear. There's a nice ivory carving in a shop window; it looks very Chinese, a nice souvenir of your visit. It costs a few hundred dollars. Would you buy it?"

I blinked. "Ivory isn't my thing," I said. "But for the right item . . . an oriental carpet, perhaps. Especially as I could

probably buy it in Hong Kong for rather less than in the
States. I could easily spend a few hundred dollars, even a
thousand, for a nice trophy of my trip."

"An *objet d'art*. You would have no way of knowing that
the ivory carving was actually poorly done by the standards
of the craft, its subject trite to any Chinese connoisseur. Or
that the poor bastard who carved it had received the equivalent of ten dollars American."

"I suppose," I said. "Wage scales in China are still rather
low."

The manager breathed out smoke slowly. "A Yank in Hong
Kong might spend a thousand bucks; an alien on Earth might
plop down a thousand *gosh* on a nice piece of pigmented
cloth, daubed by some monkeyboy that the indigenes think
highly of. You see, sweetie?"

I blinked. "Yes. But we *don't* think highly of much of this."
I waved at the black velvet, the appalling oils.

She waved her holder airily. "Since the alien ginks can't
tell the difference between a Rembrandt and a painting on
black velvet, why not sell both?"

I could only smile and shake my head.

"But you aren't here for art, are you, dear boy," the manager said. "Can I help you in some other way?"

"I doubt it," I said. "I'm here as a salesman, but I suspect
my wares would be of little interest to you. Perhaps you might
sell a few by the cash register, but it's not exactly your stock
in trade."

She shrugged, sipping gently at the cigarette holder. "So
show me."

I opened my sample case, withdrew a Mukerji Drink Valet,
and explicated its function.

She set her cigarette down and turned the Drink Valet over
in her narrow, crimson-nailed hand, giving it her full attention. "How very clever," she said. "How many units have you
sold?"

I had to think. "I believe we're up to two hundred thousand," I said.

"The retail?"

"Ten dollars American."

"Oh, no, no, no, far too low," she said, handing the Drink Valet back to me.

"But my manufacturing cost is under twenty-five cents at these volumes! Ten dollars is an extortionate markup as it is."

"Dear boy," she said, as if dealing with the mentally impaired, "you will encounter no price resistance at ten times the price." She picked up her cigarette once more.

"A hundred bucks for two ounces of plastic?"

"You will grant, I think, that I have some experience negotiating with aliens?"

"Evidently."

"Where do you distribute?"

"The spaceports. I fear we've about reached our maximum market."

"Oh, I don't think so! Alien tourists don't stay at spaceports long. New York is overrun with our friends from the stars. Paris. Chichén Itzá."

"Hmm."

"I would like to talk to your company's president," she said. "I believe I may be able to suggest a number of ways to boost your sales."

"I believe that can be arranged," I said. "I am he."

She laughed: a throaty sound. She extended her hand toward my lips, palm down. "I am Zabelle Vartanian," she said. "I'd like to be your sales director."

With some reluctance, I kissed her hand; she seemed to expect it, but I consider the gesture a nineteenth-century affectation. Her nails were long, curved, and crimson; the hand soft and veiny, the smell of her perfume overpowering at a close approach. "What about—your gallery? Don't you need to be here to manage it?"

She shrugged, tapping ash into a tray. "It can be sold. Or closed; most of the art is on consignment."

"I'm not convinced I need a sales manager," I said. "We'll be lucky to gross a million this year." That may sound like a lot, but it is not, for a small business; your corner grocery probably does better. "And while I don't enjoy sales, I seem to be doing an adequate job."

She stared at me, eyes glittering. "I'll work for no salary," she said. "Commission plus bonus. And a small equity stake."

I was taken rather aback. No salary? "You clearly believe in the product," I said.

"I'll make you a fortune, sweetie."

Well. And why not?

SHE RETURNED WITH ME TO TIJUANA.

I was a bit worried that Mauro wouldn't like her; they were such different personalities. But to my surprise, he adored her; he followed her around the office like a puppy, ran errands for her, and spent a great deal of time correcting her appalling Spanish.

The first thing Zabelle did after showing up at the office was jack up the retail price to $100. Well, $99.95. She called all of the accounts—every one of them—to explain the move and sweet-talk them around. Some of them balked, but she managed to make them happy somehow. It helped that we let them order as much inventory as they wanted at the old wholesale price before putting the new one in effect; they could sell at the new retail and make quite a margin, for a while.

I was tied up with legal preparations—depositions, pretrial hearings, answering subpoenas. I loathe the American legal system; it is so extended, requires so much paperwork, takes forever to come to resolution. Admittedly it is better than the arbitrary justice of, say, Mexico; but I would far rather try a case in Britain or Canada.

I didn't entirely ignore the business; I kept an eye on what was going on, talked to the accounts myself to ensure that they were happy with Zabelle, and spent a lot of time dealing with MuniBank. We were growing so rapidly we had continual cash-flow problems; we factored a lot of receivables. I tried to get bank finance, but we were still too new, without a record. I talked to venture capital; but no one would touch us, given our unstable legal situation. The imputed interest rate of factored receivables was absurd—though I did rather better than Captious had done, the idiot.

Zabelle showed up one day with a piece of cardboard. Around the edges ran twelve squares. Some of the squares had visible printing in them. Others did not. One was printed in such a way that the illustration—of a Drink Valet—appeared out of kilter, as if it had been printed with cyan and black plates only—no magenta or yellow.

Zabelle pointed a curved, crimson forenail at one of the squares—a full color Drink Valet illustration, with text that said: Mukerjii Drink Valet, touch for explanation.

"Touch that," she said.

I did.

The piece of cardboard spoke, though I could see neither speaker nor electronics.

"Never misplace your drink in zero gravity again! Simply insert a standard drink bulb into the clip end of the Mukerjii Drink Valet, and affix the suction cup to any convenient bulk . . ."

It jabbered on. "What is this?" I asked.

"Touch another one," she said.

I did.

"Hoot grunt whistle holler," said the cardboard. "Whistle shriek . . ."

Zabelle touched another. The cardboard began pulsing with light—first one color, then another.

"Okay," I said. "It pitches the product in what, a dozen languages?"

"That's about it, sweetie."

"How do you plan to distribute this?"

"It's the new packaging," she said. "I've got Mauro making a plastic shell; we'll glue it to the cardboard. You'll note the hole for a hook. And it's a standard rack size for the drug chains."

"But . . . Zabelle. Who makes this? How much does this cost? I could see using it as a sales tool, but packaging?"

"I sourced it from a firm in Taiwan," she said. "They bought the machinery to make it from an alien race from Xi Bootis. In quantities of a hundred thousand or more, they can deliver it for three bucks."

I choked. "But Zabelle—the whole product, with the old packaging, costs less than a quarter! You want to increase our cost of goods by a factor of twelve, for crap that gets thrown away?"

"Oh, please," said Zabelle, in a long-suffering tone. She sat back and inserted a cigarette—a lavender one, God knows where she got the things—in her holder. She lit it and breathed smoke toward the ceiling. "Our retail price is a hundred dollars. Right? Don't you think we can support a cost of three bucks and a quarter?"

"Well, yes, but how can you possibly justify an additional three dollars—"

"Johnny, sweetheart. We're not running a candy store, for goodness sakes. Our accounts pay us forty dollars for each Drink Valet we sell. Right?"

"Yes."

"We sell a hundred of them, we earn four thousand dollars."

"Yes."

"This packaging increases our marginal cost for a hundred units by three hundred dollars. To make up three hundred dollars, we need to sell just under eight additional units— eight times forty is three hundred and twenty, yes?"

"Okay, I see that."

She leaned forward and put a red-taloned, somewhat arthritic hand on my arm. "Will you take your long-suffering sales manager's personal guarantee that this packaging will increase our sales by more than eight percent?"

"Hmm. Well, yes. I take your point. But what was wrong with the old packaging? I used icons to show how to use the Drink Valet . . ."

Zabelle crossed her legs, shifted the cigarette to the other hand, and sighed again. "Sweetie, how many aliens see in the visible spectrum?"

"Um . . ."

"How many even *see*?"

"Uh . . ."

"Of those who can see in the visible spectrum, how many can interpret a black-and-white line drawing as representing a physical object? Or can follow the iconographic conventions you've used to indicate motion?"

"Okay, Zabelle. You've made your point."

"Thank you, Johnnie. You are a dear."

She stood up and kissed me on both cheeks. I held my breath as she did; I do wish she would use a tad less perfume. Or a less overpowering scent.

THE PACKAGING INCREASED OUR SALES BY CONSIDERABLY more than eight percent; the rate of sale per outlet almost doubled. Zabelle ordered giant inflatable Drink Valets, and hired actors to wander around the malls in Drink Valet costumes. We started advertising wherever aliens could be expected.

By the end of the year, we'd sold three million dollars worth of merchandise. Not too shabby, for a start-up with four full-time employees.

We got new office space; I took a very nice apartment. Things were looking up. Assuming I didn't wind up in jail, of course.

Cohen and Captious were, at my orders, doing everything they could to delay the day of reckoning; but ultimately, I would have to face a jury.

13

TALL TALE$ AND P/E RATIO$

"SIR, I HAVE A MR., UM, KUZCHEWCLICK ON THE PHONE for you," said my secretary. The "click" was the pop of her gum; I had no idea whether that was part of the name or an incidental sound.

"A mister what?"

"It's an alien, sir."

"Put him on," I said.

The vid light on the phone came on as she transferred the call, so I stabbed the button to activate the viewscreen. Mr. Kuzchewclick looked rather like a praying mantis. I tried not to flinch; the saw teeth on those long arms could take your head off faster than you could say Jack Robinson. Probably faster than you could say "Ja . . ."

"Carburetor felicitations!" said the mantis.

"I beg your pardon?"

"Carburetor?" it muttered, seemingly as puzzled as I. "Drive shaft? Piston? Ah! Manifold! Manifold greetings."

"Ah. Yes. Good day to you also."

"I am bringing you good news today, Mr. Johnson Mukerjii of Mukerjii Interstellar, Limitada. My firm, Bloknik and Bloknik, is having the good fortune to be the local arm's largest booking agent for starfaring voyages!"

It took me a moment to disentangle that. "I see," I said.

"But I have no interest in booking passage on a starship. Nor, I suspect, do I have remotely enough money to do so even if I had the desire."

"Alas, I am being devastated to be agreeing with you. Few denizens of your beautiful planet are being rich enough, with the unfortunate eventuality that my office is failing to be meeting its sales quota this fiscal quarter. But I am hoping to be persuading you of journeying to the stars!"

"Thank you," I said, "I appreciate your enthusiasm, but I'm afraid I'm not interested . . ."

"Am I to be understanding correctly that your firm, Mukerjii Interstellar, Limitada, is being a manufacturer of travel accessories for starfarers?"

"Yes, that is so, but. . . ."

"Then I am having wondrous spectacular good newses for you; Señor Mukerjii! Not far off, in star system termed in local argot 'Fomalhaut B,' is soon to be convocating a convocation! A gala sales event for manufacturers of travel accessories for starfarers! May you be in the process of experiencing pleasure at my faxing you the relevant details?"

"Er . . . Well, I suppose it wouldn't hurt to fax me the information. Do you mean a trade show?"

The mantis looked briefly confused. "Trade show? Swap meet? Theatrical exchange?"

"Trade, as in industry, business, or profession. Show as in convention, event, festival."

"Yes! I am seeing. Trade show. Fax to be transmitting momentarily. Carburetor thanks! And I am contacting you henceforth shortly for follow through. Down. Up. Follow up."

"Yes, certainly. And thank you, Mr., er, sir."

"Bon voyage!" said the mantis, and hung up.

THE FAX WAS IN ENGLISH, OF A KIND. IT HAD EVIDENTLY been translated from some alien tongue, and not terribly well. The headline read: "248th {Adjectival Form of a Duration} Industrial Carnival of {Placename} Clan of Makers of Cheap Things to Go Places With."

I puzzled it out. Adjectival form of a duration; call it "annual," albeit "annual" means "once every orbit of the planet Earth around the Sun," an absurdly parochial concept. Industrial carnival: trade show. Clan of Makers: Association of Manufacturers. Placename: some region of space, presumably, perhaps the local stellar arm.

Put it all together, it meant something like "Carina Arm Travel Accessories Show."

The flyer's information was scanty, but it did indicate that the event was to be held in Fomalhaut B; my friend the mantis had circled the star name in purple ink, and had written "Only 28 light-years from Earth!!!" next to it.

Only. Yes, indeed. Only. With three exclamation points, forsooth.

Booth space started at 500 *gozashstandu*—$25 million American, the last time I had checked the rate of exchange.

Oh, well. Too bad. It would have been nice. There was no way we could afford this.

BUT BECAUSE IT WAS INTERESTING, I SENT BRIEF E-MAIL to Zabelle about it, indicating my conclusion that we couldn't afford to go. And I thought that was that, until she marched into my office, wearing a long, black silk dress, lavender mules, and a necklace of carved amethysts, each stone the size of a bird's egg.

"Dear boy," she said, "I must see this fax at once."

So I pulled it out and showed it to her.

"I believe it means something like 'Carina Arm Travel Accessories Show. . . .' "

"I can read, sweetie," she said, and pored over the fax for a time. Finally, she put it down on the desk and sank into the deep blue plush armchair I kept for visitors. "We must go."

"It would be interesting, I agree, Zabelle, but we simply can't. You saw the price of a booth? And I haven't followed up with the travel agent, but the cost of spacefare can't be small."

Zabelle took a compact from her purse and slowly retouched her lipstick. I waited for her to complete the operation.

"We *must* go," she said, folding the compact with a click and putting it away.

I shrugged. "We can't. Look, if we're lucky, we'll hit five million in sales this year. That's a nice little company; you, Mauro, and I can all live very well off it. But there's no way we can afford to go; by Earth standards we're a minnow, but by galactic standards we're a pimple. We just can't afford the price."

"We can't afford not to," she said. "You're right, we'll hit five million, and we'll stick there; we've reached our potential market on Earth. The only customers we can reach here are the few alien tourists who bother to come to our impoverished, remote little backwater of a world. And we can make five million a year off them. But our *potential* market is enormously greater than that, if we can figure out how to sell into the galactic market. If we can get offworld. If we can get to the show."

"I know that, Zabelle. I'm not a complete fool. But *we can't afford it.*"

She opened her purse again and pulled out a folded-up magazine article. She unfolded it, and put it on my desk. It had been torn from *National Geographic*. "According to this," she said, "the population of the local·stellar arm is between two and three trillion sapient beings. Let us suppose that a mere one percent of them take a space trip each year. That's a potential market of twenty to thirty *billion* units annually."

"Zabelle, you can't squeeze money from a stone."

"You told me about an alien device you saw once at Cape

Kennedy," she said. "Something like an ice-pick with a brush at the end, right? You said we could make it."

"Yes, Zabelle, that's our next logical expansion. Start making some of the grooming aids that local stores are selling to alien visitors. With Earth's low wages, we should be able to make them more cheaply."

"But you don't know what the thing is for, how to pitch it, what language to use in the packaging, whether it's protected by some alien equivalent of a patent and whether we'll get in trouble if we make it—nothing. How do we find that out?"

"I hadn't given it much thought yet, Zabelle, it's a vague notion for the future. . . ."

"You find out at a trade show. You find out who your real competitors are, who potential distributors are, what other products are selling well. . . ."

"Zabelle, I'm well aware of the purpose of a trade show."

"You ran a hardware company in Silicon Valley before Contact. Would you have considered running one in, oh, I don't know, the Andaman Islands?"

I hesitated; I didn't know where this was going. "It could be done; satellite links make it feasible. And India isn't far away; easy to find engineers cheaply in India."

"But if you did, wouldn't you find it *especially* important to go to trade shows in the States?"

"Oh, I see. Of course, yes; in the Valley, hardware is in the air. Everyone knows what everyone else is doing. You can make hardware elsewhere, but if you do, you have to fly to California frequently, just to take the industry's pulse."

"We're running our company not from the Andaman Islands, but from the depths of the Amazon jungle, sweetie. We're dimly aware that there's a market out there, but have never been beyond the rain forest canopy. We *must* go."

"But Zabelle . . . Where are we to get the money?"

She smiled sweetly. "I'm just the sales manager, dearie.

You're the CEO. Getting the money is your department."

She opened her purse again to extract her cigarette holder
and lighter. She busied herself with them as I stared at her
and thought.

Finance was my department. Where could we possibly get
money on this scale? Bank loan? Forget it. Venture capital?
Don't be absurd. Swindle someone? I'd done it with Huff,
but there's a world of difference between swindling someone
out of a few hundred thousand and swindling someone out
of millions.

Bank robbery? International terrorism?

Absurd.

No, there was only one way to raise this kind of money on
relatively short notice.

I didn't like it. I didn't want to do it. But Zabelle was right.
We had to get to Fomalhaut B.

"We'll have to go public," I croaked.

HERE ARE THREE REASONS NEVER TO GO PUBLIC. ONE:
You run the risk of losing control of your firm. Two: Public
companies have to comply with a whole slew of regulations
privately held firms can ignore—and that applies to Mexican
companies, too, if they want listings on American exchanges.
Three: You have to deal with investment bankers.

Here's the traditional view of the market: It consists of
sober, intelligent, hardworking MBAs in sober, intelligent,
hardworking pin-striped suits. It consists of columns of gray
text in the daily newspaper, or streams of arcane numbers
running across the bottom of your screen, the result of bids
and counterbids, money flowing smoothly through the ancient institutions created at the dawning of the industrial age
and sustained and developed since: London, New York, Tokyo, NASDAQ. Wise investors calculate risk and return, the
markets move in their majestic and efficient way, pricing risk,
pricing value, growing over time, the Dow and the S&P 500

shifting with the changing fortunes of the entire world's economy. It is, so people believe, the pinnacle of the world economy, the ultimate arbiter of success or failure, the ultimate
check on management, the measure of economic well-being
or collapse, the market of markets, the *ne plus ultra* of capitalism.

Here's the truth: It's all run by a bunch of red-suspendered
frat boys on drugs. They're close to the money, and they make
a lot of it: Anyone close to the money does. Sales managers
outearn line producers; accountants do better than office
managers; investment bankers earn incomes that make Hollywood look like the low-rent district. It's not a function of
utility to society; it's a function of proximity to cash.

I have never met a more loathsome body of hail-fellow-well-
met, glad-handing, eye-on-the-main-chance, coke-snorting,
male-chauvinist, hard-partying, law-bending scoundrels than
investment bankers. These are the fellows you loathed at college, the ones who got the girls for no explicable reason, the
ones who skated through their courses on Bs, Cs, and purchased papers, who never experienced a serious intellectual
moment in their lives. And far from getting their comeup-
pance, they found a niche perfectly suited to their limited intellectual capacities, a way to make enormous wads of money
out of no greater talent than the ability to schmooze over
drinks.

I'd gone public before, of course, with MDS; this would
be my second time through the mill. It was not something I
looked forward to.

THE FIRST STEP WAS TO FIGURE OUT THE MINIMUM SUM
we needed. Twenty-five million for a booth; but that was
only the start. I wasn't clear on what other costs there might
be, but I knew how trade shows work on Earth, and knew
there'd be other costs. On Earth, booth space means a bare
patch of concrete in a convention hall. If you want carpeting,

chairs, tables, a backdrop, electrical wires, phone lines, you pay for each and every item, at absurd rates. Not to mention the cost of a bunch of union electricians, phone workers, and porters to stand around while your staff does the actual work—you wouldn't want the convention-center workers to do it, because they haven't a clue and would probably wreck expensive equipment if they tried. But you have to pay them: union rules.

The flyer gave nary a hint as to the cost of such services, but I was sure we'd have more than one nasty surprise upon arrival at Fomalhaut B. We'd better budget a bare minimum of an additional $10 million; $25 million would be more conservative, but Krishna almighty, it was going to be hard enough raising funds.

Then, of course, there was the cost of travel and accommodations. I called back Mr. Kuzchewclick.

"Carburetor greetings, Mr. Mukerjii!" he said, mandibles clashing in apparent joy to see me. "Is my faxing you piquing your interest?"

"I believe it has, Mr., Kuz, um, mumble," I said. "I'm calling to inquire about the fare to Fomalhaut B."

"Yes indeedy!" said the mantis. "I am experiencing such gratification that my sphincters are relaxing!"

I cleared my throat, not sure how to respond. "Ah, good, good."

"First-class or tourist?"

"Um, cheaper is better," I said.

The mantis hesitated. "You will require oxygen on your journey?"

"Ah, yes, I should think so."

"You are being in the future pleased to know that transit to Fomalhaut B is availing itself to you at the extremely modest charge of twenty-five million dollars.".

I gasped. "One way or round-trip?"

"One way, I am regretting."

"Per person?"

"Yes, indeedy."

I sat gaping at the screen for a long moment. I needed to go personally; I was terrified at the thought, but I wasn't going to let Zabelle go without me. And I needed Zabelle there; she was far better at dealing with aliens than I.

"Um, is there no way to cut that?" I asked. "Booking in advance? Frequent-flyer membership? Something?"

The mantis appeared to hesitate, looking somewhat disappointed. "We could be freezing you," it said.

"Freezing?"

"Suspending your animating. Putting you on ice. Stacking you in cargo hold like cordwood."

"That would be cheaper."

"Much. Ten million dollars. Per person, one way. Of course, we are finding it necessary to be obtaining the liability waiver."

"Whatever for?"

It hesitated again. "We are finding the odds of revivification very favorable."

"Am I to understand that the freezing process is not foolproof?"

"You are being new species to us," the mantis said apologetically. "Process is being very delicate. Mishaps occasionally resulting in rupturing of too many cell walls, producing failure to be reviving."

"You said the odds were favorable. How favorable?"

"At present, we are estimating in excess of ninety percent in favor of results we are desiring!" the mantis said heartily.

"One out of ten I die," I said.

"Twelve, we are guesstimating," said the mantis.

"One way."

"Yes, you are surmising correctly," said the mantis. "Two freezings for round-trip."

"So for a round-trip, one out of six I never get back."

"No, no. If you are dying on outgoing journey, you are not experiencing second freezing. So odds are one-twelfth plus one-twelfth minus one-twelfth squared, so . . ."

"Yes, I understand basic statistics," I said, a little irritated.

"Shall I be booking tickets?"

"Ah, not just yet, Mr., uh." I said. "I shall have to confer with my colleagues."

When one talks about business risk, one does not normally mean the risk of death.

A one-sixth chance of death to save $15 million. That valued my life at $90 million.

If my mere existence was worth $90 million, I was rich. At least in the same sense that Maureen used to contribute so much to the household finances by saving us money. I recall on one occasion, she saved us several thousand dollars on a single shopping trip. I had to ask her to stop being so thrifty lest she bankrupt us.

TWENTY FIVE MILLION DOLLARS FOR THE BOOTH. Another $10 million for incidental expenses. Two people at $10 million each, one way; $40 million round-trip. Grand sum: $75 million. Better try for $85 million, just in case.

Our gross for the year would be around $5 million. Our margins were high; our profit would be close to $4 million.

Stock are normally valued by what they call the price/earnings, or P/E, ratio. Add up all the shares issued by the company, multiply by the share price; that's the company's total capitalization. Divide by net earnings.

Depending on the state of the market and the industry in which a company operates, P/E ratios can range from five to fifty. A P/E ratio is only a rule of thumb, and doesn't apply to all industries; insurance companies are normally valued on the basis of the payout-to-premium ratio, banks on return on capital employed. But a typical small investor scanning the Wall Street Journal looks at the P/E column to tell him a little bit about how highly the market values a company.

I needed $85 million. The company earned $4 million annually. If we sold 100% of the company to the public, we needed to value it at a P/E ratio of about 23. Call it 25, because anyone taking us public would expect a cut.

Twenty-five is high. In a normal market, it might not be absurdly high. But at the moment, we were in the greatest depression since the fall of Rome.

When a company makes a loss, the P/E ratio is meaningless. Earnings are zero. You can't divide by zero.

I took a look at the *Journal,* ran my eye down the P/E column.

There were rather more "N/A"s than numbers; more companies with losses than profits.

It was absurd, of course. Who would pay so much for so small a company, especially one intending to blow all its capital on a single, highly speculative measure?

Raising this much money was simply impossible.

I've never known the absurd or the impossible to stop an IPO.

I TOOK THE SUBORBITAL ROCKET TO NEW YORK, TO SEE Artie Sassareno. He'd led the team that took Mukerjii Data Systems public, although he'd been at BT Alex Brown, then. Now he was working for Ponzi Churner, an investment bank specializing in IPOs and M&A; a small firm, but one of considerable antiquity, founded in the 1820s by Silas Churner. Martin Ponzi, a corporate raider, had added his name when he mounted a hostile takeover of the company back in the 1980s.

Sassareno met me at the door to his office. "Hey, Mukerjii!" he shouted joyfully. "Good to see ya, man!" His left hand grabbed my shoulder, his right came down to grasp my own in a firm, vigorous shake that Leander Huff would have envied. "C'mon in, guy!" The hand on my shoulder slipped around behind my back to urge me into the office. "Can I get you a drink or what?"

"Thank you, no, Mr. Sassareno," I said. "It is a bit early in the day for me, I fear."

"Sun's over the yardarm somewhere, Muks. And what's with the mister bit? Call me Sass! Or Artie, if you like."

I did like. It was hard to take him seriously as a mister. An overgrown and rather unruly football hooligan, perhaps. "As you wish, Artie."

The office had royal blue plush carpeting, a deep leather couch, stark ash cabinetry and table, and a huge oaken desk. In short, it was in some interior designer's decent taste, and expensive, but indicating in no way anything about the character of the man who occupied it. The desk bore the obligatory pictures: the suburban wife, the blond-haired suburban kids. Certificates on the wall attested to an MBA and a CFA.

"So tough luck about your old company, Muks, but I hear you got a new gig now."

"Quite so, Artie. And we're at the point that we need to raise considerable capital for expansion."

He grinned at me. "You're ready to cash out, you mean."

I sighed. "No, Artie, that's not it, actually. I'm not looking to take money out of the company myself. We genuinely need the cash for expansion."

"How much you need?"

"About eighty-five million."

Sassareno whistled. "What're your sales like?"

"We're on course to hit five million this year."

"How much last year?"

"Under a million."

"Great!" His face lit up. "Growth rate over five hundred percent! You might be able to get eighty-five mil."

"Our margins are good, too," I said. "Four of five million is net."

A look of shock passed over Sassareno's face. "What? You mean you made a profit?"

"Yes, and a very tidy one, too," I said with some pride.

"That's terrible! That could queer the whole deal!"

I stared at him for a long moment. "I'm not following you, Artie. Won't investors value the company more highly if we're profitable? Why should profitability queer the deal?"

Sassareno got up and fetched himself an Amstel Light out of a small refrigerator. "You don't understand the market, Muks. If you don't make money, but you're growing quick, who's to say what the company is worth? Could be worth anything, could be the next Microsoft, everyone wants to get in on the ground floor. With 500% annual growth, the day traders'll go gaga. But if you make *money*—well, then, you've got an 'E,' see? If you got an 'E,' people say, well, in this industry, the average company has a P/E of ten. Your company is worth ten 'E.' If you make money, they know how to value you. You're better off not making money—not having an 'E.' "

I thought for a time. "Well," I said slowly, "we're privately held, and the authorities in Mexico are, um, flexible. Nothing regarding our profits has appeared in print, as of yet."

Sassareno smiled, raised the neck of his bottle, and took a swig, smoothing down his Hermès tie. "Now of course," he said, "as your prospective underwriter, Ponzi Churner would have a fiduciary responsibility to future investors, see, so it would be, like, totally illegal for me to suggest that you produce financials that are anything less than one hundred percent accurate."

"I take it, however, that should we produce paperwork showing a loss, few questions would be raised?"

"Hey, not by me, Johnny." He gave me a wink. "So, tell me a story."

I wasn't following him. "A story, Artie?"

"Yeah, a story, man. We're in the business of telling stories."

"I had understood you to be an investment banker, Artie, not a—a latter day O. Henry."

"Who? Oh, some writer guy, huh? Ya gotta understand the market, Muks. What makes for a successful IPO?"

"A successful initial public offering? I'd assume a proven track record, sound financials, clear opportunity for expansion. . . ."

Artie snorted, shook his head, and swallowed a long gulp of his beer. "Yeah, right," he said. "You're saying, it's numbers on paper that make a deal, Muks. That's what most people think. But this is the stock market, it's not a convention of accountants. You know how many people give a crap about financials?"

"Um, no, Artie. How many?"

"In any given industry, about twelve. Every big investment bank has a staff of analysts—one to follow insurance, one to follow transport, one to follow defense and aerospace, like that. An analyst has to pay attention to numbers. An analyst produces reports saying, 'this stock is undervalued, buy' or 'this stock is fairly valued, hold.' And maybe a half dozen big investors actually read these reports, and look at the numbers, and pull up a spreadsheet, okay? But this is boring, and anyway, it doesn't work."

"It doesn't work?"

"Nah. Analysts have no better chance of guessing which way the market goes than a dartboard. If you buy on the basis of what the analysts say, you underperform the market. We do analysis only because some big customers want us to. Nobody else gives a crap."

"If it isn't numbers, Artie, what is it?"

"It's a story! A little razzle-dazzle, a little soft shoe. Investors are human, Muks. They love stories. And hell, it's the day traders make an IPO work, a bunch of middle-class wackos with computers and too much time on their hands, telling each other stories about new hot stocks in chatrooms on the Internet. Do they know from a balance sheet? Look, let's role-play this. I'm your broker." He pantomimed picking up a phone and dialing a number. "I call you to pitch you on a stock. Good morning, Mr. Mukerjii."

"Ah, good morning, Mr. Sassareno," I said, playing along.

"Artie, Artie. Hey, I'm calling cause I got a hot little number I think you might want ta plunk some cash into. I see you got a capital loss in your account so far this year, be nice to make some of that back, right?"

"Certainly, Artie. What do you have?"

He pulled his imaginary phone away from his head. "I'm gonna do this two ways, okay? First the numbers way. Second the story. We'll start with the numbers."

"Okay."

He put the imaginary receiver back to his ear. "I've been looking over this company, Amalgamated Consolidated, they're in the business of widget manufacturing. Year-on-year sales growth of twelve percent or more for the last five years, profits have been keeping pace. Their book-to-bill ratio is among the highest in the widget industry, but their profits were depressed last quarter by unforeseen factors, so their P/E ratio is currently well below average for the industry. Our analysts think we may see appreciation of as much as thirty percent in the stock price over the next six months."

He took the phone away again. "Now I'm going to do the story." Receiver back. "Hey, Muks, I got a hot one. Been talking to Joe Slobotnik, CEO over at Amalgamated Consolidated. The market is all screwed on them; they're selling way below other companies in the widget industry, and you wanna know why? Cause the asshole analysts can't tell their ass from their elbow, that's why. AC's net was down last quarter. How come? Cause a little old lady in Burbank slipped on one of their widgets and busted her hip, sued them and won four million bucks. You know the courts in California, right? Anyway, their stock price went sploosh 'cause their profits dived, but its purely temporary, they're goin' great guns over there at AC, got a growth rate that beats anyone else in the industry. If this baby doesn't shoot up by a third in the next six months, I'm a monkey's uncle."

He hung up his imaginary phone. "Now which one would make *you* buy," he said.

"I want both," I said. "I want your impression of what's going on, *and* I want to see the numbers."

He nodded. "You're smarter than the average day trader," he said, "but it's the story that grabs you in the first place. Numbers make you yawn. Stories tug at your heartstrings, open your wallet, get told to your friends who open *their* wallets. Give me a good story over good financials any day. A story about a plucky little company that's gonna conquer the world, about a wifty new technology that everyone and his pet dog is gonna want to buy at Kmart, about changes in society that are gonna make your product a megahit, about discovering how to wring extra bucks out of an underexploited asset. Pretend I'm a Hollywood producer, man; give me high concept. Give me a really hot story I can tell to the money guys to get them drooling."

I stared, taken aback. Sassareno waited me out, sipping at his beer. "Horatio Alger meets *Star Wars?*" I said at last.

He chortled. "I like it already. Tell me more."

So I opened my sample case and pulled out the Drink Valet.

"The alien ginks actually buy this crap?" he said, turning one over in his hands.

"At a retail price of a hundred bucks," I said.

He whistled. "Okay, so what do you need the eighty-five mill for?"

"We've about reached the maximum market on Earth. But there are two to three *trillion* sapient beings in the local stellar arm; if only one percent of them travel each year, that's a potential market of tens of billions of units annually. If we can reach galactic retailers. We've learned of a trade show twenty-eight light-years away, where we hope to make contact with beings who can expand our market by several orders of magnitude. . . ."

"Got it in one," he said, manicured fingers moving a gesture expressive of avaricious delight. "But never say 'we've reached the maximum market on Earth,' Muks. Say 'While room for continued growth in sales on Earth alone still exists . . .' Make 'em think you're gonna keep growing at five hundred percent annually, and this alien market thing is just the icing on the cake."

"Well," I said slowly, "that might be plausible, actually. Our success is built on a single product; but the basic idea behind the business is simply that Earth has extraordinarily low wages by comparison to the aliens. I've noted a variety of items for sale in venues that cater to aliens that are well within our manufacturing capacities. We can ensure continued growth even on Earth by manufacturing additional products. . . ."

"I love you, man," said Sassareno, leaning across the table and locking his head with mine, arm around the back of my neck, in the fashion of an American footballer.

I extricated myself with some difficulty. "Ah, likewise, I'm sure," I muttered. 'You insolent boor.'

Sassareno got up. "We're gonna pull this thing off, Johnny. And I can tell you, Ponzi Churner needs this. The IPO market is deader'n a cat on the BQE, but this one has all the ingredients: good story, supersonic growth. You, me, and my company'll make a killing off this little piece of crap you got here."

He tossed me the Drink Valet and went to rummage in the fridge. "This calls for the Dom," he said, finding two champagne flutes.

Overrated stuff, champagne. Overpriced soda pop. Give me a good Bordeaux any day.

14

OYSTERS AND JAPANESE

THE NEXT SEVERAL MONTHS WERE SPENT IN CREATIVE bookkeeping, lying on the phone, and general preparation for the big event. The actual business was neglected; there was too much else to do. Consider: on the one hand, a business throwing off $4 million a year. On the other, a deal that can net $85 million at a single blow. Which do you grant the higher priority?

We prepared a completely bogus business plan claiming a takeoff in sales which looked like a curve going asymptotic to the vertical. Sales were brisk enough that, with a little creative accounting, we could at least make this semiplausible. The prospectus was filled with warning language, indicating that, in essence, we made no pretense that the business plan was anything other than bogus, that everything could change on a moment's notice, and that we had only the vaguest idea what we were doing. Luckily, no one actually reads prospectuses and, anyway, such language is standard practice, designed to cover management's ass should anything untoward happen.

There were a million pieces of paper to file, many of which involved the creation of accounting records that either did not previously exist or directly contradicted previous records, which had to be discreetly redacted, with earlier versions de-

stroyed. In particular, our profit became a mysterious loss—
or rather, continuing high levels of investment, so that our
cash flow remained in the red.

A few days after I sent our draft prospectus to Ponzi
Churner, I got a call from an irate and rather red-faced Sassareno.

"Mukerjii!" he said. "Where the hell do you get off?"

Where, I wondered, was the Sassareno who behaved as if
we were bosom pals? "What seems to be the problem, Artie?"
I said, with perhaps just a little irritable stress on "Artie."

"The deal's off, Mukerjii," he said.

I started. This was wholly unexpected.

"What seems to be the difficulty?"

"You idiot," he said. "A company can't go public if any
principal is a felon."

I fear I rather gaped at him. Was Zabelle a felon? I couldn't
believe it; she was wily enough to get out of anything. Mauro?
As honest as the day is long. The only other existing stockholders were Huff and I—I'd assigned him 2% of the shares,
which he had returned to me defaced with an angry scrawl,
but nonetheless he was a stockholder of record. A law-abiding
chap, Huff. Well, largely; I recalled his cavalier attitude toward firearms.

"What are you talking about, Artie?"

"You're under indictment for wire fraud, Mukerjii," said
Sassareno. "No way the SEC will let you go public. Wasting
my goddamn time."

My brow cleared. "Ah!" I said. "I see. What if I take care
of it?"

Sassareno hesitated. "If you can get charges dismissed—or
be proven innocent—within two weeks, we can still proceed."

I smiled. "I believe there will be no difficulties," I said
soothingly.

• • •

I CALLED MAURO AND ZABELLE IN TO DISCUSS THE MAT-
ter. In truth, I was far less sanguine than I had let Sassareno
believe.

"What's the problem, *jefe*?" said Mauro. "Pay him off. We
can spare two hundred thousand."

"I've tried that, Mauro. I made an offer to his lawyers
months ago. It's a personal thing, I believe. I made a fool of
him, and he wants me to pay—not just in money. He filed
criminal charges too, remember."

"Do you know Huff well?" asked Zabelle.

"Not particularly," I said. "We've met many times at trade
shows and the like, of course. But we were never close."

"Have you read his work?"

"His sci-fi? No."

She nodded. "We must do what we can," she said. "Try
to set up a meeting with him."

"I'm not sure he'll even agree to that."

"Agree to any location or terms. If we can't get to him, we
can't persuade him."

"I'll do my best."

IT TOOK SEVERAL DAYS FOR A MESSAGE TO FILTER
through the lawyers to Huff and back. He would meet us
for dinner, at Todo Caro, a restaurant in Laguna Beach. He
would make the arrangements for dinner. We would pay for
the meal.

I went in to tell Zabelle, and found her reading *These Stars
Are Ours!* She was up to her elbows in his books—*Death
Blossoms Soundless*, *Beyond the Oort Cloud*, and *For God and
Terra*.

"Typical of an author," she murmured. "They're used to
sticking publishers for pricey meals. You can expect the tab
to be at least four figures."

I winced, but it was not material; if a thousand-dollar meal was what it took to get Huff to settle, the money was well spent. "Are you learning anything from this?" I gestured at the books.

She looked up, an unexpectedly dreamy expression on her taut, multiply lifted face. "I believe so," she said. "He is very—gallant."

"Gallant?" I said, in some disbelief. "He is an arrogant pig."

She eyed me, the look I expect to see in her eyes—hard calculation—having returned. "He has rather different values from you, Johnson. You must let me do the talking."

"That would be a vast relief," I said.

WE DROVE UP FROM TIJUANA, IN A JAG CONVERTIBLE I had recently purchased; despite the warm weather, Zabelle sported a six-foot-long silk scarf that streamed behind us as we drove up I-5. We were a few minutes early—an unnecessary gesture, as Huff kept us waiting for three-quarters of an hour.

At Todo Caro, we were led down a long, winding path from the restaurant proper. Flowers grew to either side. The path gave out on a small, rocky beach, hemmed in by cliffs, waves breaking not far away. Part of the beach was occupied by a deck, set with a single table and a number of serving stations. A complete bar, with bartender and two wait staff in white linen awaited us. We were distant enough from the coast road, and from the restaurant proper, that the only sounds were the ocean, the mournful call of the gulls, and the occasional distant roar of a suborbital rocket. The sun was still high enough above the horizon to make my tuxedo jacket rather warm; Zabelle had insisted that I wear black tie. "It is a symbol," she assured me. "Both that you, too, are a man of power, and that you acknowledge his authority." She herself wore a tight black antique Dior dress, full-length, a strand of pearls, a black hat with veil straight out of the 1930s, and gold rings on every red-taloned finger. Her body was a miracle of surgery and engineering, but I had to admit, she looked rather elegant.

It would have been a lovely setting, if I had not been so on edge. I hated having so much depend on the action of one unstable man; with his agreement, we could get to Fomalhaut B. Without it, I might well wind up in jail.

I nursed a scotch and soda—the bar's only scotch was Macallan 25, Huff's preferred tipple, as I recalled, and no doubt even more overpriced here than normal. Zabelle had a Campari and soda. We both noted the chilling bottles of wine about the table—the Schramsberg *blanc de blanc*, and a Napa sauvignon blanc that I didn't recognize but, I had no doubt, would cost me well in excess of a hundred dollars.

Huff came down the path; the usual tweed jacket, widewale corduroy trousers, dress shirt with blue stripes, a constellation-pattern tie. His tie clip was in the shape of an archaic, finned rocket ship. His lawyer accompanied him: a bald fellow well in excess of six feet, wearing a Brooks Brothers pinstripe, looking like nothing so much as a cross between Lurch and Adlai Stevenson.

Huff had grown a full beard—sand-colored hairs admixed with gray. He put my hand through the usual wringer, mouth rather grim as he did. "Mukerjii," he bellowed. "My lawyer, Bartholomew Grind."

At Zabelle's request, we had not brought counsel of our own. "This is not a legal proceeding," she had said, rather stiffly. "Let the lawyers get involved, and nothing will be accomplished."

Grind shook my hand, rather limply for so large a fellow; it was a relief after Huff.

"May I present my vice president of sales and marketing, Ms. Zabelle Vartanian," I said.

Zabelle rose and presented her hand to Huff; he smoothly

bent to kiss it, without hesitation, as if neither he nor she were conscious of the gesture's archaicism. "*Enchanté*," he murmured.

I nearly gagged. Americans should not kiss hands. I'm doubtful even that Europeans should. The typical American hand-kisser is a poorly socialized lower-middle-class fellow with pretentions to gallantry who believes that kissing hands will make him appear debonair and sophisticated; in fact, it makes him look like a nerd. The typical American woman who allows her hand to be kissed is either clueless, or good-humored enough not to want to destroy the ego of the poor sap who slobbers on her hand, at least without first determining precisely how much of a twit he is.

And *enchanté*, forsooth! Maureen, I found enchanting, the jade. A businesswoman in a business context I do not, however attractive she may be. It is not appropriate. One may be attracted; enchanted, never.

"Shall we be seated, gentlemen?" said Zabelle, rather gaily.

Huff held her seat out for her. My eyes went to the lawyer Grind; was I the only one finding this ludicrous? Apparently so, for he was merely gazing outward, at the sea.

Huff ordered a Macallan on the rocks; the lawyer requested a chardonnay. Huff turned to me. "You wanted this meeting, Mukerjii," he said. "So say your piece. I'll say no, you can either slink away in shame and leave me to have a first-rate meal at your expense, or stay and be miserable while we eat. I can't imagine what you expect to gain, but what the hell, the swordfish here is good."

"My dear Dr. Huff," said Zabelle, "I can't imagine why you insist on persecuting poor Johnny."

I could imagine all too well. "Persecuting!" said Huff, turning to her. "Do you know what this scoundrel, this con man, this palter did to me? He swindled me out of two hundred thousand dollars!"

"Your signature was on that check," I said.

"After you got me drunk! And kept me drunk until it cleared!"

"Nonetheless, you wrote it of your own free will," I insisted. "I held no gun to your head!"

"Diminished capacity," said the lawyer distantly.

Huff was getting alarmingly red in the face. "No gun! Neither did you offer any clear deal, simply spun me a tissue of lies...."

"Oh, dear, please, gentlemen," said Zabelle. "Do calm down." Huff subsided somewhat. "Admittedly, Johnny took a rather, um, unorthodox route to the raising of venture capital...."

"Venture capital?" spluttered Huff. "If it's venture capital, where's the venture?"

I cleared my throat. "The money was used to found Mukerjii Interstellar...."

Huff snorted. "You sent me shares, as I recall, and I returned them. Two percent! No venture capitalist with two neurons capable of firing simultaneously would take two percent to fully capitalize a firm...."

"Um, yes, well, if the percentage is an issue..."

"It isn't, Mukerjii. No amount of money will settle this. You're a swindler, you belong in jail, and that's where I intend to see you."

Well. That was that, then. I settled back in my chair with a sigh and tossed off the remnants of my scotch. Huff was right; I might as well leave. No point in staying and watching him masticate. I was about to ask for another drink, when waiters appeared with plates of oysters; six for each of us, three different varieties. Champagne was poured. I looked at the oysters rather glumly; I love oysters, and had never really noticed before how ugly they are.

"I see," said Zabelle. "If you were a lesser man, monetary recompense would suffice, surely."

Huff sat straight as a ramrod. "No doubt," he said, "but this man is a menace to society."

"How like a man to personalize everything!" said Zabelle. "I believe there are larger issues at stake."

Huff peered at her. "Larger issues?"

"I've been reading your work, Dr. Huff, and I perceive that you have a very clear idea what sort of society you prefer. A vigorous, expanding, optimistic society that values honor and duty."

Huff rather preened. "Precisely," he said. "I'm flattered that you have read my work."

"Surely you can see that, at present, neither Earth nor America in particular is exactly a reflection of your ideal."

"I'm afraid you're very right," said Huff. "We encountered the aliens on their terms. If we'd had a few decades more, if we had discovered the faster-than-light drive on our own . . ."

"But we didn't," said Zabelle. The oysters were being cleared, mine untouched. I found the champagne unsatisfying, and asked for another scotch. A goat cheese, arugula, and endive salad appeared, along with fresh bread and olives.

"Among other things, I read an article you wrote for *Reader's Digest*," Zabelle said.

" 'The Aztecs or the Japanese,' " said Huff.

"Yes," said Zabelle. "I was impressed by the argument. You are correct that we need to adopt alien technology in a hurry if we aren't to find ourselves the permanent equivalent of a Third World country. But the Japanese adopted more than Western technology, you know."

"They're still very Japanese," protested Huff.

"Technology is not culture," said Zabelle. "But the Japanese were able to succeed in becoming a modern technological society because they also adopted capitalism. They exported to earn the hard currency they needed to modernize."

"Well, of course," said Huff.

A cheese pastry of some kind was next. Out came the sauvignon blanc. I drank more scotch. I was feeling somewhat drunk, but didn't much care. Our friend the lawyer seemed as self-involved as I, eyes flickering occasionally to Zabelle and Huff, but otherwise on the sea, the cliffs, his meal.

"Ours is a flexible society; it has to be, technological change over the last two centuries has been too rapid. We can adapt to the alien challenge. But we must earn hard alien currency to import the technology, the ideas, the machine tools . . . We must open to the stars. We must not merely sell them raw materials and *objets d'art*. We must learn how to export to their markets, become a player on the galactic stage."

Huff smiled at her, leaning close, as if truly enchanted. "I think rather more in terms of power politics," he said.

"Money is the sinew of war," Zabelle said.

"You're quoting me," he said.

"Yes. You want Earth to be an interstellar power? Well, Japan became an international one. But only after its economy was large enough to support a modern military."

"I suppose your argument has something to do with this ridiculous Drink Valet thing Mukerjii is flogging."

"We have," Zabelle said, "a real chance of making this ridiculous Drink Valet thing Earth's first real interstellar export success."

And that's about where I lost track of the evening, I'm afraid: too much depression, too much scotch. I vaguely recall being hauled up the path to the parking lot, arms draped over the shoulders of a couple of beefy waiters.

I woke up with a killing hangover, still drunk, as we stopped to pass through customs on the way back to Mexico. "Oh God," I groaned. "It's over, isn't it?"

"Yes, dear," said Zabelle. "It's over. We're paying him back the two hundred thousand with interest, he gets ten percent of the company, and he's dropping charges tomorrow."

I sat upright, immediately regretting the gesture. Head in hands, I asked, "How did you manage that?"

She sniffed. "If you want to know, you'll have to stay sober next time."

They waved us through the border. Leaving the States is a lot easier than entering.

"You are a miracle worker, Zabelle," I said.

"That's not all, I'm afraid."

"Um. What else?"

"He's on the board of directors."

"We have a board of directors?"

"We do now. You, me, Mauro, Les, and Sassareno."

"Les?"

"Leander."

"*Fantastico.*"

"And he's coming with us to Fomalhaut B."

"You're joking."

"No. He wants to scout out the aliens' military capacities."

"At a travel-accessories trade show? They don't sell fighter bombers with luggage, Zabelle."

"It wasn't my idea, dear boy."

15

THROUGH DARKE$T NA$DAQ, WITH GUN AND CAMERA

PREPARATIONS FOR THE PUBLIC OFFERING PROCEEDED without further hitch. The SEC approved our filings, both we and Ponzi Churner sent out press releases, and I began fielding calls from the financial press.

I tried to slough off as many of the calls as feasible on Zabelle; she was far better at talking to journalists than I. Still, some callers specifically asked for me, and I took my share.

Most of the time, managing journalists is easy. They're on a deadline, they need so-and-so-many column inches, they don't give a crap who you are or what the story is, so long as you feed them enough material to fill the space. Sure, they'd be happy to write an exposé if the opportunity reared its head, but as far as the people who called knew, the IPO of Mukerjii Interstellar was routine, another start up cashing out, a page-six story in the business section running two hundred words at most.

We had a balancing act to perform, you see. We needed enough publicity to reach investors, to make people aware of Mukerjii Interstellar's existence and its potential; but not so much that anyone became truly interested, paid us close attention, realized that our financials were a tissue of lies.

There was only one who made me nervous: a fellow named Scott Daly, from the *Orange County Register*.

"MR. MUKERJII," HE SAID AFTER THE PRELIMINARIES, "what happened to the criminal charges against you filed in Santa Ana?"

Damnation! They were, of course, a matter of public record. But they had received no particular press—a wire-fraud case against a homeless former corporate exec, a lot of homeless former corporate execs around at the time. And we had certainly not mentioned the indictment in our press kit. But there had been a minor news item in Orange County, where they had been filed. . . .

"The charges were dropped," I said.

"By Leander Huff, who filed them, and who I see is a major stockholder in your firm. How much did you have to bribe him?"

"Not a penny, young man," I said. "Dr. Huff is a farsighted gentleman. He provided the initial capital for the company, and—"

"Ah! Provided the initial capital. An interesting turn of phrase, that. Voluntarily?"

"Certainly!" I bluffed. "Have you spoken to him? I believe he resides in Orange County."

"Yes," said Daly. "He said, quote, That swindler could sucker a lollipop away from an octopus, end quote, and hung up on me."

"What a jackass," I thought. The man should know better than to give anything to the goddamn press. "Well, as I'm sure you're aware, Mr. Daly, relationships among the principals of a start-up are not always smooth. Certainly, Dr. Huff and I have had our differences. Nonetheless, his confidence in our management team, and our appreciation for his business savvy, are both testified by the fact that he recently consented to join our board of directors."

There was perhaps the faintest snort from the other end of the line. "So you're saying, one of your largest stockholders only recently dropped charges of fraud against you, continues to loathe you, is disgruntled in the extreme, and yet everything is just hunky-dory in Mukerjiiland?"

Well yes, that was about the size of it.

"Mr. Daly, I said nothing of the kind. You said that. And if this hostile tone continues, this interview will shortly be at an end."

"Okay, okay. Perhaps you could explain a little about your heavy levels of investment? From your filings, it appears that you make truly staggering margins on your sole product, and your overhead is quite modest, yet the company has never made a dime. What exactly are you investing in?"

Gurk. "Ah, we're still ramping up production to meet increasing demand," I hazarded. "And, of course, we are investing in the development of further products that we hope will engender equal enthusiasm among the aliens when they reach market. . . ."

"What products specifically?" said Daly. "Mukerjii Interstellar hasn't had any patent filings since the one for the Drink Valet."

"Ah, ah, of course, ah, they're all proprietary and confidential at this point," I said. "It would be premature to reveal their nature to potential competition. When they are more fully developed, rest assured, we will seek patent protection."

Man had me a bit rattled on that one. In fact, we had only the vaguest idea what other products we might be able to manufacture, and no real knowledge of how to sell them. We had no immediate plans, no schematics, nothing in the pipeline.

"From the statements of your banking partners, it appears that the IPO for Mukerjii Interstellar will raise in the neighborhood of eighty-five million, all of which will be retained by the firm for investment purposes."

"That's correct."

"You're already pumping every penny you earn into investment. What on God's green earth can you possibly want with that much capital? It's completely out of kilter with the scale of your company's sales."

"Ah, but that's just it, Mr. Daly. Not on God's green earth, but off it."

I launched into Zabelle's spiel: two to three trillion sapients in the local stellar arm.

"Yes, yes, Mr. Mukerjii," Daly said, stopping me impatiently. "I've got all that from your press release. But Mr. Mukerjii, how much can it possibly cost to do this?"

"You'd be astounded," I said. Certainly, I had been.

And after a bit of polite chitchat for closure's sake, Daly rang off.

What worried me wasn't what he'd said, or what he'd got from me, or even from Huff. What worried me was that the man was basically on to us. And he clearly wasn't satisfied by my whitewash.

The last thing we needed was negative publicity on the eve of our IPO. The only silver lining there was that the *Orange County Register* is not exactly the *Wall Street Journal*. A goofy little right-wing rag, in fact.

"IS PLASTIC GIZMO WORTH $85 MILL?" READ DALY'S headline. It was pretty scathing, but we'd successfully stonewalled him. He couldn't actually allege anything illegal, because he didn't have hard evidence. All he could do was raise some questions.

That was enough to worry me, though. A lot. All we needed was some investigator at the SEC to read this and start asking questions. . . .

"KUZCHEWCLICK, MAY I BE ASSISTING YOU?" SAID THE mantis.

"Good afternoon, Mr. um, Kuzchewclick," I said.

"Miz," said the alien, razored forelimbs rasping together menacingly.

"Pardon?"

"I am having the honor of belonging to the female gender this mooncycle," it said.

"My apologies, Ms. Kuzchewclick," I said.

"It is being of no account," it said. "And how may this humble entity be helping you?"

"Some weeks ago," I said, "you contacted me about a trade show in Fomalhaut B."

"Ah yes indeedy! I am remembering. Are you wishing to be booking tickets now?"

"Yes," I said. "Three tickets."

"Most excellentment! In coldsleep, if I am remembering correctly," it said, with faint disapproval.

"Correct," I said.

"That will be costing sixty million U.S., round-trip," it said.

That, indeed, was what was worrying me. Sixty million dollars was the bulk of the money we hoped to scam with this IPO. And the booth fee alone was another $25 million: all our IPO money spent right there. I'd wanted a $20 million reserve, but I hadn't planned on a ticket for Huff. And I knew full well there'd be other expenses, expenses our $4 million of retained earnings might not cover. . . .

"I'll only be booking tickets one way," I said faintly.

The mantis's mandibles clashed.

"Fomalhaut B is not having any permanently inhabitable worlds," it said. "Once the event is being over. . . ."

I realized I was running a risk; but surely I could purchase return tickets at Fomalhaut B, if necessary. And I didn't want to tie up another $30 million in capital; one-way was a third of our IPO cash as it was.

"I understand," I said.

It made a complex movement I took as a shrug. "As you are wishing," it said. "How are you paying?"

"I expect to have funds to pay for the tickets on May 15," I said.

"And when are you wishing to be departing?"

"As close to May 15 as feasible."

"No, no, no," it said. "Tickets must be having been booked at least two weeks in advance."

This was unfortunate. I was worried about the SEC. I wanted to get off-planet as soon as feasible. Was there any way to get my hands on the money in advance?

"I see," I said. "Please reserve the tickets now, and I'll get back to you on the funds."

"MUKS! HOWAYA, MAN?" SAID SASSARENO, RED-FACED AND too enthusiastic. It was a bit after lunchtime in New York. It looked like the three-martini lunch was back in style.

"Quite well, Artie, thank you," I said. "Are things proceeding apace?"

"The deal is going slicker 'n a pig in poop, Muks. Already placed a shitload of your stock with some of the institutional guys."

I perked up. This was indeed good news—albeit pension funds make for more obstreperous stockholders than small investors.

"Glad to hear it, Artie. For my part, I have a bit of a problem."

Sassareno became cautious. "Sorry to hear that," he muttered. "Anything likely to queer the pitch?"

"I trust not," I said. "The difficulty is that I need thirty million dollars rather before the IPO."

Sassareno's lips pursed. "That's a hard one," he said. "What for?"

"As you know, Artie," I said, "our purpose in going public is to raise funds to reach sales outlets off-planet. Specifically, we need money to book spacefare to Fomalhaut B, for the trade show I mentioned previously."

"Can't it wait?"

It could, if we weren't in the process of committing securities fraud. I wanted to get off-planet as expeditiously as possible.

"We need to book in advance, I'm afraid."

Sassareno muttered something. "You aren't planning to skip are you, Muks?"

"Where to, Artie?" I said. "Not to Fomalhaut B, I assure you; I'm told they turn off the atmosphere there when the show is over."

He snorted. "Yeah. I dunno, Muks. Thirty mill is a lot of dough."

"See here, Artie, you've given us a guarantee price. Even if the IPO fails, Churner Ponzi is on the hook for more than that. Can't you advance us . . ."

"Yeah, but if the deal falls apart between now and then, we aren't," he said.

"I believe we could finance a loan of such magnitude even if the IPO fails," I said.

"That's not what your financials say," he said, smiling thinly.

That was certainly true; our financials claimed we were operating in the red. If true, there was no way we could afford interest on $30 million—of course, the financials bore about as much relationship to reality as the worldview of that fellow who had tried to lynch me under the impression that I was Jewish.

"Our financials," I said, raising an eyebrow.

Sassareno sighed. He knew the reality of the situation as well as I, but also knew admitting it would put *him* on the hook for securities fraud. "Look, if I go to our corporate finance guys, they're going to turn a loan down on the basis of your financials, you know that, Muks."

Indeed. "You can't secure a loan against the IPO proceeds?"

"Too iffy."

"How about against my company's equity?"

"Can't encumber the company that way; your prospectus already claims you're debt-free."

"Can't we structure it so it's secured by the IPO proceeds if the deal goes through and by the company itself if not?"

Sassareno hesitated. "I'll need to show a big return to work that one," he said.

Bastard. "What imputed interest rate do you want?" I said.

"Forty percent."

Bloody bastard. "Make it thirty-five," I said testily.

He grinned at me. "Pleasure doing business with you, Muks."

SO I BOOKED THE TICKETS AND SENT ONE TO HUFF (NOT without thinking about "losing" it somehow). And paced back and forth in my office, smoking too many cigars, worrying, while the red-suspendered twits at Ponzi Churner beavered away, preparing for The Day. I tried to take my mind off the precariousness of the situation with paperwork—and believe me, an IPO requires reams of it—but it did not suffice.

Especially when I learned that Daly was talking to our accounts.

Zabelle came into my office one day, wearing a leather skirt, a blouse with gold sequins, and heels that would have been too high on a woman half her age.

"What is wrong with you, Johnson?" she said, folding herself in a seat, knees held together, skirt riding up her withered thighs. "You're irritable and upset, and I can't for the life of me see why. Everything appears to be going quite well. Swimmingly, in fact."

"It's Daly," I said. "It's the fact that this whole thing is a house of cards. If the reality of our financials comes out before the launch . . ."

"One week, Johnson," she said. "That's all. Calm down."

"That's why I *can't* calm down."

She sighed and lit one of her long pastel cigarettes. "If you're that worried about Mr. Daly," she said, "I happen to know some people in the Russian *maffiya*."

I gaped at her. "What are you suggesting?"

She raised an eyebrow at me. "Me? Suggesting? Would I suggest something? What do you think?"

I sighed. "It's tempting, Zabelle, but I don't do business that way. Securities fraud, yes; murder, no."

She chuckled. "Everyone has their limits. I won't bring it up again."

I looked at her suspiciously. " 'Will no one rid me of this priest?' That's *not* what I'm saying, Zabelle. I won't have that on my conscience. Such as it is."

"Yes, yes, Johnson," she said smoothly, a dangerous glint in her eye.

"If we were to kill Daly, we'd deserve everything Huff thinks about us."

She hesitated for the first time, then sighed. "Yes, okay, Johnny. I suppose you're right," she said, and departed in a cloud of cigarette smoke.

What was it about Zabelle and Huff, anyway? I genuinely think she was prepared to have Daly killed until I brought up Huff's disapproval. *My* disapproval did not weigh so heavily.

THE BIG DAY FINALLY CAME.

I slept very little the previous night, woke in the darkness of morning, and went in to the office at 4 A.M. Absurdly early, of course, but I wanted to be there when the markets opened in New York—at 9 A.M. Eastern, 6 Pacific time.

I pottered about, pacing, checking news sites on the web, doing nothing much until people started drifting in. Not our whole staff, of course, but Mauro and Zabelle wanted to be there for market open also.

Sassareno called at 8:30 Eastern; one thing I'll say for investment bankers is they keep early hours. "Nothin' to worry about, Muks," he assured me. "Placed more'n two-thirds with the institutional guys, the rest has been parceled out among the underwriters, everything's set to open on target." We were issuing 8½ million shares at a price of ten bucks a share. That meant a bit over 5 million were presold to big investors, the rest parceled out to brokerages that had either presold small investors or were keeping a few shares to trade at launch.

I fired up my computer, and pointed it at the NASDAQ site. Holding, holding, ready for the market open.

Everyone came into the office; Mauro wheeled in an enormous ice bucket with several bottles of champagne. Awfully early, but if this came off, there would certainly be grounds for celebration.

Ding went the computer. Some asshole programmer's idea. NASDAQ is an electronic market, there's no opening bell. Still, there it was.

MKIL, our ticker. Ten, ten, ten and an eighth.

Up an eighth within seconds of market open.

"Simmer down, now, Johnny," said Zabelle, putting an arthritic, red-taloned hand on my arm. "We're public."

Mauro whooped and opened the champagne.

And why not? At current valuations, he was now worth mid–six figures. Not bad for someone who had been running a bankrupt plastic company less than a year before.

I relaxed at last. It was going to work. The proceeds would more than pay off Ponzi Churner's loan. Most of the rest would be converted into *gozashstandu* within hours, for use when we finally got to Fomalhaut B.

And within two days, Zabelle, I—and, God help us, Huff— would be on our way.

• • •

OUR HAPPY ILLUSION LASTED LESS THAN AN HOUR.

At 9:38 EST, Reuters ran the story: "Mukerjii Interstellar Profits Understated," by-line: Scott Daly.

At first reading, it was innocuous. It claimed we were actually very profitable. And the research was good; he'd managed to dig up our sales through a dozen major retailers. Our staff was a matter of public record. It wasn't that hard to estimate our operating costs.

It might even sound like good news, to the public: this newly launched company was making more money than it let on. Shareholders rejoice. And indeed, a quick check showed that our shareprice was up to 16—day traders churning the price skyward, the first hot IPO they'd had to handle in quite a while.

But I knew the subtext: Our SEC filings were patent nonsense, first, last, and in between. We were perjurers. We were securities frauds.

I was, I suspected, about to meet my friends Stackpole and Epstein again real soon.

I choked, read the story, and bawled for Zabelle.

"OH DEAR," SAID ZABELLE, SITTING AT MY DESK AND reading the screen. "You really should have let me take care of it, Johnson, dear."

"If only the bastard had held off another two days," I said.

"I'm sure he wishes he'd been able to file it two days *ago*," she said. "He might have been able to stop the IPO."

"What are we going to do? They'll suspend trading, Ponzi Churner will claim they knew nothing, I—and you, Zabelle, you're a director, you have fiduciary responsibility—are going to wind up in federal prison. . . ."

"I'll get my car," she said.

16

ATLA$ $HRUG$, MERCEDE$ BEND$

ZABELLE'S CAR HAD A MERCEDES BADGE ON THE HOOD.

It was long, low, like a cross between a Dodge Viper and a stealth fighter.

It floated above the ground. Antigrav, I imagined.

It had gull-wing doors.

It was candy-apple red.

"When did you get this, Zabelle?" I asked.

"Last week," she said.

"Since when does Mercedes . . ."

"It's alien manufacture," she said. "They have a comarketing deal with DaimlerChrysler. Do shut up, dear boy, and get in."

I got in. The doors closed with a chunk. It was like being in a cocoon; the street noise suddenly shut off.

"Where are we going?"

"To the Baikonur Cosmodrome, Johnny, dear; where do you think?" Our tickets were on the *Judicious Lepidosauromorph*, an alien ship on the ground at the Russian spaceport.

The car lifted another foot off the ground; Zabelle slid smoothly into street traffic.

"But Zabelle . . . That's thousands of miles away."

"About eleven thousand kilometers," she said absently,

turning at the corner and heading for the highway. "Five hours at Mach two."

"This thing can go twice the speed of sound?"

"Mach six, according to *Car and Driver*," she said. "But the skyway doesn't get up above Mach two."

She pulled up on the on-ramp and onto the highway—an old-fashioned multilane concrete monster—heading toward the ocean. We were up to 100 km/hr in seconds. Still a long way from the speed of sound.

"But . . . what about my luggage?"

She fumbled at her purse with one hand, and handed me a cell phone. "Tell Mauro to FedEx it to you," she said.

LEFT LANE FOR SKYWAY, said a sign, in English and Spanish. Zabelle pulled into the lane as I made the call.

The car's nose lifted.

Long yellow floating tubes slid past us as we gained altitude. I chatted briefly with Mauro. The coastline passed below.

The signs were long smears now, each letter elongated for miles. They read right to left, as it were, so you'd encounter the first letter first as you sped past—reading them in proper order, but curiously inverted, for people used to reading left to right. Like those signs, painted on tarmac, that are supposed to say "PED XING" but look at first glance like they say "XING PED" because "XING" is closer to you.

" . . . ENOZ DEEPS DECUDER DNE 2 HCAM TIMIL DEEPS"

After a while, I nodded off; I hadn't slept well, and we had a long trip before us. When I awoke, we were above the Pacific Ocean. There was little traffic. "Why don't you check the news?" Zabelle said, pointing to a vidscreen on the dash.

I punched some buttons, and found CNN. Some blather

about a tornado, something about some brainless starlet, and then . . .

"The Securities and Exchange Commission suspended trading in Mukerjii Interstellar, today, mere hours after it launched on the over-the-counter market," said another blow-dried announcer, "alleging irregularities in the company's financial statements." Cut to a rather red-faced fellow in a charcoal suit on the steps of a government building somewhere. "We don't know what the hell is going on," he said, "but it's obvious that Mukerjii's filings are a load of crap, and we're going to get to the bottom of this."

Back to Mr. Blowdry: "Arthur Sassareno of Ponzi Churner, lead underwriter for Mukerjii Interstellar's public offering, had this to say."

Cut. My old buddy, Artie, sitting in his office. "Needless to say, we're shocked," he said. He didn't look any too shocked. "We worked closely with Mukerjii Interstellar on their filings, and relied on their good faith. . . . Of course the financials were audited by a reputable firm. . . ."

I snarled and snapped it off.

"Well," said Zabelle.

She drove for a long moment, then said, "We better get to Kazakhstan quickly, Johnny."

Zabelle flicked a switch; the windshield filled with a heads-up display, showing everything down the road a hundred kilometers ahead. She eased the car up to Mach 4, sticking to the upper left lane. We passed other vehicles so quickly they were distant dots ahead—then suddenly, streaks beside us—then equally suddenly, distant dots behind. Zabelle steered by the display, not by the view out the windshield; we were moving too fast to make that feasible.

A slower-moving aircar appeared in the display, down the skyway from us, in the same lane as us. Zabelle slid slowly down a lane; we roared past. I wondered about the turbulence behind us; we were moving at four times the speed of sound, after all. True, the lanes were over a hundred feet across—much wider than that of a conventional road—but that was far from enough to dissipate the shock wave in our wake. Nonetheless, the vehicle we passed continued onward, rock-steady, apparently oblivious to our passing. Good engineering, that.

We roared past a vehicle painted an eggshell blue: United Nations colors.

"Oh drat," muttered Zabelle. She glanced at me. "Better put on your seat belt, Johnny," she said.

I snorted. "Why bother?" I said. "If we hit anything at this speed, we're atoms anyway."

Zabelle did a barrel roll, the aircar sliding out of the skyway and into the blue, 10,000 feet above the Pacific.

I clutched at the ceiling, trying to stop myself from falling against it until the Earth was below us again.

"Just put on your seat belt, Johnny," she said.

With shaking fingers, I did.

A voice from the dashboard spoke. "Baja California plate THX 2001, you have left the Transpacific Skyway. This is grounds for immediate license suspension. Return to it immediately." Interesting, I thought; the aircar was Mexican licensed, but it knew to address Zabelle in English.

On the heads-up display, a dot far behind us was pulsing in red.

"Why the hell did you do that, Zabelle?" I demanded.

"That was a cop we passed, Johnny," she said absently, "doing double the speed limit. If we stuck to the skyway, they'd chase us from here to Singapore."

The dash was speaking again, this time in a distinct Australian accent. "G'day, Baja THX 2001. This is Sergeant Jenks of the UN Skyway Police. You'd better climb back to the skyway, y'know; speeding ticket's a lot less hassle than losing your bloody license."

Zabelle nosed the car into a steep dive. My stomach lurched. I noticed that the speedometer was falling. Zabelle must be braking; otherwise, we'd be picking up speed with the dive, not losing it.

"Zabelle . . ." I moaned.

"We have to get below their radar, dear," she said.

"Zabelle! It's just a speeding ticket! Get back to—"

"Are you sure there isn't a warrant out for our arrest, Johnny?" she snapped. "Do you really want to talk to the nice policeman?"

I subsided, quite unhappy with this turn of events.

Soon, we were mere meters above the waves. I saw why Zabelle had cut speed. The waves below tossed drops of salt water into the air—a thin spray at surface level, but at our speed we intersected a great many of them. It was like driving through a rainstorm.

Zabelle punched another button; the heads-up display became a map of the Pacific, showing our position over it. GPS data, I assumed.

The skyway was marked in yellow. Zabelle made a course correction. We were arrowing straight across the Pacific toward Borneo, the skyway heading farther to our north, in the direction of Manila.

The voice from the dash didn't speak again.

We'd gotten away, for the nonce.

After a time, I dozed off again.

WHOOOP WHOOP WHOOOP.

The alarm jerked me out of sleep.

The car was moving straight and level, thank God. It was dark outside.

Zabelle was bolt upright, gripping the wheel with white-fingered hands.

"What happened?" I asked.

"I fell asleep at the wheel," she said, voice a little shaky.

"Johnny, I think we had better switch places."

"What? I can't drive one of these things."

"Certainly you can, Johnny, don't be a fool." She unbuckled, and started levering herself arthritically over the gearbox . . . if it *was* a gearbox.

We were in deep bucket seats. Between the seats ran the gearbox—or joystick?—and a long low ridge.

I looked at the heads-up display; there didn't seem to be any aircraft nearby.

"What happens if you let go of the controls?" I asked.

Zabelle grunted, trying to get her feet up to the level of the gearbox. "It will fly straight and level. I think."

"You *think*. Zabelle, why don't you take us up a bit? That way we'll have farther to dive before crashing."

She muttered something, but nosed the aircar up.

Soon we were high, stars bright above us, dark waves glinting below, seemingly the only object between sea and sky in all the nighttime world, nary a ship nor another aircraft in sight, amid the vast Pacific expanse.

"Okay," I said, and grabbed Zabelle's slender shoulders, trying to pull her over the central obstruction.

I'm not that strong, I'm afraid. Not exactly a weight lifter. Zabelle's feet scrabbled, her crone hands grabbed at me, we both grunted and panted. . . . I shifted position, heaving at her.

"Watch what you're doing, Johnny! I'm not a girl anymore!"

"Zabelle," I grunted. "This is not your best idea."

"Shut up and pull. AAAAAAAAGH!"—this last as the aircar suddenly began to roll, the stars spinning past in some crazy gyration.

She was hurled partway across the partition, legs still over the plastic barrier between the seats. Somehow I managed to drag her the rest of the way into my lap—bruised several times by amazingly sharp elbows.

"Get over there quick, Johnny," she yelled. "We've got to get the car under control!"

"I know that, you silly old bat!" I shouted, trying to dump her against the door, off my lap, trying to clamber over the central obstruction. Never mind that Zabelle was rather peevishly pushing at me, that there were scant feet between the obstruction and the roof, that the foot wells were entirely separate, that I had to drag my whole body over the gearbox; the sky was spinning, I was desperately afraid we'd start to tumble, and heaven knows what would happen then, at supersonic speeds. I was acutely aware we could die; my stomach lurched violently, my body, too, as the craft spun.

I managed it, somehow I managed it, at the cost of a blackened eye. I grabbed the wheel and tried to turn against the motion of the roll. By mistake, I pushed the wheel *in* as well as turning it.

I hadn't realized the wheel moved in and out. The car I'd rented in Orlando didn't do that. In response, the aircar began to yaw dangerously, vibrating back and forth, while traveling well over Mach 1, more than the speed of sound.

"What the hell do I do, Zabelle?" I shouted.

She was preoccupied, blood pouring from her nose, a lace handkerchief pressed against it. But she grabbed the stick with one hand.

"The brake, Johnny! Works like in a regular car. The brake. Left, pull up . . . no up, you moron! How did you ever get to run a company?"

I desperately wrenched at the wheel, trying to follow her instructions, the world whizzing dizzily about. "If you hadn't been speeding on the goddamn skyway . . ." I shouted, struggling with the wheel.

"I had to, you imbecile!" she screamed, leaning over to grab the wheel with her free hand, blood from her nose spattering my trousers. The aircar was shaking like it was going to come apart at any moment.

"You didn't have to! You didn't have to drive to bloody Kazakhstan, either! What the devil are you doing? Give me that wheel—"

"Let go of it! You have no idea what you're doing!"

Well, that was true enough. I let go of the wheel and let her struggle with it.

Slowly, the world's gyrations began to subside, enough that I began to realize what was happening outside. We were diving straight toward the sea, rolling slowly as we did . . . Slowly, Zabelle pulled back on the wheel . . . Slowly, the aircar nosed up, but we were diving still . . . It was hard to decide how far above the water we were, in darkness, nothing below us to give a sense of scale . . . And just as we achieved level flight, there was that sudden spatter of rain against the windshield—

Not rain, the spray above the ocean. I shuddered, realizing how close we had come.

"Haven't you ever played a flight sim?" Zabelle asked in disgust, turning the wheel back over to me. "Push to dive, pull to climb."

"Twitch games," I told her with some dignity, pulling the wheel back experimentally and climbing a few hundred feet. "A complete waste of time."

She snorted—and coughed; snorting is a bad idea with a nosebleed. "And I am not an old bat," she said.

"Nor am I an imbecile," I said.

"If not, you play the role well," she said, fumbling for her purse and a packet of tissues.

AFTER AN HOUR OR SO OF SLEEP, ZABELLE WOKE UP AND began clicking through a series of maps on the heads-up display, making disapproving clucking sounds.

"What is it?" I asked.

"I've taken us around India," she said, "but we shall have to go in either over Pakistan or Iran."

"And?"

"Both are quite mountainous," she said. "I don't fancy trying to keep under radar in such rough terrain. Neither of us is exactly a great pilot."

"That's an understatement."

"We shall have to rejoin a skyway," she said.

"But surely our license has been revoked," I said.

"Yes," she said. "But perhaps if we go via Iran . . . They're still awfully prickly about cooperating with international organizations, perhaps they won't track on our plates."

" 'Perhaps' is a lot to risk our futures on," I complained.

"Offer me another option," she said.

WE ENTERED IRANIAN AIRSPACE NOT FAR FROM THE PORT of Bandar Beheshti, flying very low. A skyway ran from there to Tehran; Zabelle found a dusty country road close to the city, and landed on a deserted stretch. In ground mode, we approached the skyway on-ramp.

We attracted some odd glances, to be sure; not too many candy-apple Mercedeses with Mexican plates driving around the south of Iran, I suspect. But nobody stopped us, and soon we were aloft again, driving just under the speed limit.

We passed another of those strangely inverted signs:

". . . CIMALSI EHT OT EMOCLEW
NARI FO CILBUPER
SNOITALOIV GNIVOM LLA
HTAED YB ELBAHSINUP"

I swallowed. And I had thought California state troopers were bad.

NATURALLY, WE OBEYED THE TRAFFIC LAWS. TO THE DOT. Keeping down and right, and always under the speed limit.

We got across Iran in just under an hour, up to Kerman on the main Tehran road, then taking the exit for Mashad and points north. The road signs were in English, Russian, and Arabic, as well as Farsi. Between us, we could read two of the four.

And we had no problems across Turkmenistan or Uzbekistan—perhaps ten minutes apiece, amazing how geography is compressed at twice the speed of sound.

Coming in toward Tyuratam, the eastern sky began to turn rose with impending dawn. We'd outflown the terminator, starting in the California morning, flying into Pacific night, but had spent some time flying north, now, and the morning had caught up with us.

In the heads-up display, I noticed two vehicles pacing us, twenty kilometers back or so. At first I thought: of course, they're at the speed limit, too; but no one else was under the speed limit, except for people entering or leaving at exits. Typical; if the speed limit is fifty-five miles an hour, everyone goes sixty-five; if it's Mach 2, everyone goes 2.4.

I pulled to the lower right land, and cut back to 1.7. They cut speed, too—not taking the same lane, but pacing us still.

Clearly, we had been identified. Sometime in the last hour, a computer search had found our transponder on this skyway. And someone—UN traffic cops, Interpol, perhaps the Khazars—was tracking us.

The exit for Baikonur was no more than 200 kilometers ahead of us—perhaps ten minutes at our current rate of speed. Surely they must suspect we were heading there. What other business could we possibly have in Kazakhstan?

"Here we go," I told Zabelle, praying that two hours in the seat of the aircar had given me enough experience.

I peeled down, past the yellow markers, out into uncontrolled space.

"What are you doing?" screeched Zabelle.

The same automated voice sounded from the dash, warning us to get back in lane.

I watched the heads-up display as the dots representing our followers slid out of the skyway, too.

"We're being followed," I said.

From the Baikonur exit—visible on the display as yellow lines in cloverleaf shape—a dozen or more vehicles exploded, darting from the skyway, too. They had been waiting at the exit to intercept us.

I glanced at Zabelle; she clutched at the dashboard for dear life, no doubt mistrusting my abilities as a driver. Not unreasonably; I mistrusted them myself.

I dived toward the desolate Kazakh lowlands below us, "virgin lands" the idiot Reds had developed for farming, long since salted up and abandoned, desiccated soil unfit for much of anything. We needed to get below the radar—if that was even possible, in this flatland.

Tense with the danger, I flattened mere decameters above the ground—realizing my mistake as I did, the shock wave of our passing kicking up dust, leaving a highly visible contrail behind us. I nosed up the aircar a bit, until the contrail disappeared.

It didn't help. It wasn't long before three aircars were pacing us, one above, two just behind us and to either side. The vehicles were painted black; red, blue, and white tricolors on the side made clear they were Russian.

Kazakhstan's independence is fairly notional.

"*Gospodin* Mukerjii," said a pleasant tenor voice. "Please to land immediately."

The vehicles looked rather less sleek than ours, but rather more dangerous. A roof rack held what were clearly missiles.

"Uh, yes, certainly, um, Officer," I said. I began to cut speed. They paced us.

"What are you *doing*?" Zabelle demanded in a whisper. "We're just minutes from the Cosmodrome!"

Just minutes from finding out what it's like to be an expanding ball of flame, actually.

Ahead, I could see a river; I switched the heads-up display to show us satellite imagery of the surrounding area. There *had* to be some better cover than this flat plain. The river was the Syr Darya, a trickle, one of the few rivers feeding the Aral Sea.

I mashed a foot onto the accelerator suddenly; a few moments later, began sawing the wheel, yawing the craft back and forth, hoping a zigzag might prevent those missiles from striking us. I dived down toward the river, feeling the spray of water against us—not as thick as over the ocean, but something at least, something that might hide a heat signature. If those missiles were heat-seeking. God knows what they were. Nobody understands half the technology we buy from the aliens.

Silent explosions blossomed momentarily before us, and were gone—silent because we outpaced their sound.

Mach 3. Mach 4. My God, Mach 5.

I peeled away from the river, rolling the aircar, zagging as much as I dared, feeling the vehicle rattle like a VW Bug trying to make seventy miles an hour. Zabelle was whimpering with fear.

Suddenly, a dozen dots appeared on the heads-up display, from a ring around the Baikonur Cosmodrome—my God, they were using antimissile defenses, probably built when there was still a Soviet Union.

"You'd better start braking," said Zabelle shakily.

"Another minute," I gasped.

"Now," she said, "you can't shed this much speed in an instant. . . ."

I saw her point, slammed on the brakes. I had no idea how it worked; there didn't seem to be any ailerons; if the aircar used reaction mass, I saw no evidence of it. We were slammed forward, hanging in our seat belts, Zabelle's purse flying from her seat and plastering itself onto the windshield. I could see the Cosmodrome ahead, the hulking postmodern sprawl of CosmoMall, the Museum of Heroic Soviet Space, the parking structures . . . and beyond, the launchpads themselves, a dozen or more, filled with a staggering variety of ships.

The antimissile defenses either couldn't fix on us, or our driving was too erratic . . . whatever the case, I saw dots arc past us on the display, flashes of light in the distance. I hoped no one was getting killed; it would be foolish to kill people over one stupid securities fraud.

"Which one is our ship?" I demanded.

Zabelle had anticipated me; she had some kind of web page on the display: a map of the Cosmodrome, the alien ships neatly labeled in Russian.

"That one," she said.

It was a sphere, supported by six squat legs, each ending in tripodal fingers. It was gunmetal gray; bulges scattered across the sphere looked like nothing so much as enormous rivets. It did not look like my idea of a judicious lizard.

It was coming up too quickly, I hadn't shed enough speed. I arced around the *Judicious Lepidosauromorph*, headed away from it again, desperately braking. . . .

Explosions blossomed around us. Black Russian craft looped crazily by, trying to intersect us. I heard the sudden rumble of sound as we broke back down below Mach 1, aircar shaking . . . an alien craft like a cathedral looming before us . . . rolling just to its left . . . path still arcing . . . coming back to the *Sauromorph* . . . the car shuddering, still slowing . . . diving under the ship . . . trying to land . . . plowing into the tarmac, the Mercedes flipping over and over, Zabelle screaming . . . feeling myself held utterly motionless by some force as my ears were assaulted by crashes, my stomach by crazy lurches, the world outside a mess of yellow polluted sky, black tarmac, gray gunmetal. . . .

My guts still reeled, but the world outside was motionless. My door was half smashed in; we hung upside down in our seat belts. The car had flipped onto its roof. Zabelle and I both appeared to be alive.

Mirabile dictu. Or no miracle, perhaps; simply good safety engineering. . . .

Zabelle got open her door, undid her seat belt, fell to the roof of the car with a grunt, and crawled out onto the tarmac.

I managed to scrabble across the roof to follow her.

A crazed maniac wearing a tweed jacket, urban camouflage pants, and combat boots was running toward us, cradling a submachine gun. "This way!" he shouted.

I almost crawled back into the aircar for cover before I realized it was the damnable Leander Huff.

"Coming, Les!" shouted Zabelle, scrambling to her feet and making considerable speed, for an old lady in high heels.

I tottered after them, realizing it had been decades since I was in anything like decent shape.

One of the Russian aircars roared toward us, aiming to pass below the *Judicious Lepidosauromorph*, strafing the ground, guns spitting from either side of its headlights.

Huff rattled off a stream of bullets from his submachine gun, but they seemed to have no effect.

Twin lines of bullets streaked toward us as we ran . . .

And suddenly, cyan light streamed out from one of those curvatures on the alien ship's hull, passing close enough to us that I felt the heat of it, smelled the ionization of the air in its wake. The beam intersected the Russian car . . . which vaporized instantaneously.

We reached one of the alien ship's legs. Something like a cross between a ladder and an escalator was there, metal links rising swiftly up the leg to a hatchway far above us. Huff helped Zabelle onto it—she stepped onto a rung, clung to it, lifting swiftly upward. I followed.

As I rose, I could see emergency vehicles clustered on the tarmac, black Russian aircars swarming over the spaceport like angry bees. Soldiers in tan-colored uniforms began firing at

us—Huff letting off a long blast from his SMG in response—
until their officers evidently ordered them to hold fire.

Someone had some sense. Firing indiscriminately toward an
alien ship is not something *I* would want to do. Especially
not one that had just swatted an aircar out of the sky like a
bug.

The rising ladder pulled me through the hatch of the alien
ship; I leapt onto a long, gunmetal deck. A dozen aliens
awaited us: centaurlike, four legs ending in three-hooved toes,
two arms ending in four-fingered hands, green, lizardlike skin,
narrow skulls, many-toothed mouths above eyes set at the
side of the head, like those of a horse. They wore tool belts;
their flanks were painted with abstract patterns.

"You are more trouble than you are worth," said the box
at the belt of one of the aliens. Only the translator box made
noise; I assumed the aliens communicated among each other
via something other than sound waves.

"I'm sorry, sir," Huff replied with some dignity, still pant-
ing from his sprint. "It seemed necessary."

"I get in trouble with human authorities for what?" the
alien said—disgust evident despite the affectless translation
of the device at his belt. "Three steerage passengers."

He spat on the deck, a surprisingly human gesture. The
spittle dissolved the paint on the deck, leaving a spot of shiny
metal behind.

"Give me your weapon," he said to Huff. Huff reluctantly
surrendered it.

The alien turned it over in his hands. "Shoots slugs?"

"Yes," said Huff.

The alien handed it back. "Take out cartridge."

Huff pulled the cartridge of bullets from the stock.

The alien took the Uzi back, and took a bite out of its
barrel. Something sizzled inside that fanged mouth; an acrid
gas escaped from his lips.

"Not bad," said the alien, chewing contemplatively.

• • •

THE ALIENS TOOK US DEEPER INTO THE SHIP—GRAY metal everywhere, they seemed to decorate nothing other than their own bodies—and led us to a room that was clearly designed for human visitors, outfitted with cheap furniture and a bar. They fed us: take-out Chinese. It figured; they probably had no facilities for preparing human food.

We talked as we ate. Huff had heard the news about the SEC, and had taken a somewhat earlier suborbital rocket to Baikonur than he had planned to take. He had no problems; the SEC didn't want *his* head on a platter.

Not yet, at any event. He *was* a board member, of course.

A point of which he was acutely aware. "If you think I'm going to the federal pen with you, Mukerjii, you're off your nut," he told me. "I plan to testify like a snake-chunker at a revival meeting."

"I knew I could rely on you, Dr. Huff," I muttered around a mouthful of egg roll. The food was wretched; well, we were in Kazakhstan, what did you expect?

"In the meantime," he said, "we'll just have to hope our good captain doesn't turn us over to the authorities."

It wasn't until I had finished eating that the enormity of my situation hit me. Here I was on an alien vessel, an outlaw—wanted worldwide, on the lam from the police.

Right. Jesse James, Bonnie and Clyde, the Unabomber, and portly Bengali me. I sighed.

I retired to the couch, shaking and silent, letting Huff and Zabelle coo at each other.

Sometime later the door opened, and one of the aliens walked in; perhaps the one who had eaten Huff's gun, I couldn't say—no doubt those flank markings were individual, but I had trouble telling them apart. "You must meet with pigs," quoth the alien.

We all looked at him, rather taken aback.

"Pigs? Coppers? State authorities, yes?"

"I see," I said, sitting up. "What is the purpose of this meeting?"

The alien looked at me. "They demand we surrender you. We tell them: urinate off. They say, they are humans, law-breakers, must talk to us. We say, you may talk. They send pigs to talk to you. We don't want more trouble. You talk."

I shrugged. "We'll talk to them," I said. "Are we free to stay with you afterward?"

"You pay, you stay," said the alien.

I trusted he meant that I *had* paid and *would* stay.

"STACKPOLE," SAID STACKPOLE. "EPSTEIN," SAID EPSTEIN. The flashed their badges. "U.S. Secret Service."

Black suits, white shirts, standing on the deck of the alien craft.

"Good afternoon, Mr. Mukerjii," said Stackpole, "nice to see you again. I have a warrant for your arrest, I'm afraid."

"What, again, Agent Stackpole? No great surprise," I said. "However, I'm afraid I shan't be accompanying you."

"I'm afraid you must, sir. And you, too, ma'am. We have approval from the Kazakh authorities." He held out the warrant.

"This ship is sovereign territory of Tsoonchai Nation," said the alien captain. "Your puling monkey laws do not apply here."

Stackpole turned to him. "Mr. Mukerjii is accused of second-degree murder as well as securities fraud, sir," he said apologetically.

"Murder?" inquired the captain, turning to me, teeth clashing angrily.

"I've never killed anyone!" I protested.

"Captain Kirilov of the Russian Internal Security Force was killed while pursuing you, sir," said Epstein. "I believe you can plea-bargain the charge down to manslaughter."

The captain's translator made a dangerous chirring sound.

"*I* kill one of your savages," he said, "not this one. Any craft that approaches my ship, guns firing, I kill also."

Stackpole and Epstein exchanged glances. Suddenly, they had their guns out. One was trained on the captain, the other on me.

Before I could so much as twitch, one of the aliens had plucked Stackpole's gun from his hands, while the other had pushed Epstein out the open hatch, hitting him with a shoulder like an American footballer.

The alien with the gun ate it.

I hoped Epstein was okay.

"Get off my ship, pig," the captain demanded.

Stackpole blinked, and backed slowly to the ladder.

THE ALIENS LED US TO A ROOM FILLED WITH GUNMETAL gray machinery, and left us there for some time. After a few moments, a gentle "thrum" went through the ship. One curved wall of the room turned transparent; through it, we saw the Earth dwindling below us, the terminator slicing Europe in half at about the longitude of Berlin, western Europe's cities shining brightly through scattered clouds, central Europe brown and green in the day. That "thrum" was all we had felt of takeoff; presumably gravitational generators had prevented us from feeling the strains of acceleration.

The image shifted; I realized we were not looking downward, that the image we saw was projected by the ship to display things of interest. We soared past the scarred moon, and out-system.

For a time, nothing could be seen but the distant stars; but then, a reddish dot grew at screen center. Soon, we were able to see the bands and whorls of Jupiter, its moons about it, gnatlike in comparison. Except that—Jupiter appeared to have ears. Gradually, I realized they were the plumes of gas I had read about, rising into orbit.

"Look," I said.

Huff and Zabelle crowded about me, peering at the image. As we neared and the disk grew larger, we could see that the gas was coalescing into a ring about the planet. "What are they doing?" wondered Zabelle.

Huff grunted. "Your guess is as good as mine," he said. "Astronomers have noticed it before. Building some structure in orbit around Jupiter, apparently. And look at Callisto."

Something stuck out of one of the moons, like a toothpick stuck in an olive. "Orbital elevator," said Huff. "Used to transport stuff into and out of Callisto's orbit much more cheaply than launching by spacecraft. We know about the principle, but don't have the technology to build such a thing ourselves."

"What's it all for?" I wondered.

"Haven't you noticed?" Huff said. "Almost all the 'alien' products we buy are made in the Jovian system."

I recalled the aircar one of the engineers had bought when I still ran MDS; it had been made on Callisto, possibly lifted into orbit by that elevator before being launched toward Earth. We watched in silence as Jupiter slid past and began to diminish. I wondered, though; the aliens seemed to be plowing quite a lot of capital into developing Jupiter. Could it merely be to produce things to sell to our own impoverished species?

A chill struck me, along with a new thought: Perhaps they did not expect humanity to be their only customers in the solar system. Their financial resources were enormous, by our standards; if aliens wanted to start moving in, all they had to do was buy up property. Resistance would be futile, of course; if any national government was foolish enough to prohibit real-estate sales to aliens, a show of force would be enough to make them back down. . . .

We *could* end up like the Aztecs, I realized. Or perhaps more like the nineteenth-century Chinese, controlled and dominated by alien colonies on our own soil.

"You were right about selling Jupiter," I told Huff. He merely snorted, as if to say that any idiot could see that.

A door snicked open, and one of the centaurlike aliens entered. "Now," it said, "you go on ice." One four-fingered hand pointed to three coffins, or so they appeared.

I shrugged; it was time, surely.

"Freeze us?" Huff asked, turning to me.

"Yes, Dr. Huff," I said. "We're traveling in coldsleep."

He frowned. "Whatever for? This is no generation ship."

"Is cheaper," said the alien.

Huff snorted. "Pinching pennies, Mukerjii?"

"They are," I pointed out, "your pennies, Dr. Huff; you *are* a stockholder." I went to lie down in one of the coffins. It was quite uncomfortable, but I imagined I wouldn't care long. I watched Zabelle and Huff take their places.

The alien unexpectedly stuck a piece of glass in my arm. I yelped—some kind of injection, I assume. The others took theirs.

It occurred to me that of course Huff didn't know the whole story. I smiled.

"I'm told the odds of surviving coldsleep are quite good," I said. The world was spinning a bit.

Huff's head came sleepily up. "What? What do you mean?"

"Better than ninety percent," I said, my own voice coming distantly.

"You son of a bitch," I heard, before I blacked out.

17

YOU GET WHAT YOU PAY FOR

THE CAVERN THROBBED. ABE LINCOLN SAT MOTIONLESS, an enormous bulk looming above us: gray stone, grave and somehow menacing.

No, it wasn't Abe Lincoln. It was an alien, a gargoyle, or something like one; taloned feet and claws, horns, enormous eyes with vertical slits that sphinctered slowly, head glacially turning to examine us. His posture, and his chair, bore a resemblance to the Lincoln Memorial in Washington; my muddy brain had taken a moment to realize the difference.

Muddy was the word; my thoughts tried to slog across a springtime steppe, neurons firing as slowly as that creature before us moved. I was vaguely aware that the centauroids had pried us from our coffins, fed us dreadful coffee, pressed our luggage into our hands, and led us to this place. Recovering from coldsleep was evidently not an instant process; I felt unrecovered still.

The cavern throbbed. Though the creature before us appeared to be of stone, the room we occupied was curiously organic, walls curving into ceilings and floor—grayish green, pulsing slightly, here and there pipes or capillaries or veins throbbing as liquids passed through them.

Throb.

Welcome to the Carina Arm Travel Accessories Show. Please state your planet of origin.

The words were not spoken; they came unbidden into my brain.

Those eyes sphinctered. I felt as if I were in the presence of a god: that enormous form sitting before us, subsonics throbbing through us, words coming into my brain. I suppressed a fleeting desire to fall to my knees.

"Earth," said Huff crisply, looking rather put out. "Terra."

Throb.

Yes. This is not an attack. We are taking genetic samples for identification purposes.

Something plopped onto my shoulder from above; I jumped, shrieking a bit, I fear. It was a hairy spider the size of a dinner plate, or something like one. It bit my earlobe, leapt from my shoulder to Huff's, then from his to Zabelle's.

I put a hand to my ear; there was a small puncture. My hand came away with a few drops of blood, but the pain was slight.

Your booth is A3C89$_{b12}$. One thousand seven hundred twenty-eight gozashtandu *have been deducted from your account. You have not purchased any accommodations or fittings. Do you wish to do so at this time.*

Throb. Blink.

I glanced toward Zabelle; the black-plastic cases containing our marketing displays and materials rested on the floor nearby.

"We . . . we will need power," I said.

How many gigawatts?

Blink.

Gigawatts? Good lord. "Um, a hundred kilowatts should be ample."

We will supply power. There will be no charge for drawing

power at that level. The cost of setup will be one hundred forty-four gozashtandu.

Throb.

A quick calculation; a tad under a million dollars. Just for wiring the booth?

Do you wish atmosphere?

"Ah . . . I don't quite follow . . ." I said.

There was a long silence that I somehow intimated was compounded of irritation.

You breathe an oxygen/nitrogen mixture. There are no permanently habitable bodies in this system. We will supply your booth with atmosphere for the duration of the show at a cost of one thousand one hundred fifty-two gozashtandu. We can partition your booth into separate atmospheric zones at an additional setup charge of eight hundred sixty-four gozashtandu plus one thousand one hundred fifty-two gozashtandu per atmospheric type, if you wish to accommodate customers who breathe a variety of different fluids or gases. Alternatively, we can lease you space suits in a wide variety of models. . . .

"An oxy/nitro mixture will be fine," said Huff.

You will then be wanting gravity. At your planetary normal pull.

"We have to pay for *gravity?*" I demanded.

Irritation. Throb. Old Abe was not happy with me. I was an obtuse lad.

Gases are not known for their propensity to stay in the vicinity of small orbital bodies in the absence of gravity. Gravitic generators are installed in the booth. Turning them on requires the services of skilled union technicians. Powering them does not come without cost. The charge will be five hundred seventy-six gozashtandu for the duration of the show.

I was beginning to comprehend. Trade shows the world over nickel-and-dime you to death; it was the same offworld as well apparently with a few added wrinkles.

Convention centers back home had never had the gall to charge you for *gravity*. Or the air you breathed. It was a new dimension in greed.

"Earth-normal gravity will be fine," I said resignedly.

Very good. Radiation shielding is recommended for carbon-based species; it will cost one thousand seven hundred twenty-eight gozashtandu.

Abe was throwing me for a loop again. Radiation shielding?

"Yes, of course, we will need that," said Huff.

"Why?" I demanded.

He looked at me with as much contempt as Old Abe. "We might be okay without it," he said. "Or the local star could have a major solar flare while we're here. Then you'd find out."

I still wasn't getting it. Oh, I got that they were suckering us into spending like water the money we'd committed securities fraud to get. But Christ on a stick, radiation shielding?

Well, hell. The odds were good we were never coming back from this show anyway. Why not gamble a little more with our lives? Seventeen hundred *gosh*, a cool seven and a half million dollars?

Still, Huff was better on the technical issues than I. "All right, we'll take the shielding," I said with a sigh.

Have you made arrangements for accommodations.

Blink.

Abe had my attention again. "No, uh, we reserved no hotel room."

Our facilities are booked up. However, I can arrange for sleeping pallets to be erected on your booth. And for the water and carbohydrate-protein mixture your species requires to be supplied to you on a periodic basis that is suitable for your metabolism.

My, that sounded appetizing. "How much?"

One thousand one hundred fifty-two gozashtandu.

I did a quick mental calculation: 6480 *gosh* in total; call it a little over $32 million American. Six times our annual gross, just to kit out a goddamn trade show booth.

Plus the $30 million for our spacefare. We'd gone public for $85 million, and Ponzi Churner had nicked $4 million on the deal.

We were down to $19 million dollars before we made sale one.

Not enough money to pay return fare.

"In addition to our own dietary needs," I said, "it would be useful to be able to offer refreshments to visitors. Is there some standard package that provides small quantities of comestibles for a variety of species types?"

Certainly. The cost per day will be one hundred forty-four gozashtandu per dozen anticipated visitors.

I sighed. "One such setup will be fine," I said.

Very good. I will state a variety of other services we offer. Please interrupt if any are of interest. Program advertising. Launch party sponsorship. Nuclear warheads. In-system . . .

"Nuclear warheads?"

For advertising/light show use. In-system vehicle rental.

"Ah . . . Are there taxis we can use instead?"

Yes. But you will then need access to the systemwide communications network in order to call a cab. The cost is modest: one hundred forty-four gozashtandu.

Modest my foot. "Yes, we'll take that."

Furniture. Recreational drugs. Additional computer hardware and office supplies. Hyperlink communications across the Carina Arm and indeed both spinwise and antispinwise from the Arm. Mercenary military . . .

"I believe that will be all," I said, noticing Huff perk up at the mention of mercenaries.

Very well. Good day. Complimentary transport to your booth will be provided. Have a pleasant and profitable time.

Sphincter. Throb.

There was a sucking sound behind us; part of the wall had irised open, displaying a pulsating, organic tunnel. Uncertainly, I led the way toward it.

As I did, another tunnel opened up to our left, and four mantislike aliens carrying boxes and wearing porkpie hats appeared.

As we entered our own tunnel, Old Abe addressed the newcomers.

Welcome to the Carina Arm Travel Accessories Show. Please state your planet of origin.

Throb.

I realized what I'd done, of course. We would die here, light-years from home, unless we wrote enough orders to be able to pay our return fare.

Come back with your invoice or on it, as it were. Move product or die.

THE TUNNEL DISGORGED US INTO ANOTHER ORGANIC cavern, this one open to space. Despite this, it was filled with a breathable atmosphere; some kind of force-field technology, I assume, prevented the atmosphere from escaping.

A line of vehicles floated above the surface of the cavern, extending toward the opening. The closest vehicle pulled toward us.

It resembled one of the aircars I'd become familiar with, except that the front seat was encapsulated, a transparent bubble over the driver. As it pulled toward us, the rear of the craft reshaped itself into seats suitable for humans.

The driver looked like nothing so much as a black furball with compound, insectile eyes. Four limbs extended from its shapeless body, all four grasping a wheel.

"Where to, mac?" it said.

We climbed in, and a transparent enclosure swept up from the right and left sides of the craft, coming together above us with a click. I looked upward; there was no visible seam between the two.

Zabelle pulled out a translucent tablet about the size of a sheet of paper and several inches thick. She examined it. "Booth . . . ten-three-twelve-eight-nine," she said.

"You got it," spake the driver.

The craft slid smoothly across the cavern and out the opening—into the void.

As it did, gravity fell away. We were in free fall. I gulped as acceleration pushed me back into the seat, fumbling for seat belts, which suddenly appeared as I thought of them.

"HERE WE ARE, MAC," SAID THE DRIVER.

"Here" was a rock. A cratered rock, slightly longer than it was wide, with a big chunk gouged out from one side. It tumbled through the void, slowly turning. Our craft began to roll, stars turning above us, until it matched the rock's rotation.

We slid forward; then the craft flipped over until the rock was below us. As we neared our destination, gravity suddenly switched on again; down was toward the rock.

We settled on it, and the transparent enclosure slid away to either side.

"This . . . this is it?" I said. "This is our booth?"

The driver punched something on the dash, checking, I guess. "You got it, mac."

Zabelle and Huff got out; the driver popped the trunk. Huff began unloading the equipment, and I went to help him.

Soon, the three of us stood under alien skies, stars wheeling above us as our booth tumbled through empty space.

"It's nothing but a rock," I complained. "In the middle of nowhere. A rock."

Huff knelt and examined the asteroid, took out a penknife

and scraped at it. "Fine-grained diorite," he said. "An inch and a half of regolith."

"Thank you, Mr. Science," I snarled.

There we were, on a chunk of rock, bare as creation except for the three of us, a wisp of atmosphere to let us breathe, a set of big black-plastic cases, and our luggage.

"I think we have a problem, Johnny," said Zabelle.

"You *think*? I damn well know we've got a problem."

"What did you expect?" said Huff.

"Not this," I said.

"There's no floor traffic if there's no floor," said Zabelle.

I nodded gloomily.

"Ah," said Huff. "You mean—no one will wander by, because there aren't show floor aisles to wander."

"Yes, Les," said Zabelle. "And we don't know who the big accounts are. We have no contacts. We have set up no appointments with prospective clients."

"Maybe I should have bought some nukes," I said. "Letting off a hydrogen bomb might be the only way of attracting attention."

Zabelle opened her purse and extracted a long, brown cigarette.

"I think I'd better spend the last of our money on a program-book ad," I said glumly. "It's about the only thing that might help."

So WE SET UP THE DISPLAY. IT TOOK US A WHILE TO FIG-ure out how to plug it in; we found a brown icosahedron sitting in a crater. On top of it was, I swear, an old-fashioned Princess phone. In pink.

I picked up the phone. There was a hum, a click, and a voice said, "Operator. Can I help you?"

I was startled enough to hold the receiver away for a moment and look at it.

Well, we had paid for a telecommunications setup. Of

course they would try to tailor things to suit the myriad species attending the show. A Princess phone was certainly familiar by the standards of *my* culture.

I realized I did indeed wish to place a call. "Could you connect me with the program-book advertising department?" I asked.

In moments, I was another $2 million poorer. But maybe the ad would attract *someone* to our booth.

Another call to technical support revealed where our power supply was located; the icosahedron *was* our power supply.

Experimentally, I held the plug from one of our lighted displays up to the thing; the material of the icosahedron flowed about the prongs of the plug. And once it had done so, flipping the switch turned the display on.

Fine. Whatever.

We turned to unpacking and setting up the display. It had set me back a pretty penny, on Earth, although by comparison to what the aliens charged for things the cost now seemed trivial. I thought it was rather spiffy. There were enormous lighted panels. There was a giant rotating Drink Valet, light by spots and uplights. There were touch-screen displays that could make sales spiels in a dozen alien tongues. There was even a holographic display running a continuous ad, depicting a drink bulb tumbling across a ship in null gee, hitting a bulkhead, and squirting liquid.

Too bad there was no one around to see it.

Zabelle was studying that translucent tablet of hers. "What is that?" I asked.

"The program book," she said. She handed it to me. It began to describe the wonders of some kind of animated luggage, showing scenes of sluglike critters in a tropical setting, obviously having a good time.

"Is our ad in there?"

She fiddled with it for a moment. Our ad was indeed in there. It looked pretty tacky, and ran a quick ten seconds.

I shrugged. It was there, at any rate.

"The show begins in about eight hours," she said. "Let's get some sleep."

I looked about. I could have used a drink—but if Fomalhaut B had any nightlife, it wasn't obvious where.

So we turned in.

I HAD THE DEVIL OF A TIME SLEEPING. THERE WAS NO night to speak of; or rather, there was night every few minutes, then day, as the asteroid tumbled. The gravity might be Earth-normal, somehow, and the air quite breathable, the cot not dissimilar from my bed at home; but the ever-changing light and dark emphasized the alienness of our surroundings. Ultimately, I put my head under the pillow to try to gain some respite.

And when I arose, I realized we had no way to bathe.

Another call, another million dollars.

BREAKFAST WAS KIBBLE. PURINA PEOPLE CHOW, IF YOU will. It had the consistency and taste of cat litter. I longed for the gourmet delights I'd prepared as a chef for that shantytown by the Bay. *Thon pour chat* was a taste treat by comparison.

But it contained, so we were assured, all the nutrients required to sustain human life.

It was, I suspected, going to be a long show.

But by the time the show began, we were all bathed, dressed, fresh-faced, and ready to go.

To go nowhere.

We stood about under the alien sun, watching the stars go by.

After an hour or so, Huff gave a disgruntled grunt and opened his own luggage, taking out a large and, to my ill-educated eyes, apparently powerful submachine gun. He began stripping and cleaning it.

I goggled. "Dr. Huff! What the devil is that?"

He glanced at me briefly. "An M-16 carbine, Mr. Mukerjii."

"Dr. Huff, we are here to make sales. Not war."

He peered down the disassembled barrel at me. "I've never known a little firepower to hurt," he said mildly.

"If you kill any of my customers, I'll . . . Well, I certainly shan't buy you a return tickets."

That got his attention. "We don't have return tickets?"

"No. And what's more, we don't have enough money left to buy them."

He put the gun down and got up, brushing regolith from his trousers. "Let me get this straight. At the end of the show, they turn off our air and gravity. And we've got no way to get home."

"Right you are, Mr. Board Member."

Huff turned a dangerous red, then sighed, turning away. "What a fate for a science fiction writer," he said. "To be a desiccated corpse, drifting through space around an alien star." He turned back to me. "As a member of the board, I strongly urge you to make every effort to, ah, achieve a level of sales that would permit the continued existence of Mukerjii Interstellar's highly talented executive team."

I snorted. "As CEO of Mukerjii Interstellar, I can assure you that I have a strong personal stake in doing so."

"Do you have any sales leads at present?"

I looked about the deserted asteroid, "Actually, no."

Huff sighted down the disassembled barrel of his gun at me. "Better develop some. Fast."

"Easier said than done," I said, somewhat sadly.

18

ANON(ITE) MEET$ HI$ MATCH

DURING THE SHOW'S FIRST CYCLE, WE HAD PRECISELY one visitor. It looked like an animated hand: a central neck, two upward-stretching limbs on either side, and a heavy torso, on which it walked by pogoing. "Friendly greetings," it—or rather, its translator—said. Zabelle went to meet it, and I hung back, not wanting to give the impression, however truthful it might be, that we were desperate for customers.

"Good aftern . . . ah, greetings," said Zabelle. "May I tell you a little bit about the Mukerjii Drink Valet?"

"Maybeso. But no buy I," said the creature. "Am slave of UNTRANSLATABLE Travel. Please have brochure." It handed one to Zabelle, who took the tablet gingerly. "Am visiting booths of competitors. Am doing market research. Please may have I catalog of yours?"

"Yeah, yeah, sure," said Zabelle, and gave it one.

"Many obsequious noises," said the hand. "Come up and see me some time."

"What?" said Zabelle.

"Sorry? Poor translation. Maybeso come see booth of ours. Number one-zed-zed-eleven-four. Anytime wish you."

HOURS PASSED. I SAT, DISCONSOLATELY SWILLING WATER, watching Zabelle pace, furiously lighting cigarette after cigarette as the dispassionate stars wheeled overhead. Huff had gone to the other side of the asteroid and let off an occasional blast with his submachine gun. He had brought his own entertainment, it seemed.

At last, I rose. "Zabelle," I said, "I believe I will take our competitor up on his offer and go see his booth."

"Absolutely not," she snapped. "I forbid it. I need you here to deal with this amazing press of customers."

"Right," I said.

"Go, go," she said, waving at me. "It can't hurt."

So I went to the Princess phone and called a cab.

THE BOOTH OF UNTRANSLATABLE TRAVEL WAS EVIdently a lot grander than ours. It was no asteroid, but a small blue planet.

It was, I presume, smaller than Earth, since we'd been told there were no permanently inhabitable worlds in the Fomalhaut system. Yet it seemed vast enough, as the cab approached, as we entered the atmosphere and came down for a landing. Large enough, certainly, to support weather systems; wisps of clouds were evident from orbit.

The largest continent looked remarkably like a suitcase, albeit one with a handle not designed for a human hand.

Now *there's* a technology to think about: one that can sculpt an entire continent into the shape of a product.

We landed on what seemed to be a wooden deck, built near a beach. Waves curled lazily onto bright sand from an azure sea. As the transparent enclosure of the cab slid back— letting in a fresh, ocean-scented breeze—the air was suddenly filled with the strains of John Philip Sousa. "The Washington Post March," to be precise.

I looked about, but there appeared to be no band. A woman stood nearby, however: a very American blonde, at least five-foot-ten, long straight hair, brilliant blue eyes, dazzling smile; red lips, long red nails, a one-piece bathing suit, and high heels. A vision straight out of Miss America, in fact, and obviously someone's erotic fantasy, if not mine.

I found that reassuring, actually; they knew enough about Earth to proffer cheesecake, but weren't reading my mind.

She waved. "Hi there, Mr. Mukerjii!" she said, walking to the cab and helping me out. Gravity was a little less than Earth-normal. "It's a pleasure to welcome you to Foo Travel."

I let her take my arm, and we strolled across the deck to what was clearly a bar. "Foo? One of your sales agents visited our booth and gave us a catalog; he called it Untranslatable Travel."

"I guess," she said, giggling, hip brushing mine. "Portable translators aren't as good as the stuff we've got here. Let me see." A vague look came into her eyes, then she said, "Foo is a metasyntactic variable; since our name is indeed untranslatable, we use it as a sort of placeholder. Untranslatable sounds, I don't know, too funky." Giggle.

She vaulted onto the bar, lay on it, head by me, eyes peering up at me, red lips smiling, one leg bent, high heel on the bar.

"Can I get you a drink?" she whispered, arching her back, breasts moving disturbingly under that bathing suit.

John Philip Sousa had, I noted, faded away into some kind of suitably tropical steel-band tune.

This was a bit much, I thought. Still, ah, I did appreciate the sight. "Piña colada," I said.

She reached below the bar with one hand, and pulled out a frosty drink. There was no blender sound, no apparent effort involved—just stick a hand down there somewhere and, presto, a piña colada.

I took it; her fingers brushed mine as I did, she smiling lazily at me. The drink tasted a bit off, actually, but I don't imagine there were any real coconuts within two dozen light-years.

"I assume that you are not, in truth, human," I said.

"Depends!" she said sunnily, one red-nailed finger playing with the cuff of my shirt. "Genetically human, engineered for the show because they knew there'd be some of your species here! But no time to raise a kid; I've got no brain, just hardware up here." She tapped her forehead.

I must have looked a little disturbed at that. She pouted up at me a bit, withdrawing her hand. "I know you humans have some taboos about stuff like that," she said, "but don't worry about it. You'll get over it."

Very reassuring, I'm sure.

"C'mon!" she said, vaulting to her feet again. "We'll miss the floor show."

I almost choked on my drink. I looked about; there was nothing but blue sky, this bar, the deck, the sea. . . . Certainly no soundstage or showgirls. "The what?"

She took my arm again and drew me to the edge of the deck, picked me up, and set me on the sand. "C'mon," she said. "Walk with me." And we walked along, arm in arm, her body alarmingly close to mine.

The steel band faded away. A small flock of birds ran up and down the beach, not far from us, toward the sea. They moved in unison; flocking behavior, although it did somewhat resemble choreography. No, they weren't birds, really, but birdlike creatures, scales rather than feathers. They began to whistle. In unison.

I realized that their movements were not semirandom, the way those of sandpipers on a beach seem to be. Choreography was indeed the word: the flock was moving back and forth almost like . . . Rockettes.

There was a bass sound—something between a cough and a whistle—from the ocean. A marine creature was there; I saw nothing other than its back, sliding whalelike into the water. Another sound; and another; there was a whole pod of them out there, surfacing, blowing, sliding into the waves.

The sounds they made were rhythmic, a beat. It was, I realized, a bass line, provided by whales, or something like them.

From the dunes ran two dozen or more little furry creatures, something like six-legged weasels. They ran in lines, one after the other, curving into arcs, figure eights . . . darting about us, and the birds, humming in high-pitched little voices.

I stopped and stared.

Miss America put an arm about me, nuzzling my ear. "Like it?"

I pulled away; she pouted. "It's entertaining," I said, "but what's it all about?"

She put two fingers to her lips and whistled.

Four green-skinned creatures rose from the water at the beach, water dripping from their hair. Their torsos were those of walruses, their faces rather birdlike; and each had a pair of humanlike arms, which they clasped over their chests.

From over the ocean, a dozen objects flew. They skipped toward us, and flew over our heads in a circle.

They were travel bags, in a variety of decorator colors, flying gracefully about us, lids opening and closing in time with the music.

The green-skinned creatures began to sing audible English words.

Pack it to the fullest, pack it to the brim
Press a little button, pack some more again
'Cause it sends your clothes and items to dimension X
Twelve dimensions in your bag means nothing is excess!

One of the bags flew up above the others; its lid opened, clothing fell from it to be snatched from the air by the other bags.

Throw it from a spacecraft, watch it tumble down
Gravinertial stabilizers lower to the ground
Though it falls for kilometers, it will be intact
But whatever you have packed may smash upon impact.

As the verse was sung, one bag flew up high in the air like a rocket, leaving a faint sonic boom in its wake—then plunged back to splash into the ocean some distance away, zooming back toward us, the bag still glowing red-hot from reentry. It gradually cooled with a ping, seemingly no worse for wear, rejoining the other circling bags.

It's a miracle of engineering
You'll find it most endearing
You'll never go without again
Your suits will never sag
'Cause you'll pack half your kingdom
In this old kit bag.

I glanced sidelong at Miss America. She was smiling and swaying with the music. It *was* rather catchy. She caught my eye and winked.

Try to lift a planet, feel your muscles strain
But lift our patent luggage, never feel a pain
Forget about those wheelies, think antigravity—
The lift repulsors in your bag could float the Zuider Zee!

Several of the pieces of luggage—not, thankfully, the one still cooling—swooped down to beach level and under us, picking us up; one under my bottom, another supporting my back at a slant. Miss America was picked up, too, and flew through the air, laughing, long, bare legs kicking. I tried to retain my composure as we flitted through the air.

Never lose your baggage, at the carousel
Watching all the luggage, circling pell-mell
The brain inside your bag is smart enough to know your
      tune
Just give a little whistle and up to you it zooms.

Miss America whistled again, and all the bags, save the ones supporting us, clustered around her, lids opening and shutting in a curiously endearing way, like puppies begging.

It's a miracle of engineering
You'll find it most endearing
You'll never go without again
Your suits will never sag
Cause you'll pack half your kingdom
In this. . . . oooooold . . . kiiiiiiit . . . baaaaaaaaag!

With the finale, the singers slid away back into the ocean, and the furry creatures ran back to the dunes. The suitcases carried Miss America over to me—and formed a staircase in the air, from our height down to the beach, each step a bag. She took my hand and led me down the stairs, stepping carefully with those high heels.

"What do you think?" she said.

"Too silly for words," I said.

She giggled. "Yes, but how many would you like to order? Or would you like me to introduce you to other items in our line of fine travel items?"

"I think after that I need another drink," I said somewhat weakly.

She giggled and took my arm.

I WAS, I ADMIT, A TAD INEBRIATED BY THE TIME I RETURNED to our booth. And perhaps a bit disheveled, my tie undone.

"Our booth looks like crap," I said as I pulled myself out of the cab.

Zabelle looked at me rather sternly, arms folded. "So do you, Johnny," she said. "What do you mean? It's not bad."

I sighed. "It's quite spiffy by terrestrial standards, I suppose," I said. "They've sculpted entire continents in the shape of their main products. They've engineered entire ecosystems to make sales pitches. And they've refined the business junket to a fine art. You can sit on the beach and be plied with piña coladas by nubile young women as long as you want, if you don't mind being subjected to an unremitting sales spiel."

I pulled my new luggage from the seat of the cab.

"Piña coladas?" she said.

"Or a reasonable facsimile thereof," I said. "The lobster was good, too."

Well, the boiled arthropod. I know of no terrestrial organism with three claws.

"I'm glad to see someone was having a good time," Zabelle said icily. "What's that?"

I looked at the bag. "Ah, a piece of luggage."

"I can see that. What did it cost you?"

I winced. "A hundred *gozashtandu*."

"Half a million dollars," she said sadly. "Johnny, what *am* I going to do with you."

"Not material," I muttered. "We need thirty mil to get home. And . . . It's got antigrav . . . The interior is dozens of times larger than the exterior, multidimensional something . . . practically indestructible."

"Oh, shut up, Johnny," Zabelle said irritably. "The show closes for the cycle in a few minutes. Go clean yourself up."

"May I see that?" said Huff. I handed him the bag.

While I was in the shower, I heard the sound of gunfire again.

When I had cleaned up, Huff handed me the suitcase back. "Very impressive," he said. "Do they make body armor?"

I inspected the case, but there was nary a scratch on it.

19

ALE REP$ FROM THE TAR

I SLEPT POORLY AGAIN, IN THAT EVER-CHANGING NIGHT and day, but soon enough the Princess phone was ringing. Zabelle tumbled out of her own cot and picked it up, listened for a second, and cursed, slamming it down. Our wake-up call.

Another day cycle, another dollar. Actually, another day, no dollars; another day of the three before the show ended, and they turned the gravity off, and our bodies were flung into space by the rotation of the asteroid, our fluids to boil away into the vacuum of space, our corpses to drift for all eternity through alien skies.

A cheering prospect.

I groaned, rolled out of bed, and went to stand under a hot shower for a good long time. It didn't help.

More kibble for breakfast. And, thankfully, a steaming hot cup of some bitter black liquid that, whatever its culinary drawbacks, did seem to contain a stimulant.

I donned my suit. Savile Row; I could afford such niceties again, on the basis of cash put up by our foolish investors, cash unlikely ever to see a return. Perhaps pointless to don a suit, and yet doing so made me feel faintly better, putting on my armor as it were. At least for another few days, I was a businessman; I would not abandon the pretense before it became necessary. I knotted the tie severely and went to stand by our display.

Waiting. Regolith beneath my feet, black sky and stars above. Giant inflatable Drink Valet spinning, its electric motor whirring faintly. Backlit displays blazing away. Zabelle pacing in flat heels, lighting cigarette after cigarette. I hoped she had brought enough; there was no corner store where we could acquire more. And Zabelle without nicotine was not something I hoped ever to have to face.

Huff was dressed in khakis, tie, tweed jacket. He had the program tablet, perusing it; not much else to read or look at. I'd looked through it myself the previous day; there were thousands of companies here, God knows how many products. A lot of business was being done at the show—but not by us.

Waiting.

For hours.

We had nothing better to do, but wait. Wait for the inevitable end.

When MDS had gone under, that was wrenching enough. But at least that disaster had not been a direct threat to my life. I spent a lot of time contemplating what I'd done with my existence; I had no children, no wife, nothing to mark my passing. No company to pass on, no heritage.

Electric motors whirring, Drink Valet spinning: my only monument.

HOURS PASSED.

And then, I noticed a speck of light above us; noticed it because it had a perceptible disk—it was no star. It grew larger, approaching, gradually resolving into the shape of an in-system craft: not one of those cabs we'd used coming in, but a sleek teardropped item in silver with red, arcing stripes and gull-wing doors.

A customer. I began to sweat, called over Zabelle, pointed it out. She stubbed out her cigarette and straightened her dress.

The vehicle came in for a landing, and one of the gull-wings opened with a sigh of air. A tall, skeletal biped stepped out: skin blue, two vertical gashes across the face that sphinctered slowly—breathing, perhaps. Below was an elongated eye, an ovoid running horizontally from side to side; two dots, pupils I believe, were at opposite ends of the single eye. It wore trousers, of a kind, ending in boots with three large toes, and a frilly white shirt that would not have been out of place on an eighteenth-century Englishman. A translator box was affixed to its belt.

Zabelle and I descended on the alien like attacking sharks. Any pretense that we were not desperate for customers had long since departed.

The alien made lugubrious hooting sounds, in stereo, from its facial orifices. "Greetings, great lords," translated the box. "This worm apologizes in advance for any breach of your business customs, as he is not familiar with the etiquette of your species." He went to his knees, and knocked his head against the regolith.

"Oh, please get up, sir," said Zabelle. "We are quite an informal species, and you need not address us in such obsequious terms."

The alien stood up. "Oh good," he said. "We're pretty informal, too, but you never know." Three-fingered hands brushed regolith off his knees.

"We normally shake hands on greeting," I said, offering my own. He took it gingerly with three fingers, and we shook.

"Greetings, then," he said. "And now what?"

"We introduce ourselves. I'm Johnson Mukerjii, president and CEO of Mukerjii Interstellar. This is my vice president of sales and marketing, Zabelle Vartanian."

"Pleased to make your acquaintance, President Johnson Mukerjii, Vice President Zabelle Vartanian," said the alien. "I am yclept Manbrachfalbraitlinogishwitz."

"Oh, call me Johnny," I said. "Everybody does."

"I see," he said. "Then call me . . ." He hesitated. "Manny."

"May I show you our product and demonstrate its use?" Zabelle said.

"Of course," Manny said, "but I have to tell you I'm not a buyer."

Zabelle snorted and stalked away to have another cig—rather rudely, I thought.

I sighed. "If I may," I said, "why did you come to see us, then?"

"I saw your ad in the program book," Manny said. "I was intrigued by this Drink Valet. May I see it?"

So I took him back to the display and broke out a Drink Valet and a squeeze bulb to demonstrate, giving him my practiced spiel. The suction cup stuck nicely to the lighted glass panel of the display.

I'd used a full drink bulb, and it fell off after a few seconds. Embarrassing. "But," I said, "of course in space there's no gravity to put torque on the shaft of the drink valet, so it should remain fixed for some hours, until air infiltration under the latex destroys the suction."

"Quite clever," said Manny. "Does it work in other atmospheres? Chlorine, say?"

I blinked. "I have no idea," I said. "I imagine some atmospheres might react with the components . . . but we could probably design something that would work in chlorine. Temperature is an issue, as well; too cold and the latex becomes rigid, too hot and the plastic will melt. But . . ."

"Still," said Manny, "that leaves us a lot of potential markets."

Us?

"I think I could sell this," he said.

"I'm afraid I'm not following you," I said.

"I'm an independent commissioned sales representative," Manny said. "I rep six or seven travel-accessory lines . . . I cover a section of the Carina Arm, roughly from Wolf 629 to Procyon."

I felt the hair at the back of my neck stand up, a jolt run through me. "I take it," I said slowly, "that you have existing relationships with a number of accounts in your territory?"

"Of course," he said. "That's my business."

"Do you think you could sell any of them on the Drink Valet?"

"Yeah," he said. "I think it's a slam dunk."

I could have kissed him. I restrained myself.

"Well," I said, "what kind of commission do you expect?"

"Oh, the usual," he said.

Annoying, that; it meant I was forced to reveal my complete ignorance of the standard practices in this industry. "And, um, what *is* the usual?"

He peered at me, both pupils sliding to focus on my face. I suspect he found me as unreadable as I did he. Expression may be a universal among humans, but he and I were the products of alien evolutions. We seemed to talk business easily, enough, though: Genetics is not universal, but money is.

"It's 12/144th, of course," he said. "You've never dealt with sales reps before?"

"Of course I have," I said, "on my homeworld."

He was silent for a moment. "You have no offworld sales?"

I winced; I really hated revealing our weakness. "That's right," I said.

He looked about our bare booth.

"You know," he said, "I have a lot of friends who rep other territories. Would it be okay if I got some of them to drop by?"

"It would be more than okay," I told him, with perhaps a touch of desperate eagerness. "It would be lovely."

I packed him into his craft with a gross of samples and some of our promo sheets, and watched him dwindle again into the void.

I found Zabelle sitting on her cot, slumped, shoes off, a bottle of something in one hand.

"What's that?" I asked.

She looked blackly at me. "Armenian brandy," she said, and took a swig from the neck.

"You brought a bottle of brandy all the way from Earth?" I said.

She got up and opened a bag. There were a half dozen.

"Good stuff," she muttered. "I figured to entertain accounts."

"You may have the opportunity," I told her.

IN A WAY, THE WAITING THAT FOLLOWED WAS EVEN MORE difficult. Before, it had simply been a matter of stoically awaiting the end. Now, we had a wild, desperate hope—but our fate was utterly out of our control. There was nothing we could do until Manny returned—if indeed he did return. And even then, our fate was in his three-fingered hands.

But we hadn't that long to wait; about four hours after Manny left, he was back, followed by a flotilla of other vehicles—no cabs, I noticed. I guess it was more efficient to rent a vehicle for the show, if you had meetings across the system, than to take cabs everywhere.

An astonishing variety of creatures poured out of the vehicles: some kind of levitating fluffball with amazing teeth and a single large eye; an entity in an iron lung, much like the one I'd seen outside Huff's house in Orange County; something that looked like nothing so much as a chimpanzee with a cigar, which it lit without so much as a by-your-leave; and a sluglike fellow with eyestalks and extravagant ropes of garnet jewelry.

Manny introduced each of them, and all did their best to

shake my hand, adapting themselves to human business customs—a necessity, I guess, for salesmen who deal with a multitude of cultures. And Manny had them gather round while I explained the Drink Valet and its use.

"What are your merchandising plans?" asked the slug.

"Ah . . . I'm afraid we don't have any, really," I said apologetically. "We just aren't familiar enough with the interstellar market. We do have a co-op advertising program in place that could perhaps be adapted, but other than that we're open to suggestions."

"What is the retail price?" asked the chimp, through a cloud of blue smoke. It smelled, to my nose, somewhat like rosemary; not an unpleasant scent.

"Ah, a hundred dollars in our local currency," I said—an astoundingly high price for a little plastic dingbat, but the aliens at the duty-free malls on earth didn't seem to bat an eye at it. "About 3/144ths *gozashtandu.*"

There were mutters and squonks. "Far too low," grumbled the fluffball.

"We had thought, actually, that it was remarkably high," I said. "Our manufacturing cost is a trivial percentage of that—"

"Sure," interrupted Manny, "because you come from some hick world where people work for air and a pat on the head. But look, I'm the buyer from, say, the Eekratkoi Mercantile Clan. You're trying to sell me on this thing. I look at it; one SKU, takes up maybe a square decimeter of shelf space, retails for 3/144th *gosh*. When headquarters looks at sales reports, I know they want to see sales of at least 144 *gosh* per SKU per cycle, and I know our store managers aim for at least 576 *gosh* per square meter. Unless the thing sells like lead jockstraps in a solar storm, there's no way I can meet those numbers. It's just too cheap an item."

"What do you suggest?" I said.

"One *gosh*," said the fuzzball to a murmur of agreement.

Roughly $5000 American.

"But who'd pay that?" I said.

Manny's slits sphinctered rapidly. I think he was startled. "Anybody," he said softly. "It's a negligible sum. Nobody thinks twice about paying a *gosh* for something."

Ye gods. It was like a dollar at home. You can sell almost anything under a buck. . . .

"Gentlebeings," I told my reps, "you're the experts. A *gosh* it is. You really think you can sell this at that price?"

"At that retail," he said. "You want to set a wholesale price of about 60/144ths *gosh*."

"Yes, of course," I said. "We'll have to modify some of our sales materials, but that should be no great problem."

"Keep selling it however you want on your homeworld," he said. "You know that market better than we do."

"You're obviously reaching a small market at the moment," said the thing in the tank. "How quickly can you ramp up production?"

"Pretty quickly, I imagine," I said. "There's a lot of surplus industrial capacity on Earth at the moment."

"How many units can you produce in a year if you have to?"

Good question. Given a wholesale price of something over $2000 for a tiny plastic doohickey, I could afford to purchase just about Earth's entire plastic extrusion capacity, if I had the orders. "If we had to, I think we could produce a billion units," I said.

"That should do for a start," said the tank.

For a start?

"You really think you can sell a billion units?" I asked in bemusement.

"Personally," said the tank, "I don't believe in an order until I see the invoice, and maybe not until I get payment. But yeah, I think I can move a few million myself."

None of the others seemed to think this was unreasonable.

Zabelle winked at me. I flashed on a Warner Brothers cartoon—Daffy Duck diving into a pile of gold and shouting "I'm rich, I'm rich, I'm thocially thecure."

Yes. However, as our non-oxy breather pointed out, don't count your sales until your invoices are hatched.

"Ah, your commissions are based on the wholesale rather than retail price, I assume," I said, a little weakly.

"Sure," said Manny.

ZABELLE CALLED UP A MAP OF THE LOCAL PART OF THE galaxy on the program tablet, and the reps outlined their territories. There was some overlap between the regions they wanted to cover, but we managed to divvy things up. Soon, we were represented across most of the Carina Arm, and sections of the stellar arm coreward.

And then we broke out the multispecies refreshment pack for which I'd paid so dearly—as well as Zabelle's brandy. It transpired that all but the tank-confined fellow enjoyed the consumption of ethyl alcohol, and when our new sales representatives departed, they did so in a haze of bibulous good fellowship.

20

ALL MERCHANDI$E FOB EARTH

WHEN THE BROWN ICOSAHEDRON ON WHICH OUR PRIN-
cess phone rested first gave a bullfroglike "blaaat," I was startled; investigating, I saw that a sheet of thin plastic, covered
with English letters, was slowly extruding from the brown
surface.

It fluttered to the ground, and I picked it up.

Clearly, the icosahedron functioned as a fax as well as
power supply, for here was the evidence: Our very first order,
for a dozen gross. Huff was actually pleased enough to slap
me on the back.

The icosahedron began to "blat" with fair frequency. Orders began trickling in: a gross here, a dozen gross there.

I began to think we might get home. And as I did, it occurred to me that I had best check on the availability of transport to Earth; airplanes get booked up, and so might transport
out of Fomalhaut B.

I picked up the phone, and asked the pleasantly modulated
voice to connect me with a starship operator who could get
us home. It did so almost immediately, to my relief. I inquired about fares; they were rather higher than the fares we'd
paid to get here, because we were booking at the last minute:
3456 *gozashtandu* each for coldsleep, 5184 for tourist class.
So we needed either 10,368 or 15,552 *gosh*, depending on

whether or not we wanted to run the risk of dying again. Taking the cheaper option, at our new wholesale price we needed orders for about 25,000 units.

We had that within the cycle. I decided to wait a bit, and book the more expensive fare; a one-out-of-twelve chance of dying was worth avoiding.

Zabelle was practically dancing; I hadn't seen her so cheery for months. Even Huff was smiling. For my part, the fear of death was merely replaced by a somewhat more remote fear: I knew we'd be facing the SEC when we got home.

If we got home. An invoice is not the same as cash on hand, and the starcraft line quite rightly wanted cash in advance. I knew how to solve this problem, though: It took me only four calls to find an alien banking syndicate to factor our receivables.

I slept much better when the show recessed at the end of the cycle.

THE NEXT CYCLE, MANNY SHOWED UP IN HIS SLEEK LITtle spacecraft and practically leapt from the door. "Johnson!" he said. "I got an appointment with Grishneg."

"With what?" I replied.

His slits sphinctered rapidly. "You guys really are cubs in the swamp, aren't you?" he said. "They're the largest retail group in my territory: 1,372,438 retail outlets in the stellar arm alone."

I swallowed. This made Wal-mart look like the newsstand down the block. "You want me to come?" I asked.

"Have to," he said. "Grishneg is a *zdeg*-race outfit."

"So?"

He sighed, and pulled me toward his craft. "I'll explain en route. Come on."

"I want to come, too," said Huff.

I glared at the man; he'd dressed in urban camouflage today, for some reason: irregular rectangles of black, gray, and white. Take him to a meeting dressed like that? Well, I suppose; the aliens wouldn't know our customary business garb, they'd think nothing of it.

"We're going to make sales," I told him, "not war."

"I appreciate that," he said dryly. "But I did come to try to find out something about the aliens, and this may be my only opportunity to get off this rock."

"Whatever," said Manny. "Make it quick. Our meeting is in 2/144ths cycle."

About fifteen minutes. I swallowed. "Right," I said. "Let's go. Yes, you too, Huff."

We piled into the spacecraft; the gull-wing doors closed with a snap. The seats were more like racks than bucket seats: back and thigh support, but not much in between. Uncomfortable, but I could manage.

"The *zdeg* are incredibly arrogant, incredibly bloodthirsty," Manny said. "Used to be a warrior race. They have some very elaborate sales rituals."

"Ah . . . I say, old BEM. What if I make a botch of the ritual?"

"Don't even think about it," he said. "Told you they were bloodthirsty, didn't I?"

"Interesting," said Huff. I heard a metallic click, and turned to look at him, sitting in the rear rack. He had a pistol out and was cleaning it with a handkerchief.

"Great," I thought. "Wonderful. Dandy. I'm off to sell plastic to ultraviolent aliens with touchy customs, in the company of a heavily armed right-wing loon who happens to be my largest single shareholder."

I didn't even say anything to Huff. What was there to say? He was going to get us all killed.

MANNY BRIEFED US ON THE WAY. I TRIED TO ABSORB AS much as I could, but there was little time. We headed toward a starship that, from afar, looked rather like a triangular waffle iron: protrusions and hollows spaced evenly across its surface. As we drew nearer, I began to feel like I was in a *Star Wars* flick; it was enormous, filling what seemed like half the sky. The protrusions were gun emplacements, the hollows cargo bays. A cloud of other spacecraft moved like gnats about it. I imagined a John Williams theme.

More than once, I had flown out to Bentonville, Arkansas, to try to sell Wal-Mart on one of MDS's high-tech products. They were arrogant in a peculiarly middle-American way. Bentonville was literally in the middle of nowhere, a four-hour drive from the nearest airport. The town itself consisted mainly of motels catering to business travelers who were in town to grovel to Wal-Mart. If you wanted to sell to the world's largest retailer, you made the trip, to East Dogmeat, Arkansas, drove for hours, stayed at a fleabag motel, and went to kiss the ring of Sam Walton's vicars on Earth. They *wanted* you to do that. They *wanted* you to abase yourself before the Bubba King.

It occurred to me that Wal-Mart was a bunch of pikers compared to Grishneg.

The spacecraft's vidscreen lit up with something that looked like a grasshopper in war paint. "Identify yourself or be destroyed!" it said.

"This worm grovels in abject fear," said Manny in an off-hand tone. I was glad one of us wasn't nervous, at any event. "It begs to bring a potential vendor on board, in the dim hope that Grishneg will find our dull merchandise of some minor interest. My registration number follows."

After a moment, the grasshopper gave us an approach vector, and told us not to deviate from it if we valued our lives. Manny switched off the screen.

As we made the final approach, he said, "By the way— Mukerjii Interstellar isn't a limited liability corporation, or anything like that, is it?"

"Why . . . yes. Of course. That's the standard form of business organization on Earth . . ."

He made a loud sucking sound through his slits. "Uh-oh," he said. "We're in trouble."

I HAD NO TIME TO WONDER AT THIS DIRE STATEMENT. WE were on board the alien craft. Our ship sailed into a cargo bay; we jerked as we passed through a force screen. As at convention reception, the bay contained an atmosphere even though it appeared to be open to space. We landed, and those gull-wing doors rose.

As we stepped out, nine giant grasshoppers appeared in three ranks of three, multileggedly marching with military precision. They all bore war paint, carrying brightly colored weapons that, on Earth, I would have taken for air-powered water pistols. I had no doubt they fired something more lethal than a stream of water. I looked at Huff out of the corner of my eye, and was relieved to see that his gun was not visible—hidden somewhere under his cammos.

They halted before us. One of the grasshoppers made a sound like a violin. "Ooh, yuck," said his translator. "Mammals. Kill them."

I bent over and touched my toes, offering my posterior to them in the ritual gesture of submission. Manny was doing the same. Huff hesitated and then, with an annoyed grunt, assumed this humiliating position.

"Better not, Sergeant," said one of the others. "It seems to be sapient."

The sergeant made a whining noise like a muted buzz saw. There was an irritated pause. "These are decadent times," it said at last. "Very well. You. Mammals. Where are you going?"

We stood up. Manny grunted, and popped something gumlike into one of his sphincters. "This creature begs leave to escort his revolting companions to open commercial negotiations with the noble house of Grishneg."

The sergeant quivered with suppressed loathing. "Bah," it said at last.

"WHOM ARE WE GOING TO MEET?" I WHISPERED TO Manny as the soldiers marched us along.

"The CEO," he said. I swallowed hard. I was about to meet the chief executive officer of the largest retail operation in the stellar arm. I'd better not botch this sales call.

I glanced over my shoulder at the formidable warriors behind us, and remembered Manny's admonitions. No, I had better not botch it indeed.

Huff was gazing alertly about. His gait had changed; not the confident stroll of a successful Orange County bourgeois, now, but a pantherlike tread, knees bent, on the toes, as if ready to sprint or dive for cover at any moment. His eyes kept going to the guns our escorts carried. He was making me dreadfully nervous.

"Why the CEO?" I whispered.

"To the *zdeg*, a business relationship is a military alliance. By ordering from you, they pledge that they will pay their debt to you with their lives and their sacred honor. Alliances can only be formed at the highest level of the command."

I digested that. It occurred to me that alliances run both ways. I had no desire to pledge my life, nor my sacred honor, such as it was, to a bunch of overgrown bugs.

THE MOUTH OF THE CHAMBER WAS THE MOUNTED HEAD of some great beast. In life, it must have been as large as a blue whale. We stepped over the lower jaw, the upper one arching high above us as we entered.

The chamber itself was lined with innumerable grasshoppers, all perfectly motionless, all painted, all holding weapons before them like Marines presenting arms. For a moment, I wondered if they were living, they were so very still; but I saw one antenna twitch. I recalled that mammals are unusual among life-forms for the constancy of their activity; most creatures have far less active metabolisms.

Along the walls, the curved floor, and the ceiling were draped fabrics, colored indigo, violet, and darkest blue; fabrics of every conceivable texture, from satin to cotton wool to deep shag rug.

In the center of this cocoon of cloth lay a giant slug-grasshopper, tens of meters in length, without war paint of any kind. Other grasshoppers massaged its abdomen; it extruded gooey, whitish eggs. The eggs were carried off from time to time. The giant's egg-laying did not seem to affect her other activities.

As we approached, we skipped three paces to the right, turned around, offered our posteriors once more, then fell to our stomachs and wormed our way into The Presence—all according to ritual. Huff looked disgusted, but followed Manny's lead.

The—queen? CEO? both, I guessed—did not notice us at first; she was occupied with other business. A grasshopper stood stiffly at attention before her.

"I regret to report, my queen," it said, "that sales volume in my division has dropped below seven billion *gosh* in this fiscal quarter. I know the penalty for my failure, and await your judgment."

"You have failed your race, your House, and your queen," said the giant grasshopper-slug. "Pay now the price." She reached out one huge chitinous leg, grabbed the smaller insect, and tore him to shreds. Greenish insectile ichor splattered about the chamber. She popped bits of him into her mouth, and chewed.

Nice people, the *zdeg*. I began to have second thoughts about this. Maybe third.

Manny spoke up. "This miserable one approaches in hope of audience."

The queen swiveled a compound eye to look at him. One of her assistants whispered at her leg . . . I presume her auditory orifice was there, and that it was briefing her. "Manbrachfalbraitlinogishwitz," she said, after listening for a moment. "We see you."

"Your courtesy to this one is overwhelming," said Manny, still on his stomach. "I beg leave to present one Johnson Mukerjii, whose commercial enterprises this worm has the dubious honor of representing, and his slave Leander Huff."

"What do you wish, Johnsonmukerjii?" said the queen.

Despite Manny's briefing, I wasn't sure how to respond, although elaborate courtesy seemed to be the order of the day. "This one, whose race has barely achieved multicellular status, grovels piteously before your beauteous and munificent highness," I said into the carpet. "My starveling and barely sapient subordinates have created a tawdry and essentially useless piece of commercial gimcrackery which we have the appalling gall to believe may find a place in your veritable palaces of enterprise."

"At least you have good manners," said the queen. "Proceed."

"I have in my case a sample of the pustulant puffery we pedantically pronounce our product," I said. Huff glanced askance at me—not a fan of alliteration, evidently.

Still on my stomach, I hauled my sample bag up to my face, and opened it. . . . "Click click," went the latches. Instantly, three grasshoppers stood around me, the barrels of their weapons pointed at head, midriff, and crotch: unsure where my vital organs were, I suppose. I froze.

"It's okay," whispered Manny. "They were startled by the sound, that's all. Take it out. Slowly."

Shaking, I reached into the bag and found a Drink Valet. I saw Huff was in a fetal position, facing toward me, on his side—one hand under a pant leg, at his ankle. He slowly relaxed. I got the impression he'd almost drawn his weapon, the idiot.

I offered the Drink Valet to one of the grasshoppers, who took it, examined it carefully, and brought it to its queen.

"As your glory surely knows far better than my own scumlike species," I said, "zero-gravity travel entails certain discomforts for many. One such, trivial to be sure, but nonetheless to be considered, is the difficulty of setting down one's beverage. In the crude and fumbling way common to humans, this worthless one has embarrassed himself at times by losing control of his squeeze bulb which, tumbling across space, has spattered liquid onto godlike superior beings, to this abashed worm's unspeakable regret. The simple, indeed, absurdly lowtechnology item you hold is designed to ameliorate this difficulty; one end clips to a drink bulb, the other is a suction cup, which may be affixed to a bulkhead. Thus even repulsive endoskeletal creatures such as myself are able to arrange our affairs so that our betters are not bothered by our clumsiness. . . ."

"Yes, I see," said the queen. "A device the invention of which displays a certain primitive mammalian ingenuity. I believe we could sell a few."

I sighed into the carpet with relief. Then, another grasshopper spoke: "My queen, it is a device simple to manufacture. Why should we ally ourselves with this sack of protoplasm when we can easily make it ourselves?"

True. All too true. And if the aliens had any concept of patent law, I had yet to encounter it, and certainly we had not filed for a patent with the appropriate authorities. Nor did we have any lawyers versed in interstellar law, and we certainly hadn't an iota of the firepower evident here. If they wanted to rip us off, there was squat we could do about it.

The hell with the sale; I only wanted to get out alive. But Manny came to the rescue.

"Your magnificence," he said, "the Mukerjii Drink Valet, as we term it with such absurd grandiosity, is indeed a simple device, and we have absolutely no doubt that the eminently superior *zdeg* race can manufacture it, indeed to far more exacting standards than we.

"However, if I may be so bold, may I say that I find it hard to believe that the time and effort of bold *zdeg* warriors should best be spent devising and producing so trivial a property—especially when my client's miserable and impoverished species can manufacture it and provide it to you at a cost that can only be described as tiny."

"Indeed?" said the queen. "What is the wholesale on this?"

"O beauteous one," I said. "Know that the Mukerjii Drink Valet is available in quantities of a dozen gross or more at the modest cost of 60/144ths *gozashtandu*."

The grasshoppers twittered a moment in surprise.

"A very reasonable price," said the queen. "Does that include freight?"

"Your supremacy," I said, "this pustule on the universe's face regrets to say that all merchandise is FOB Earth."

"Very well," said the grasshopper queen. "Are you ready to swear to uphold and defend the honor of the House Grishneg, and to fulfill, without fail, all terms and conditions of your contractual arrangements with our House, and to pledge your life, your property, and your honor, and those of your vassals, employees, subordinates, slaves, partners, shareholders, and investors, and the heirs, successors, and assigns of same to this end?"

What? What was she talking about? Manny hadn't mentioned this.

"I am," I said weakly.

"Very good," said the Queen. "Done by me, Queen of House Grishneg, this 3,568,342nd cycle of my reign. This agreement shall be construed under the laws of the *zdeg* race, and shall inure to the benefit and be binding upon the heirs, executors, administrators and assigns of both parties. Sealed and signed. Give him a printout."

THE GRASSHOPPERS ESCORTED US BACK TO MANNY'S craft. Huff was scowling, eyes darting down every corridor. I was sweating; God knows what I'd just agreed to, and Huff's behavior was making me nervous again. "Let's just get out of here, Les," I said.

He only grunted at me, and cast a glance at the warriors behind us.

We got back to the cargo bay and climbed into Manny's vehicle. Manny got clearance from a grasshopper to depart, and we rose up, then slid through the forcescreen back into space.

There was a momentary hissing sound from the backseat, followed by a metallic clunk. I turned.

Huff had folded the backseat down, and was crawling into the trunk.

"Huff! What the devil do you think you're doing?" I demanded. Manny craned to see what was going on.

"Good-bye, fellas," said Huff. "See you in hell."

He slammed the backseat closed, locking himself in the trunk.

"Huff! Get . . ." I began.

Through the rear window, I could see the trunk suddenly open explosively. It wasn't until later that I wondered why the entire craft hadn't decompressed; I guess there was an airseal between the trunk and the backseat.

Huff tumbled out of the trunk and into space. He grabbed the vehicle to stabilize himself. He was in vacuum without a space suit. His eyes were closed, blinking open for a fraction of a second to catch a glimpse of space.

"He's insane," I told Manny.

"He can survive a few seconds in vacuum," said Manny.

Huff had his gun out. He fired it soundlessly, away from

the *zdeg* battleship. The recoil sent him flying toward the ship. I hadn't known you could fire a gun in vacuum. I guess the explosive contains its own oxidizer.

"This is bad," said Manny. "If the *zdeg* get upset . . ."

Huff sailed away from us, toward the *zdeg* ship. A second shot could be seen in the distance, a brief bloom of flame—a course correction.

Huff's body sailed into one of the cargo bays, close to the edge. There was artificial gravity on the other side; I could see him fall a short distance, pick himself up, and dash away into the ship.

"What the hell do we do?" I moaned.

"We get out of here quickly, or we inform the *zdeg*," he said. "I prefer not to trust to their mercies."

"Maybe we should wait for him. . . ."

"We have no idea what he's doing," said Manny. "I don't think it wise to hang around. Pretty soon they'll start asking questions."

He picked up speed, heading away from the warcraft.

"What if they capture him? Or kill him?" I said.

"We hope they can't identify him," he said. "Otherwise . . . do you understand what the alliance you just swore means?"

"Not entirely," I said.

"It means," Manny said, "that if you can't ship product or can't meet any debt, they can seize you, everything you own, and everyone and everything associated with your company. And God forbid one of your people should be caught spying on them."

"WHAT?"

"The *zdeg* are a warrior race," he said. "They pledge their lives and their honor to the fulfillment of all debts. They will not deal with vile cowards who refuse to do the same."

I stared out the viewport, feeling an incipient ulcer. Two cycles previously, I had been a dead man, without a *gosh* to my name, ready to die at the end of the show. Yes, I would be willing to pledge my life for an order the size of one Grishneg could give us. "But I can't speak for my stockholders," I said. "They just bought a stake in the company—they're not partners. They're only at risk to the value of their stock. By the law of my planet, creditors can't recover money from them."

Manny snapped his "gum." "That won't stop the *zdeg*," he said.

"What do you mean?"

"If you default, a Grishneg dreadnought will appear off your planet, enslave all your stockholders, and seize their property. Your employees, too. Given what you tell me about your planet, I doubt resistance would be any use."

"And if they catch Huff? And link him to us?"

His facial sphincters practically vibrated.

"The *zdeg* secure malefactors with an organic fiber," he said, "then implant eggs in their bodies, thus providing a living foodstuff for the hatching larvae. I'm told it is quite painful."

BY THE END OF THE CYCLE, WE HAD AN ORDER FROM Grishneg for fifty *million* units. Worth close to a hundred *billion* dollars, at current exchange rates.

It occurred to me that the exchange rate was going to change. Trying to exchange that many *gozashtandu* for dollars would inevitably bid up the price for dollars.

Well, why do so? *Gosh* were much more useful on the interstellar market. And perhaps I could buy futures to lock in the current exchange rate for a time.

We turned in, after a celebratory brandy. I slept miserably, again, thinking of Huff, darting down the corridors of an alien spacecraft, armed only with a primitive terrestrial slug-thrower, surrounded by bloodthirsty warriors.

I fell asleep briefly—to dream of little grasshopper larvae bursting from my chest. I awoke in a cold sweat.

THE NEXT DAY, ZABELLE AND I PACKED UP THE DISPLAY. We exchanged a last round of phone calls with Manny and our other reps, making arrangements to keep in touch from Earth. And then we called a cab to take us to the starship that would take us home.

We received no word from Huff, or from Grishneg, before our starship began to accelerate away from the Fomalhaut system.

No news was good news, perhaps. Maybe they'd blown Huff up into so many pieces they couldn't identify the remains; maybe we wouldn't be linked to the fool.

Or maybe it was just a matter of time before Grishneg dreadnoughts darkened Earth's skies.

21

EARTH NEED$ WOMEN

I WANTED TO START CALLING EARTH AS SOON AS POSSI-
ble; but it wasn't possible, I learned, to do so from hyper-
space. So I had to wait until we reentered normal space—not
far from the Moon's orbit, but on the opposite side of Earth
from that body.

At my request, the ship's crew easily linked into Earth's
communications net through satellites. At our distance, the
lightspeed delay was less than a second—and decreasing, as
we closed with humanity's old blue planet.

Accomplishing my task took me a half dozen calls—but
no more than that. It's astonishing what a few million dollars
in the right places can do.

THE POLICE WERE WAITING FOR US AS WE LANDED AT
Kourou, along with my old friends Stackpole and Epstein.
Zabelle and I stepped out into the sweltering heat, to be met
by a squad of gendarmes in EU blue.

"Mr. Mukerjii?" said Stackpole.

"Good day, Agent Stackpole," I said.

"I have a warrant for your arrest," he said. "I trust you and
Ms. Vartanian will come quietly?"

"We will certainly offer no resistance," I told him, "but I

fear you cannot arrest us without risking an international incident."

"I'm . . . sorry, sir?"

I pulled my faxed credentials from a suit-jacket pocket. "I am the Prime Minister of the Republic of Tuvalu, you see," I said. "And Ms. Vartanian is our ambassador to the European Union."

Stackpole, Epstein, and one of the gendarmes studied the paper in some confusion. At last, the gendarme said, "You will please come with us nonetheless, *monsieur et madame.* We will have to clear this up."

"Of course," I said.

They escorted us across the tarmac and toward the spaceport administrative offices.

A lovely place, the internationally recognized and sovereign state of Tuvalu. Nine tiny coral atolls in the South Pacific, and a population of less than 10,000. Rich men and women every one of them, as of today.

I'd wanted to be head of state, but had to settle for Prime Minister; King Charles still had the honor, and changing *that* would have required the assent of the British Parliament, which would have been a rather more expensive undertaking.

STACKPOLE, EPSTEIN, AND THE LOCAL FRENCH PREFECT sat on one side of the table. Zabelle and I sat at the other. The tropical sun shone dimly through smoked-glass windows; the decor was Swedish modern, enlivened only by a bust of Charles de Gaulle at one end of the table. The occasional roar of a suborbital rocket taking off could be heard from outside, but other than that, the only sounds were the background thrum of the air conditioner, and our voices.

"You can't claim diplomatic immunity, Mr. Mukerjii," said Epstein. "The crimes you committed . . ."

"The crimes I am *alleged* to have committed, Agent Epstein," I corrected.

"Yes, sir, the crimes are you are alleged to have committed occurred before you became Prime Minister of Tuvalu." Good, so they had at least confirmed that much. "Diplomatic immunity applies only to actions taken while on state business."

"Correct," I said, "yet I believe the people of Tuvalu and small nations everywhere would be outraged should you seize their head of government, as well as their ambassador to the EU."

The prefect cleared his throat. "While the Union does, of course, have an extradition treaty with the United States," he said, "I'm not sure Brussels would be happy if I permitted American agents to arrest the Prime Minister of a friendly power on European soil."

I smiled.

Stackpole sighed. "Mr. Mukerjii, I believe it would be in your best interest to come back to the States with us to clear up these charges—"

"Not on your life," I said. "I have business in Mexico, and that's where I'm going."

"I'm afraid we can't permit that," said Stackpole.

The prefect wiped his brow with a handkerchief. "I'm afraid I will have to contact Paris, and Brussels as well," he said.

"Yes," I said. "And perhaps you fellows might contact Washington? Ms. Vartanian and I need some decisions made and frankly, the people in this room are too low level to make them."

Epstein and Stackpole looked at me, mirrored sunglasses even in the filtered light of this overly air-conditioned room. "Who do you want?" Epstein said at last.

"The president," I said.

Stackpole chuckled. "I don't think the president is going to talk to someone charged with securities fraud, even if you are a past campaign contributor," he said.

"I think he will," I said. "Take this number down; it's my bank account number at Banamex. It contains six billion dollars at present—in hard alien currency."

Stackpole swallowed, but wrote the number down as I dictated.

"What you fellows fail to appreciate is that Mukerjii Interstellar, Limitada is now a Fortune 500 company, or will be the next time *Fortune* magazine gets around to listing them. And I fully expect us to be the largest company on the planet by the end of the next fiscal quarter."

WE HAD SOME TIME TO WAIT.

The French Guianan authorities put Zabelle and me up in a very nice suite, rendered less nice by the twenty-four-hour guards on every door and the squad of military police around the building.

We returned to the same conference room in the middle of the morning on the following day. The president was waiting for us, along with a hatchet-faced gentleman in his seventies who wore a severely tailored suit. Brooks Brothers, I think.

"Howaya, Muks," said the president, a little more subdued than he normally was. "Want you to meet a buddy of mine. Dwight Draconian, Secretary of the Treasury."

"Pleased to meet you, Mr. Secretary," I said. "I'm Johnson Mukerjii, Prime Minister of Tuvalu, and this is Zabelle Vartanian, ambassador to . . ."

"Cut the horse puckey," spat Draconian. "So you bribed a bunch of grass-skirted Polynesians: don't mean squat to me. The point here is, your IPO was the most blatant example of securities fraud I've ever seen on a major money market, and I don't give a flying crap how much money you've got in the bank."

The president sat back down, wincing, looking out the window. Zabelle and I sat down, as did the French prefect, making Draconian look faintly ridiculous, on his feet, an angry glint in his eye.

"Yes, I see, sir," I said. "As president of Mukerjii Interstellar, I can only offer my apologies if there were irregularities in our public offering, and promise full and complete restitution to any shareholder who feels ill served. I doubt that many will want their money back, however. When you permit my company to resume trading, I believe the share price will soar by a factor of a hundred or more."

"Your company will never trade on an American exchange," said Draconian.

I shrugged. "If you like," I said. "I suspect the management of the National Association of Securities Dealers will have something to say about losing a listing for the largest and fastest-growing business in the solar system, of course. I prefer to list on the London Stock Exchange anyway; the reporting requirements are less onerous."

"What load of crap is this?" said Draconian. "I don't know how you got that six billion in Banamex, but that don't make you the largest business on Earth. . . ."

"No," I said. "It doesn't. Most of our funds are out-system, on deposit in the Tsitschau Financial Collective, which is headquartered in Tau Ceti. They're not where you can seize them."

"Look, Muks, I don't grok it," said the president. "The treasury guys say you broke a bunch of SEC regulations. Did you or didn't you?"

"Oh please, Mr. President," I said. "I believe there's something in the Constitution about incriminating yourself."

"Yeah, yeah, don't do the lawyer thing with me," he said. "Point is, if it's true, well, hell. Sorry, but you'll be out of the federal pen in a few years, it's not that bad, you know, look at Milliken. . . ."

"I take your point, sir," I said. "But let's look at it another way. Some people put up money because I lied about my business? Okay, that's fraud, I grant you, but I'll pay them all back. With interest. I broke some regulations? Okay, I'll pay a fine, no problem. But put me in jail? I'll tell you what happens if you put me in jail.

"One, I have a hundred billion dollars in orders I haven't fulfilled. I've factored the receivables; I have the cash in hand, the Tsitschau Collective has the invoices. If I'm in jail, the orders don't get filled, the retailers don't pay Tsitschau, Tsitschau comes looking for its money. You want to talk to a bunch of aliens with fantastically advanced technology about why they're not getting paid?

"Two, a hundred billion dollars worth of hard alien currency *doesn't* get pumped into Earth's economy. Half the people in America, maybe two-thirds across the globe are out of work. You want to explain to the American people why you closed me down?

"Three, this is just the beginning. One trade show, one product, and I've got an order that's a substantial percentage of the gross world product. Give me ten years, and Earth will be on the rise again. Close me down, and maybe someone else will take up the slack . . . but are you crazy? This is the planet's first major export success, what the hell do you think you're doing?

"Four . . . the *zdeg*. Let me tell you about the *zdeg*."

Draconian placed both fists on the table and leaned on it, glaring at me fiercely. "I don't want to hear about the smeg, whatever that may be," he said. "I've heard enough. Let me tell *you* something. It's so important for your order to be filled? Fine, we'll find people to run your company, a court-appointed management team, we'll get that order filled. But *you* are guilty of securities fraud and *you* will go to jail. America is a country of laws, not of men. And we will not be blackmailed, or bribed."

There was silence for a long moment. The president was looking out the window, but was not demurring.

Zabelle spoke up, in a soft purr. "A billion dollars, Mr. Secretary. Think about it. The wealth of a Gates. And think about your grandchildren. . . . Think of what it would mean to them."

He looked at her, jaw dropping. "A bill . . . Are you trying to bribe me?"

"Is the amount insufficient?" said Zabelle sweetly.

WE RENTED THE ENTIRE HAWAIIAN ISLAND OF NIIHAUA—admittedly a small one—for our conference, and flew our vendors in by suborbital rocket. We had luaus on the beach, and unlimited free booze, golf, sailing, whatever they wanted, all expenses paid. I wanted this to be a junket to remember. Or rather, I knew our clients would remember it for unpleasant reasons, so I wanted them to have a few good memories, too.

We packed them into the ballroom at the Hilton, each in a comfortable chair, an enormous flat screen at one end of the room for our audiovisual display. Zabelle and I got up on the dais.

"Good morning, people," I said, "and thank you all for being here today." I surveyed the audience; they were in business dress all, and sober for the occasion. They may have been frolicking, but this, they knew, was what I had brought them here for. And sensibly, they had treated the occasion with due seriousness. In this single room, I had the most important executives of the largest plastics manufacturers on the planet—Dupont and Exxon Mobil and Saudi Petrochemicals and dozens of others.

"As you know, Mukerjii Interstellar has, at the present time, orders for two hundred billion dollars' worth of our main product."

Applause and cheers.

"And as you know, our first major order, for fifty million Drink Valets, is due to be shipped in seventy-two days.

"Some of you have expressed some concern about the tightness of the schedule. I know each of you is working to ensure that we meet it . . . but I have already heard from some of our vendors that they do not expect to be able to meet their quota.

"I'm here to impress the importance of meeting that deadline on you."

I picked up the clicker from the lectern and pressed the button. The enormous screen behind me filled with an external shot of a Grishneg outlet, three alien suns behind it, chrome and green glass shining in the sun, a constant stream of lemurlike sapients passing through its doors.

"Our order is from the House of Grishneg, the largest retailer in the stellar arm—over a million stores within five hundred light-years of Earth. We want to keep good relations with these people, folks. They make Wal-Mart look like the corner deli."

Laughs.

"But not only because we can expect to make a lot of money from Grishneg in the years to come."

Click. A *zdeg* warrior, in Grishneg paints, holding a weapon.

"House Grishneg is a *zdeg*-race firm. The *zdeg* are a warrior race. They have not fought what *they* call a war in several millennia. They don't have to."

Click.

"This is a *zdeg* dreadnought. It is sixteen kilometers from stem to stern. It packs more firepower than the Strategic Air Command and the old Soviet Strategic Rocket Forces combined—when they were at their height, before the fall of the Berlin Wall and the disarmament that followed. In other words, this ship alone is capable of obliterating all life on Earth."

No laughter this time. *Click.*

A combat scene, the bass of explosions rocking the entire

room. Small, furry, rather centauroid aliens galloped in terror toward the camera—three adults and a child. Out of the smoke behind them came disciplined *zdeg* warriors. They fired. The centauroids screamed as they fell, one falling in such a way as to protect her child. The *zdeg* ran up; one paused to bayonet both mother and child to death.

"This is footage from the Rape of Epsilon Eridani. According to the Grishneg, this was not a war. It was seizure of assets in repayment of a debt. The Eridanians had failed to keep current on their credit-card bills."

Click. The interior of a queen's chamber, much like the one I had visited. Ranks of *zdeg* warriors, the enormous egg-laying queen.

"The *zdeg* consider all business arrangements a matter of personal honor. They do not accept the concept of limited liability. They consider Mukerjii Interstellar bound to fulfill the order they have placed with us. They consider you, every one of you, bound to fulfill the orders we have placed with you. Should Mukerjii fail to ship fifty million Drink Valets in seventy-two days, they will consider not only my firm, but yours, in default of its obligations. They will use whatever force they deem necessary to restore their honor and repay the money they will lose by our failure to fulfill our obligations."

Click. A bound and terrified alien, this one much like a puce giraffe; a *zdeg* spat liquid from between its mandibles, gluing an egg to the giraffe.

"The *zdeg* will consider my life, your lives, and the lives of every one of our employees and stockholders forfeit."

Click. The same giraffe, still bound, much thinner; the egg hatching; the larva began to feed as the giraffe screamed in pain and terror.

"Here's one use they make of their slaves."

I let the sequence run for a few seconds, until it became so repulsive I could no longer watch. I clicked the screen off.

I turned back to the audience. "So, people, I think we're all on agreement about this, yes? Fifty million units in seventy-two days. Let's see a little mammalian ingenuity, here. We can get the job done.

"Otherwise . . ."

I clicked the video back on for a brief second.

I'd never seen more white faces in my life. Some of them had fainted.

I like to think of myself as a people manager. Motivation, that's the trick.

NEEDLESS TO SAY, WE SHIPPED ON TIME.

IT WAS EVENING ON THE BEACH AT FUNAFUTI, TUVALU'S capital and the new headquarters of Mukerjii Interstellar. Above us, on what passed for a hill on this low-lying coral atoll, was our new headquarters, still under construction. It was a fairly modest affair, I thought, modeled on San Simeon and Lucas Ranch.

Zabelle, Mauro, and I were taking a stroll along the beach, another frenzied day of phone calls and teleconferences at an end. A soft tropical breeze blew from offshore; the setting sun shone gorgeously gold and umber and saffron in the distance. The sand was cool under our bare feet, gentle waves breaking not too far distant.

A sudden crack of thunder broke across the world. A roar of jets sounded coming in from offshore. I hit the beach as a matte black craft roared above us, over the hill, turning.

Mauro had dropped like me, but Zabelle stood watching the craft as it turned, slowing . . . red flames playing about it.

It slowly dived toward us and landed on the beach.

It was black as night, almost invisible somehow, absorbing the light that hit it. It was angular, but simultaneously streamlined, like a Stealth fighter. Stubby wings protruded from the sides. At the front, where engine cowls might have been on another craft, were enormous cyan cylinders, glowing with internal light, the glow gradually dying with the declining whine of its engines. Missiles clustered in racks below the wings.

Atop the craft was the curve of a cockpit, its contents invisible beneath the matte black surface. With a hiss, the cockpit slowly opened, rising back on a hinge at the rear.

Leander Huff—unshaven, eyes bloodshot, clad in filthy urban camouflage—pulled himself unsteadily from the craft. Zabelle ran to him to help him out and down.

I got up and brushed sand from my suit.

"What is this, Huff?" I asked.

Zabelle half supported him as he staggered toward us. "*Zdeg* Starmantis," he said hoarsely. "Range of twelve light-years, firepower enough to destroy the Sixth Fleet."

I moaned. "You stole a warcraft from Grishneg."

He flashed me a grin. "Took some doing, too."

"They'll trace you. We're all dead meat."

"Nah. Stupid bugs. Got clean away. I need food, Mukerjii. Haven't eaten in a week. And that was grubs."

"This way, Les," said Zabelle. "Chun-Yi has Asiatic prawn on the grill."

I followed them glumly up the beach. Mauro had his cell phone out. "What are you doing?" I asked.

"Better get someone to watch the fighter," he said, dialing

"What are you going to do with it, Les?" I asked, catching up.

He coughed, and spat. I noticed for the first time that his left arm was cradled against his body, and his left hand was gone, ending in a cauterized stump.

"Earth needs weapons," he said. "If we're to compete . . ."

"Horseshit, Les," I said, with affection that surprised even myself. "Earth needs industry."

"No," yelled Mauro from the starfighter, where he waited for someone to come relieve him. "Earth needs women! Save a margarita for me!"